Saving Septic Cyril

Sara Alexi is the author of the Greek Village Series.
She divides her time between England and a small village
in Greece.

http://facebook.com/authorsaraalexi

Sara Alexi

SAVING SEPTIC CYRIL

oneiro

Published by Oneiro Press 2015

Copyright © Sara Alexi 2015

This edition 2015

ISBN-13: 978-1519686237

ISBN-10: 1519686234

Also by Sara Alexi

Chapter 1

On top, the laminate is peeling away in strips and the plywood underneath now soaks up the rain, but the old wardrobe has served as a very practical porch and it will be good for another year or two. The interior bristles with half-sunk nails and on these metal spikes hang plastic bags, of various colours and branding, containing treasure he has found – things other people have lost, things discarded, things broken.

With the wardrobe door open just a crack, Cyril can peek out without being seen. The sky outside is full of puffy white clouds and a kestrel is hovering over the verge at the bottom of the cobbled lane, its movements mesmerising. With the tips of its wings fanned, it hangs there, making small rapid flaps and twitching its tail to fine-tune its position, keeping its head motionless, suspended over the long grass below. But the bird is not the reason for Cyril's caution. There are two unfamiliar people walking up the road towards him. He shuts his eyes hard for a second but when he opens them the people are still there. With one foot in front, one behind, he begins to rock, his forehead tapping against the wardrobe frame. One of the dogs pushes its snout into his hand, whimpering, understanding.

'They're coming, Coco,' Cyril whispers with a shudder. His rocking increases in intensity and he cannot look away now. The patterned blue of the woman's long-sleeved dress is so vivid, the purple of her loose trousers in high contrast. Her sandals are sparkling, golden, and over her head a scarf lifts in the breeze from the moors to reveal her shiny dark hair. She is like a bird in a picture album he once saw as child – a book thrust into his tiny hands as a

3

bribe to keep quiet whilst she was in her room. He stares with intent at the woman, trying to remain in the present, but the connections have been made, he has no control, and the world before him darkens. His twitching and rocking subside, and he becomes quiet as he rushes back.

'Here, Cyril,' Mother said, thrusting the book into his hands without a hello. 'Say thank you to the man.' As he glanced up from the book at the man, tears pricked at his eyes, blurring his vision. He stepped forward to touch her, just to feel her hand, or smell her perfume, but he was too slow and they had gone into the other room, where he was not allowed. Clutching the book, he retreated into the dark and the warmth of his wardrobe, his personal nest, with his thin legs curled underneath him on the lining of blankets and pillows.

The wardrobe was a discarded piece of furniture that had been in the alley at the back of the building when they had moved in. His mum had said it would be useful and she had walked the wardrobe to the back door. It was flimsy, cheaply made, and Cyril had thought the way it moved was comical, like a fat man rolling from foot to foot. He had tried to help, but his mum had just grown cross at him for getting in the way, and at the wardrobe when it did not slide easily over the cracked lino in the kitchen. Finally, they had manoeuvred it to stand next to his bed that abutted the kitchen sink; she said it would have to do. There was no room for it to go anywhere else anyway.

The house was originally a shop in a line of terraced houses built for the mill workers when Bradford was the wool centre of the world. The shop, its trade long gone, had spent years boarded up but had been converted into a tiny apartment and was now rented out separately from the living quarters above. The large shop window was painted white for privacy, and it let a worthless light into the room, which emphasised the drab conditions. The first day there

4

they had shared an iced bun with four candles on it. That day, the day of the bird book, she had shouted at him in the morning to behave like a big boy and then left him crying. Next week, she had said, he would be five. But when the day came there was no iced bun or candles.

With the bird book in his lap, he wrapped his orange-and-white stripy towel around his head, pressed his hands against his ears and did his best to concentrate on the pictures. The dull light from the unshaded bulb hanging from the cracked ceiling sent a shaft of light between the wardrobe's ill-fitting doors. The book, spread across his knees, was a riot of vivid colour and the pictures waltzed in and out of the light as he rocked and hummed to block out the noises, the groans and the moans.

He followed his usual sequence, staring at the picture book and letting the images sink deep inside his head, somewhere behind his forehead but high up in the top of his brain. Sometimes it seemed like he was straining his eyes, which felt like they were rolling back in his head to see where the pictures had gone. But he would continue, the colours or shapes filling his mind, and then all of him would follow them in there and the magic would happen. That day, first one came, iridescent wings of green spread wide and engulfing, then a tiny blue one leaped from the pages, flapping its gossamer feathers, making a sound as soft as silk against glass. Cyril's hands dropped from the towel as the creatures surrounded him. A black one with an orange crest sat on his knee, then butterflies, each wing the size of a grown man's hand, appeared and painted whatever they touched in colours like those in the puddles by the petrol station on the bypass. The inside of the wardrobe glowed with lustrous hues, and flowers began to bloom and blossom around him, their stems rushing upward, lifting him to a sky of blue that went on forever.

'Oh, there you are.' His mother had yanked open the wardrobe door; behind her was the bulk of the man.

'What's he doing in there? Is he soft or something?' the man said.

'He likes it,' his mother defended.

'Bloody stupid place to read, he's no light.'

'What's it to do with youse anyways?' she said, taking the book from Cyril's knee and pulling at his arm. 'Come on, Cyril, Arnold's going to tek us for fish 'n' chips.'

'Does lad 'ave to come?' The man's hands fidgeted in his trouser pockets, jangling coins.

'Well, I can't be leavin' him 'ere alone again, I were owt most o' day again.'

'We'll only be ten minutes, leave t'lad 'ere.' The man sounded cross.

'Oh, okay, you'll be alreet won't ya, Cyril? Can he keep t' book?' She turned to the man.

'Books cost money,' he said, and reached out to take it.

The front door shut behind them and Cyril's empty stomach growled.

The memory recedes, and when Cyril opens his eyes the daylight is wincingly sharp, and the woman in the lane is still there. She is even more beautiful than the birds and butterflies of that book from long ago. Cyril takes his hand from his stomach, feels again for the dog that dutifully returns to her position, muzzle in his palm. The woman moves as if she is dancing, more graceful than swallows, the light glancing off her tunic and shoes. Her step is so light she might float away with the clouds and the birds and never land. He could meet her high up in the sky of blue. They could float, look down on the world, watch the people rushing about like ants below; the warmth on their backs would reach through to their bones, their heads would feel light and the sun would fill their minds.

The man, who was walking behind her, catches her up. He is carrying two suitcases and wearing a rucksack.

He stops to adjust the weight. The woman turns to him, repositions the bundle she is carrying and holds out a grasping hand, an offer of help. The man is small, not much bigger than the woman, who herself is thin and not very tall. He takes a firmer grip of both cases, shakes his head at her offer, stands a little taller, and continues up the cobbled road unaided.

Cyril hopes they will continue, will pass the 'to let' sign outside next door. Maybe they are only visiting someone at the top of the lane, staying very briefly.

The man speaks, and Cyril stops rocking, listens. The words are unintelligible, foreign. He frowns at the gibberish, his round glasses slipping down his nose. Pushing them back up with one finger, he curls his upper lip in a brief grimace to keep them there.

Coco, seeking attention, takes her muzzle from the palm of his hand and pushes against her master's leg. He falls forward against the interior of the wardrobe, his face briefly buried in the cluster of hanging carrier bags. Something sharp in one of them digs into his cheek. It is a Tupperware lid, and somewhere, in another bag, he has a box which it might fit. He turns the lid so it lies flat. From a hole in the bottom of another bag falls a bright red plastic lighter. He has checked this one and knows it no longer works. He leaves it where it fell.

Coco senses his agitation and, whimpering, slinks inside as Cyril resumes his vigilance. The couple have paused at next door's gate and are looking up towards him. Holding his breath, Cyril makes no sound as he steps backward.

An unsettling noise begins to sound from the little bundle of bound cloth that the woman is carrying. The man and woman both turn their attention to it.

'A baby!' Cyril tells Coco, who is back by his side.

The woman speaks to the man. 'Now we are in England I think we must speak English to this little one,' she says, her delicate face now almost touching the bundle.

Her accent is slight, and interesting. She looks at the man.
'It is better, don't you think, Aaman?'

Chapter 2

The back of the sofa is smooth to the touch. As she runs her nails across the surface she watches the indentations they make. A luxurious fabric. It is a moment she wants to take her time over, so as to make a more permanent impression and to savour their fortune.

The light from the window casts a square on the big flat stone slabs laid side by side, visible around the edges of the room, but mostly covered by a thick rug.

'As she is sleeping, why don't you put her on the cushions so you can look around?' Aaman suggests, putting the two suitcases down and wriggling out of the straps of his rucksack.

The short, dark, shiny hair on the back of her sleeping daughter's head feels as soft as the sofa's padded seat. Saabira lays her Jay gently on the velour material, arching her fingers back so her nails do not touch the child's skin. The baby sleeps on, her tiny mouth pulsing, sucking as she dreams. A well-placed cushion ensures she will not roll off.

With loosely hanging arms, Saabira shakes her shoulders, shrugs and then blinks slowly. A heavy sigh rids her of the last of her tension and she allows herself to shake off the stresses of the journey – the journey that began at five the previous morning is finally at an end. She has seen the inside of one taxi, two planes, two trains and a bus and spent twenty hours in the surreal, sterile, luxury of the Dubai airport hotel room where she dared not touch anything, where the air-conditioning was too cold, and where Jay fretted for hours before she finally cried herself to sleep only to wake an hour later and begin the whole process again.

But now they are home. It is a new home, and Jay is sleeping peacefully and she can touch everything. Her fingers feel again for the back of the sofa, partly to steady herself but also to reassure herself it is still there.

In front of the sofa the fire grate is laid with wood and coal ready to light. Against the opposite wall Aaman is fiddling with a solid metal piece of furniture painted light cream, which has four doors on the front, a black top, and two shiny metal upturned bowls, hinged at the back and with handles at the front as if they are designed to be lifted. It is obviously a stove but Saabira has never seen anything like it before. It is huge.

'The notes say that this will heat the water in the taps, and the radiators.' He looks at the booklet he holds in one hand and then around the room. With a boyish bound he is by the window next to the front door. 'This is it,' he says, stroking the radiator beneath the casement. A little shiver runs visibly up his arm; it must be cold. He returns to the stove and becomes absorbed in the written instructions.

As he crouches to open one of the stove doors he is hidden from view by the scrubbed wooden table and four chairs. Saabira continues to look around, to take it all in, make it real. Along the back wall on Aaman's side of the room are a sink and cupboards, standing on the floor or hung on the wall. A door is centrally placed, opposite the front door, and to the left of this are a shoe rack and a tall fridge. The back left-hand corner of the room is boxed off with some wood panelling and another door that is partly open, showing a carpeted staircase. Carpeted! In total the downstairs space is about the same size as their home, back in the village, just outside Sialkot, but here there is a second floor, and this house is for just the three of them, not shared with Aaman's parents and grandparents.

Everything is so different. Nothing is at floor level, everything is at different heights.

'It is exciting, is it not?' Aaman's head pops up behind the tabletop. His eyes are shining but they have sunk a little as they do when he is fatigued. He strikes a match inside the bottom left-hand door of the cream stove. There is a burst of light and he withdraws his hand quickly.

'It is tremendously exciting.' Saabira turns to look behind her and pauses at the picture over the fireplace. It is a photograph that looks like the countryside they passed on the bus from Keighley. Beautiful, romantic, and slightly bleak – wave after wave of flatly cushioned hills.

Aaman has left the stove to squat by the open fireplace where he strikes another match; it blazes quickly and illuminates his open and even features. Saabira reaches out to ruffle his hair.

'You will be needing a haircut before you start your new job on Monday,' she says, and pulls at his fringe. He yanks his head backward and the hair falls in his eyes. Her stomach turns in on itself and her cheeks glow hot with the effect he still has upon her. Looking at the picture distracts her, allows her to retain some control.

'It is called moors,' he says, standing by her side to admire the photograph with her, his hands reaching, fingers spread to feel the warmth of the barely lit fire.

'Yes, Emily Brontë wrote a lot about it. I could almost believe I could observe Cathy proceeding across the wilderness out of the bus windows.' A small giggle escapes her. Turning from the picture she surveys the room again, drinks in the creams and the whites of the decoration, the cleanliness of everything, the lack of dust and sand. There are no pegs in the wall to hang things on. The door in the back wall intrigues her. Is there another room? A key hangs from a nail by the brass handle. Aaman is behind her, and his hand slinks around her waist.

'I love it when you say such highly educated things like that. Say more,' he mutters into the hair behind her ear.

'If you read English books yourself I would not need to say them,' she teases. He has parted her hair and is kissing her neck.

'Do as I say, wife.' He kisses her shoulder, pulling away her shawl.

'Read more.' She reaches out for the key but as her fingers touch the cold metal Aaman snatches it away.

She turns on him, her hand held out, eyes wide.

'If you are a good and dutiful wife you can have the key, but if you are bad and disobedient you will have to come and get it.' He dodges away, putting the table between them, all tiredness gone, mischief in his eyes.

'If you wanted a good and dutiful wife you should have picked someone who did not have the intelligence to answer you back!' Saabira puts both hands flat on the table, widening her stance, ready to dodge one way or the other to catch him.

'Shh, my beautiful and intelligent wife, you will wake the baby,' he whispers in return. Saabira turns to look at the sofa, the back of which blocks her view of Jay, but all is silent. Aaman uses the distraction to dodge back around her and put the key in the door.

'Come, wife, let us explore together,' he says softly, holding his hand out towards her, inviting her to turn the key.

As she twists the handle the wind blows the door open, pushing Saabira back.

'Oh!' Saabira grabs at the handle, and Aaman takes the strain. 'That is quite a wind.'

'Our back door opens onto the moors!' Aaman looks thrilled. Puffy white clouds rear into the sky as if the monsoon is gathering. The sun, where it bravely breaks through, casts slanting rays across the purple heather.

There are no buildings or any signs of civilisation all the way to the horizon.

'It is so beautiful,' Saabira breathes, pulling her shawl more tightly around her. 'Beautiful but cold.' She shrinks back inside.

'I suspect we will not be using that very much.' Aaman acknowledges the slatted wooden table in the small concreted backyard. A knee-high wall marks the border and the curls of fern tops peek over. To the left, the neighbour has stacked boxes to head height on the other side of the wall, and, to the right, trelliswork that supports a mass of greenery is mostly obscured by a neat stack of ready-chopped wood. The sight of this is very reassuring.

'Come in, Aaman. Let us keep what heat we have inside.' She beckons him and, with a last look, he helps her with the door, forcing it against the stiff breeze.

'It smells like warm earth and green leaves,' he says as they close the door. 'Gritty and comforting but also sharp and with a crunch.' He has never quite understood what she means when she asks him to explain smells with flavours. Never having had a sense of smell, she has never missed it and when her mother once described a smell to her as the taste of burnt oil she knew there were times when she was better off without it. Amman's description helps a little but his odd explanations are often no use at all. But he makes the effort, and she kisses his shoulder as the door shuts.

Together they approach the door in the corner that opens onto a narrow flight of stairs. On the next floor they discover a bathroom, where the radiator is slightly warm, a bedroom with a high English double bed, and a smaller room with a bed that is far too big for Jay and where the radiator is cold.

'She can sleep with us,' Aaman says, gently trying to push Saabira backward onto the double bed in the larger bedroom.

'We cannot,' Saabira protests. 'Jay might wake up.'

13

'Then we will hear her.' They fall together onto the soft mattress and Aaman becomes lost. Saabira would like to lose herself too but a part of her is alert, the invisible cord from her heart to her sleeping daughter an ever present safety net.

Chapter 3

The baby wriggles and whimpers.

'I must feed her.' During the night Saabira has found extra blankets in a cupboard, and she pulls these around her and nestles Jay to her breast. Aaman groans and pulls at the covers.

After a few minutes he heaves himself up. His hair is sticking upright and he has dark circles under his eyes.

'Maybe I did not stoke the stove enough.' He stands and pads with shuffling steps to the radiator. 'It's cold.' With a blanket from the bed around his shoulders he thumps down the stairs, and Saabira can hear him rattling the grate.

She wraps her scarf over her head. 'Today, Jay, I think it is only right that we say hello to our neighbours. We will introduce ourselves, show we are good neighbours.'

Aaman reappears and shrugs off the blanket, reaching quickly for his shirt. He catches sight of Jay as she unlatches, her soft lashes closed, a look of bliss on her little face. His pupils widen; his movements slow and soften as he takes the infant, his mouth dropping open a fraction. Saabira ruffles his hair but he does not stop staring at the bundle he holds.

'So beautiful,' he murmurs. 'Just like her ammi.' He sits, continuing to rock her. 'So beautiful.' He repeats the words but it is as if he does not hear himself, he is so hypnotised.

'I think today we will introduce ourselves to our neighbours. What do you say? It is good manners.'

But he does not appear to hear her. He is singing softly, staring lovingly.

15

'And we must get some groceries.' All they have in the house are some dry wafer biscuits from the plane. Neither of them ate much the day before. The food on the flights had a strange rubbery quality. Aaman shovelled most of his in – his adventures have made him an unfussy eater – but Saabira could not manage to swallow hers.

The thought of Aaman's adventures, as they call his time away from home – a term they both know is designed to make light of all he has been through – closes her throat, and she struggles a little for breath and her heart starts pounding.

'Are you alright?' Aaman looks up and is by her side, one arm holding their child, the other around her shoulders. His touch loosens her tension. 'Your cheeks are red – are you feeling alright?'

'Yes, I am fine,' she lies.

He passes Jay to her and her heartbeat returns to normal. She studies Aaman's face. Jay's long eyelashes come from his side. 'Like kohl,' she mutters, and Aaman kisses her briefly and continues to put on his shirt, but without looking away.

'So, groceries and then neighbours. But we take it slowly. We are tired from our travels and we have a lifetime.' He is grinning now, his voice full of energy.

When they arrived the day before she was so confused by the odd hours she had slept and the strange times she had eaten that she was not sure if she was hungry or tired or both or neither, and in her confusion she did not really take in much about the house.

It is what the English call a terraced house, one of a row, each butted up against the next. Outside, the light is a dull grey and the wind whips Saabira's scarf from around her shoulders as she surveys the house. It is crouched low to the ground and the weathered stone of which it is constructed gives it an air of austerity. The squat front door and small window downstairs and the two square windows

16

above have solid stone surrounds. The shallow-pitched slate roof is edged with a bright green moss. Each house has a narrow front garden behind a low stone wall. The lane is made of thousands of rounded blocks of stone.

'Cobbles,' Saabira whispers to herself, recalling that the Brontë sisters lived in a village with a cobbled street. Where has she read that?

She looks around. Being in England after Pakistan is like seeing a film at the cinema in Sialkot and then watching the cricket on a cousin's black-and-white in the village. The light is so dull it is as if the colour has been leeched out of everything. Except the trees, like the one behind the wall opposite their house, which glows greener than the deepest emeralds and towers over them, rustling in the wind. Above it the sky is mostly grey with only patches of blue, and it is cold. She pulls her shawl around her and her baby. She is not sure she will ever get used to the cold.

'Oh my goodness, what is that smell!' Aaman wrinkles his nose and looks around him.

'What is it like?' Saabira asks.

'Oh, it is disgusting! Worse than Jay's nappies, acrid like burnt oil smoke.'

Saabira is glad she cannot smell it, but she is aware that all smells are particulate and she draws her shawl over Jay's face and her own nose.

She turns first one way, then the other. The hairs on the back of her neck rise. It is as if someone is watching her.

The house adjoining theirs looks even darker than her own. The single downstairs window is black as if something is against it inside, and there is so much dirt on the outside that the glass does not shine. Where the door should be stands a wooden structure, like a closet, with double doors that are open just a crack and a tiny key in the lock. Near the bottom, in patches, the wood shines as if it was once polished, but near the top it is black and strips of veneer are peeling off. At home it would have gone white, bleached by the sun. Everything is so different. She shivers.

The feeling that she is being watched subsides but she pulls her daughter in closer all the same. The direction of the wind changes and Aaman takes his hand from over his nose and mouth, his brow smoothing. He had appeared almost in pain.

Up the street the cobbles only extend a little past the house with the strange front door. At the top of the road is a short terrace of houses – no more than two or three - built at right angles to the street. Opposite her own gate, a high wall runs from the corner of these houses back down the street. Halfway along, there is a break in the stone, with a grand pillar either side. The cobbles continue through this entrance, almost as if it is public, but somehow not. Further along, the wall ends and another terrace of houses leads the eye down the slight slope that ends at the bottom where the main road cuts across. Past this, over a rough stone wall, are the moors, as far as Saabira can see. Yesterday the bus dropped them in the next village, and it was a thirty-minute walk up this lonely, isolated road, with nothing but moors on either side. 'There's no bus stop in Little Lotherton,' the driver had said, eyeing their bags and frowning. 'But it'll not rain before you get there,' he had added.

Chapter 4

Cyril watches the couple leave through a crack in the door. The woman is wearing pale-grey trousers today, which are nipped in around her ankles with a stiff pink hem that touches the shiny gold of her sandals. She doesn't have a coat on; instead, she has wrapped a magnificent purple shawl around her.

'Like a queen would wear,' he whispers to Coco. Shifting his stance allows him to observe the man too. They turn and look back at the houses, his house, and then turn again, and the woman points to something in the tree. Cyril follows the line of her finger. Often there is an owl sitting in that tree but it is not there now.

Her sandals click as she walks down the cobbles and the man walks with a light step, at one point even hopping round to face her to say something, and walking backward for a step or two. They talk and laugh.

At the bottom of the lane they turn onto the road that leads to Greater Lotherton, and to Keighley and Bradford beyond that. It seems strange that such a small town should have such a grand name. Mrs Pringle from number two, who always says, 'Call me Christine, duck,' comes out to her gate, her shapeless grey jumper merging with the dark stonework of her house and a pink hairnet over her white hair in sharp contrast. A cigarette dangles from her thin colourless lip as she shouts, 'Spike!' She is holding a tin, banging it with a fork. A small black-and-white cat runs out from the old mill house opposite, its tail high, whiskers forward. Mrs Pringle turns and goes back inside, and the cat follows her. It's Saturday today, so it's quite likely that no one else will come or go now until later when Mr Dent from number seven comes out and knocks

19

on the door of number five, and the two of them will wander into the village to play darts in the Black Horse. If Cyril passes the Black Horse at the weekend he can see them inside the window, playing darts or sitting on one of the old wooden captain's chairs, ankles crossed on the stretcher of the table, resting the bottoms of their pint glasses on the curves of their bellies.

Coco nudges him.

'Alright, Coco. I have some scraps.' He leaves his hiding place and stumbles over his own doorstep into the cluttered room. The bulb has gone but it doesn't occur to Cyril to replace it. Bulbs cost money – almost as much as a tin of dog food – and use electricity. Besides, he only passes through the downstairs room when he goes in or out of the house, or when he feeds the dogs in the kitchen area by the back door. Even though, or perhaps because, he does not use this space, over the years the room has become filled with useful pieces of furniture. People are so wasteful; it is amazing what they throw away. The light from the single window at the front of the house is blocked by a bookcase that leans against it. In the gloom, with his back against the front door, Cyril can still recall how the room used to be. Archie's dining table on the left is still there, in amongst everything else. Now it has a child's crib perched on top. There is also a set of matching pottery jars with cork lids he found. The baby's bed is held in position by a corner cupboard that is jammed up next to it. Behind that, against the wall, is a bureau with a chest of drawers on top. This is where, if he can reach over, he puts the smaller things he has found: dummies, bottles for recycling, newspapers that he might look at one day. On the right of the room, balanced on the sofa, are the pieces of the collapsible bunk bed that someone at the bottom of the street threw away. He took it to use as firewood but it seemed such a waste to burn something that was still functional. Maybe, one day, someone will want it. Then there is a matching pair of tall wooden plant stands, one by the sofa and the other by the long-disused fireplace. He still considers that it was very sensible of him to leave a clear walkway from his front door through to the back door. The kitchen area is only differentiated from the sitting room area by the change in floor covering. Here the carpet ends abruptly and the lino begins.

As he passes the bureau, a rogue nail, one of many that are holding the back panel on, catches his sleeve. He yanks his arm away, and the nail tears at his shirt. He inspects the damage in the dim light. Coco whimpers.

'Alright, alright.' It feels sticky underfoot as he makes his way to the oven. The latch mechanism of the oven door does not work perfectly. It's an old model with legs, and the back ones are on the wooden floor while the front ones are elevated on several layers of lino that have been laid in the kitchen, tipping the whole cooker back at an odd angle. It might be this slant that has made the latch stick. He has not cooked in the oven for years, but it is a good place to keep scraps for the dogs. As he pulls it open, Coco's whimpering gets louder. Zaza jumps down from her place under the bunk bed wood on the sofa, and the new, as yet unnamed dog crawls out from behind the bureau. Blackie Boo slinks from somewhere near the front window. Multicoloured Teddy Tail's nails can be heard clicking as she trots down the wooden stairs from the bedroom. Gorilla Head, with her stripy markings, bounds out of the shadows formed by a stack of brooms, mops and shovels by the back door, and Mr Perfect, whose coat is nearly orange, comes out from the cupboard under the stairs. Blackie Boo hangs back. The new dog tries to befriend Coco but Coco snarls.

As Cyril turns his back to divide the scraps into the dishes, one of the mongrels snaps at another and there is a tussle in the shadows.

Ignoring the fight for dominance, Cyril opens the back door for light, just a crack, and jams it with a brick he keeps there for the purpose. When the dishes are full he turns to the dogs, who take their lead from Coco and sit. The new one hesitates, looks at the others, and copies them. Cyril puts a bowl in front of each. Coco, who is the best behaved, has to wait until last. Once she is served, Cyril gives the command and the dogs descend on their food.

Within seconds the dishes are clean, and he gathers them up and uses each in turn to scoop dog biscuits from a big sack behind the back door. When he has finished, he folds over the top of the sack and weights it with more bricks.

The dogs snort and chomp into their dishes, leaving Cyril free to go out into his overcrowded backyard.

Outside, his home-made cages are stacked one above the other, from back door to the moor gate. There are six in total. Between the end cage and the low stone wall that keeps the moorland plants from growing all the way up to his house is a stack of wooden boards. There are also wire trays from an old fridge, baking racks from an oven, bits of hardboard and a roll of chicken wire, as well as a saw and a bag of nails. He proudly surveys his handiwork. Last week he tacked a plastic rubble sack onto the end cages to protect them from the rain and the hard driving winds of the winter to come. The cardboard boxes he once put inside the cages as sleeping quarters have long since been eaten away. And a fox perhaps, or one of his dogs, has chewed at the edge of the roof of one of the top cages.

If he could just get the number of rabbits down a little, free up at least one cage, he could repair it and then move them all around and repair the next. But they breed so fast!

The rabbits watch him, noses twitching. Flop, the big rabbit with a cage to himself, lifts his head. That is about all he does these days; he's so fat he can hardly move. The rest of the rabbits are born and released so fast he no longer takes the time to name them.

He lifts the lid off the dustbin in which he stores the rabbit food. It is almost empty. Coco is scratching at the inside of the door. The dogs all need walking but he must feed the rabbits first. It is Saturday so he does not have to go to work today, leaving him plenty of time to walk them all.

As he sets out with Coco, Zaza, the new dog and Blackie Boo, the wind picks up and the heat that has been stored deep in the peat underneath the moors all summer gives off its warm and comforting smell. The lapwings sing out their lonely, haunting call and as the sun breaks through the cloud Cyril unzips his jacket. This takes him a moment or two, as the pull is long gone and the zipper head keeps getting stuck. The edge of the material against the zip, where his fingers have passed on so many occasions, is shiny with use.

He does not linger today and, on his second outing, this time with Teddy Tail, Gorilla Head and Mr Perfect, he follows the Pennine Way. This narrow trail of bare peat through the heather cuts across another, stonier path after some minutes of hiking. This is a good place to double back. There is a sign here, an upright stone that has carved into it *The Pennine Way. 286 miles. The spine of England.*

Ever since first reading this sign, Cyril has visualised the countryside with a spine. And why not? He has one, the dogs have one, why not the hills?

As he is about to turn for home Gorilla Head finds an area of bog and, with open mouth, tongue hanging and her tail wagging, she lies on her back and, wriggling, covers herself with mud.

'No!' Cyril makes a dash to grasp her collar, but she twists and leaps away, leaving him overbalanced with one soaking foot and a muddy jacket. On the way home he encourages her to roll in a stream, which gets off the worst of the mud.

At home there is no choice but to resort to taking a bath, not something he does very often. As the water drains away, sucking and swirling down the plughole, the colour of it is startling.

He pulls at the thread on the 's' of *Highroyds Hospital*, embroidered onto the pocket of his dressing gown, where the stitching has started to unravel. He could try to sew it, or maybe he could glue it. For now he wets his finger and presses the thread into the towelling loops of the material. With the curtains closed and the light outside fading, it is not easy to see if this has made a difference. Maybe it is not as bad as it seems. Laughter floats up from the street, and Cyril tentatively pulls back a corner of the curtain to peer out. The man and woman who have moved in next door are returning. The man no longer has a bounce in his step but he is still smiling. His rucksack sags, pulling on the shoulder straps, and he carries distorted shopping bags in each hand, things poking out of the top, ready to fall. The woman has a shopping bag in one hand, and the other supports her baby. The man puts his bags down outside the house next door and fishes in his pockets.

'Hurry up, Aaman, it is cold,' the woman says in English. In the half-light the cuffs at the bottom of her trousers appear black, but her sandals glint under the single street light, the one outside the gates of Mill House.

Their front door is opened to more laughter and then they quietly close it behind them and the street is silent. No wind moves the tree opposite, and the houses could be a drawing. The emptiness makes Cyril feel lonely and his mouth pulls down at the corners. Coco puts her nose into his hand but it brings him no comfort. Pushing her away, he throws himself onto the narrow bed, pulls the covers over his head and tries to block the world out. The present can be shut off, but it is the past that he struggles with.

Chapter 5

In the dark under the covers, he can picture the colour of her mustard tunic and then her pale-grey trousers with the pink cuffs; the intense purple shawl and all these colours spin in the pink of his eyelids. He rolls his head from side to side as the colours intensify. Mauves and soft reds, pale reds and rich warm yellows... Others come to join them – lime greens and oranges, swirling and spinning in his mind.

And he is back in the suitcase, his mother's clothes all around him, her aroma masking the less welcome smells in the room he is not supposed to go in.

He did not plan to go in there. It was the puppy's fault. All the previous day, the puppy whined and whimpered in the alley at the back of the flat.

'Why do they have to abandon it outside our back door?' his mother complained as she got ready to go out.

'What does "abandon" mean?'

'Left. No one wants it.' She smeared colour around her mouth, pressing the metal case hard against her lips, which meant the lipstick was nearly all used up. Her intent gaze in the mirror did not look like her: the pupils large and black, the white parts yellowish, and her cheek muscles tight, as if in a panic. Not all her face showed at once in the little mirror, which hung above the light switch by the front door. The cream wall was black with fingermarks around the light switch and below it.

'Someone's left it?'

He understood being left. He cried sometimes when he was left, and now she was putting her coat on.

There was a tear under the arm and the grey lining showed. She had bought it from the shop on the corner that smelt funny and was full of other people's clothes.

'Right, I'll only be half an hour, be good.' She always said she would only be half an hour.

Halfway round the kitchen clock was half an hour, but it always went all the way round at least once, and often more than that. Now the battery had run out and she hadn't put a new one in, and in a way this was better.

The puppy was crying again and he turned to see, and then the front door banged shut. The puppy seemed louder than before. All yesterday he had wanted to give it some scraps but his mother said they shouldn't encourage it.

'Encourage?' It was a long word, but she hadn't explained it, and the animal had cried all day and then, after she came home and he was in bed and she was in her room, it had cried all night.

And it cried again now, and he tried to ignore it. There was no radio in the house to drown the noise out, like they had in the chip shop. Nor was there anything to distract him. She had said that they would fashion a wheel for the one that snapped in two on his wooden car but that had never happened. His pot of Play Doh had long since dried out and his drawing book had been full for months; besides, his coloured pencils were down to nubs and they were hard to hold now. With nothing to do, the minutes passed slowly and the dog's pitiful whines seem to grow more anxious.

To his joy, his mother did return sooner than he expected, and he ran to her and hung on her coat, breathing in her scent, seeking her hand, his heart beating a little faster.

'Get off, I can hardly breathe. Look out, you'll squash the cake.'

'Cake? Really?' He backed off and looked to see what she was carrying. He trailed after her into the kitchen and watched, wide-eyed, as she pulled a rather battered box out of her shopping bag and cut a slice of cake.

'Right.' She did not take off her coat. 'I have to go out again. I might not be back for lunch so I suggest you save that right? Eat it later, then I'll bring something in for tea.' And she was gone, the door bouncing on the lock once as she pulled it shut behind her. Cyril's attention was on the cake. He would do as he was told and leave it for later, but perhaps just taste it, try a tiny bit of icing. He knew if tasted it there was a chance he would eat the lot. His stomach growled. He didn't realise you could eat first thing in the morning, or that these meals were called breakfast, until he went to the Home. As long as he didn't think of food he was usually alright till lunchtime. But the cake sitting on the side drew his attention to his stomach.

Then the dog started crying again and it distracted him. He opened the back door a crack and could see the puppy sitting on a piece of wet cardboard. It was raining, as usual. Having nothing to offer it, he closed the door again and the cake pulled him towards it. He felt his will weakening so he opened the back door again. The rain was cold on his skin, but not unpleasant. He squatted over the dog, and looked at it, but didn't stroke it yet.

'You hungry?' he asked the pup, who whimpered and shivered. 'You cold?' He tried to make his voice sound soothing. But the pup didn't answer. Its eyes, large and black and reflective, looked at him sadly. 'I'll take you inside, but just for a bit, to get dry,' he told it in a matter-of-fact voice. As he picked it up, with his hands around its little belly, it wriggled and squirmed and tried to lick his face, and he dropped it on the kitchen floor, unable to hold it any longer, where it immediately weed on the lino.

'Oh, you bad dog!' he scolded. 'What have you done?' And he bristled and grew silent, giving the dog withering looks and tutting and sucking through his teeth to show his displeasure. The cloth on the side of the sink was grey and crispy and smelt bad, but he didn't hesitate –

she could be back at any moment. But in the time it took him to clean up the mess, the puppy had pushed over the bin and was eating the paper that last night's fish and chips came wrapped in. It also ate a lump of mouldy bread and a rock-hard piece of cheese. Then it jumped up onto Cyril's bed, turned a circle three times and promptly went to sleep. Cyril stared at the new mess on the floor.

'What have you done now!' he shouted, recognising his mother's voice in his own mouth. 'You wicked, wicked dog,' he told the puppy, and he smacked it on its rump, making it whimper.

'Sorry!' he said then, as it cowered from him. 'Oh, sorry, sorry, little dog.' And he scooped the animal into his arms and kissed it and stroked it until it licked his face again. Its breath smelt of fish, but he didn't mind.

Mum might be back soon, though, so he tried to clear up the mess from the bin as best he could. Apart from some bits of onion that stuck to the lino, he thought he had done a good job. Then he sat next to the puppy, which was asleep again, and stroked its ears. The softness was thrilling, the warmth comforting. He put his head on the puppy and listened to its heart beating, and felt his own heartbeat with his hand and it was almost as if they became one. He wrapped his arms around his furry brother and squeezed, pushing his nose into its fur, then released the animal that was now awake and kissed it ever so gently on top of its head and wondered, if he asked nicely, whether Mum would let him keep it. Then he remembered the cake.

It was still there and he took the plate off the sink side and sat with it on his knees on the bed. It was misshapen but the icing looked buttery. He sniffed it and just as he did so the puppy woke up and in a moment it was on its feet, its mouth open, begging for a piece. What a dilemma! How he wanted to feed that pup, watch its tail wag, accept its heartfelt licks of appreciation. But his own stomach growled loudly and this was not bread or chips – this was cake!

Cyril stood, considering the choice he had to make, with the plate in one hand. The puppy jumped to reach the tempting morsel and then sat and started whining again.

'If you can't behave and ask nicely, you won't have any at all. Now sit still and wait your turn,' he told it, but the animal continued to whine.

'Be quiet, like a good boy,' he said, but the words had no effect on the animal.

'Just shut up and leave me alone!' he shouted, and stormed into his mother's room and shut the door. He hadn't meant to go in, but once he was there he found he didn't need to be angry at the puppy any more, and that felt better.

It was strange to be in her room with the door closed behind him. The air was stale and smelt of sweat that was not his mother's, and a strange salty smell. He curled his upper lip and screwed up his eyes, trying to identify the source of the stench. There was nothing in the room but her unmade bed, a waste bin full of tissues, and her suitcase, which lay open on the dull lino floor by the bed, an assortment of muddled clothes filling both halves. There was nowhere else to keep them.

He could not resist. Putting the plate on the bed he took a handful of her clothes and brought them to his face. It smelt completely of her, like when she had held him close when that woman had come round and asked lots of questions and wrote things in a book.

It was a big suitcase and before he knew it he was curled up in one half, nestling into a shiny blouse, with a flowery orange dress pulled over him. Silent tears squeezed from the corners of his eyes and he lay still, basking in her smell and the softness of her fabrics until his stomach growled and he remembered the cake. With excited energy he decided to sit in her clothes and eat his cake. What a treat that would be.

He carefully took the plate from the bed and then… Well, he wasn't sure what happened, but suddenly all the cake was gone, he had chocolate icing all around his mouth, and to his horror the icing had also dripped onto Mum's blouse and her orange flowery dress.

His mouth dropped open. She would know he had been in her room. Worse than that, he had ruined her clothes. His heart, banging against the inside of his chest, felt as if might explode, and his legs started twitching and he rocked himself backward and forward, staring down at the mess he had made. The remains of the cake caught in his throat and he thought he might cry. He had to do something.

Grabbing the spoilt items, he opened the door to the main room. The puppy was asleep again on his bed but he did not pay it any attention. He must try to fix what he had done before she came back.

The tap ran cold and he pushed the first stain into its stream. The blouse cleaned easily and his pulse slowed. Soon all traces of the chocolate were gone, and he began on the orange dress; it was heavy and the weight of it made it difficult to keep the sticky area under the tap. The chocolate did not want to be removed and he rubbed it with his finger, but this just spread the mess over a larger area.

For once he hoped that his mum would not come home soon.

He kept rubbing at the mark; it took a long time to get the dress reasonably clean, and when he had finished most of it was wet. Mum dried the clothes in a big machine at the launderette where it was warm and she pretended to be nice to him because they were out and other people could see. But he couldn't go there now, so he returned the blouse and dress to the suitcase and hoped they would dry by the time she wanted to change her clothes.

As he closed the bedroom door he could hear the key turn in the lock.

'Chips,' she said, handing him a half portion of cold greasy potatoes wrapped in newspaper. 'No money for fish.' She sat on his bed to take off her shoes and rub her feet. Then Cyril remembered the puppy in amongst his tangle of sheets. His mouth went dry and the chips stuck to his mouth like the cake had earlier.

'I'm knackered,' she said and walked towards her bedroom door pointing at her back. This was his cue to pull down the zip of her dress far enough so she could reach it by herself. The door closed and Cyril wondered if he could chase the puppy outside before she came out again. But he had not even processed his thoughts before he heard her scream, 'You dirty little bugger!' and her bedroom door flew open. She had her orange dress in her hand. He frowned. Food spills were usually 'messy', not 'dirty'.

The puppy woke up at the noise and whined. The movement distracted her and she screamed again.

'What the heck? Ahh, no! I don't know if that's better or worse. Have you let that little bugger in while I've been out?'

Cyril's mouth hung open and he struggled to make sense of what she was saying. In two strides she was across the room, grasping the puppy by the back of its neck. It whined and wriggled as she threw it out of the front door into the road, shouting after it, 'Out! You pissy little runt!' She slammed the door shut to the sound of screeching brakes outside in the road. The look she gave Cyril made him step backward and his arms lost strength, his cold chips sliding from the newspaper wrapping to the floor.

She didn't come out of her room for the rest of that evening, and as he got hungry he collected the chips off the floor, and then curled up in the bottom of the wardrobe to go to sleep.

31

He is grateful that sleep takes him now as his neighbours quieten on the other side of the wall and are no longer a distraction.

He is not woken by Zaza licking his face the next morning, as he usually is. His legs are pinned down as normal by Coco, but what has roused him is the sound of laughter through the walls from next door.

It disturbs him but entices at the same time. He wants to bang on the wall and shout at them to stop and but he wants to listen too, laugh with them. The merry sounds grow fainter and move downstairs. Cyril throws on his dressing gown and follows. In the darkness of his sitting room he pushes aside a folding table, a wooden chair with a missing leg and an old suitcase with no handle, to clear an area of the adjoining wall. He finds a glass in the kitchen and puts it against the wall, just as he once saw in a film he watched with Matron Jan.

He cannot make out the words, but every sentence is interspersed with the tinkle of her laugh and the chortle of his agreement.

Normally on Sundays he spends the day walking on the moors – basking in the sun in the summer, ploughing through the snow in the winter, pulling his hood up when it rains or his scarf around his ears against the wind. No matter what the weather out on the moors, he is free, away from people, just him and the dogs and the wonder and power of nature, and the world seems beautiful.

But today he does not feel like striding over the moors and it is only the insistence of the hounds that makes him pull on his jacket. Today he is not out for long, and as soon as he is back inside he takes up his vigil with his ear against the glass.

Chapter 6

The house seems very empty after Aaman has left for work, and it crosses Saabira's mind that hers is arguably the harder job. He will have so much to talk about with his boss, his distant cousin Tariq whom he hasn't seen since they were boys. Tariq's mother, whom Aaman addresses as 'Auntie', has given him many photos of new nephews and nieces Tariq hasn't yet seen. Last night she and Aaman tried to remember his last visit to Pakistan, but neither of them could.

Also, Aaman will make friends with all his colleagues. How can he fail when he will be working with them every day? But she must create a whole new life from nothing.

It is a thought that brings the village near Sialkot to mind and with it all the people she has left behind. Saabira scrapes baby food from around Jay's mouth with a plastic spoon. Jay has almost eaten the whole pot. She looks at the label on the jar. The baby on the label has smooth blonde hair and blue eyes, and it is smiling, with puffed-up, overly rosy cheeks. Saabira smiles.

Yesterday she bought many jars of baby food in a shop on a corner in the next village, Greather Lotherton. Once she is more settled she will make her own food for Jay but for the moment it makes life so much easier.

The walk to the next village was very pleasant yesterday, in the sunshine. Aaman carried Jay, laughing and joking all the way, and teased Saabira gently. The shop was laid out with shelf after shelf of food in packages, and a small and rather sad-looking selection of fruits and vegetables. The boy behind the counter was from Pakistan, but he did not speak Urdu, or any language

33

other than English, and he kept apologising for the small selection he had to offer.

'But I will expand into next door next year!' His accent was strange. It was a relief to Saabira when his father came out from the back of the shop and greeted them in Urdu. He explained that his grandson's accent was Yorkshire and they spoke about Pakistan for a long time.

Then Saabira inspected the shelves full of jars and packets: jars of ready-made curry, packets of ready-made chapattis, and rice in brightly coloured cardboard boxes, with a photograph of a dark-skinned man smiling out at her, who was neither Pakistani nor Indian.

'Nine'y seconds tha',' the grandson said with a smile as she picked up a box of rice to inspect it more closely. 'Bung i' int' microwave, nine'y seconds 'n' boom! Ya dun.'

Saabira doubted herself, listening to the boy. After four years at university, and with a string of letters after her name, she still could not understand a word this young man was talking about.

Jay pushes aside the last spoonful of food and takes to playing with a toy Aaman bought her in the corner shop. It is a ring of fabric, and makes a crinkling sound if you squeeze one side and squeaks if you grab the other. Jay bites on one side and squeezes the other, and manages to produce both sounds at once.

It's too early to start cooking and she has already swept the floor, made the bed and washed yesterday's clothes, and hung them on the rack over the Aga, which is what the big metal stove is called. She looks up at the clock, calculating how many hours Aaman has left at work. There are no eggs to collect, no buffalo to feed, no vegetable plot to tend, and no neighbours to pass the time with. Perhaps she should introduce herself to the neighbours here. That would be the real start to her new life.

Jay is fighting sleep but Saabira wraps a shawl around her; her long eyelashes flutter and her face takes rest. With the baby asleep this would be a good time to find out who is living either side of them.

With Jay nestled in the crook of her arm Saabira pulls her heavy shawl over them both.

The house below theirs has a grey front door and the front is freshly painted a bright white. Containers of flowers sit on the lower windowsill and there is a tree in a wooden bucket either side of the gate. These details make it look more inviting than any of the other houses in the street.

The metal knocker echoes a little inside but as she waits there is no sound of footfall. Perhaps they are at work.

The house on the other side of hers is darker than all the rest, the windows dull, with no signs of life, and her heart sinks a little. Saabira examines the makeshift wooden porch and wonders where or how to knock. Should she open this outer door and tap on the inner one, or should she rap with her nails on the thin wood veneer?

Coco whimpers at the tapping, which brings Zaza out of her hiding place, curious. The two dogs huddle around Cyril's legs. The new, as yet unnamed dog also ventures towards them. Zaza growls, and the nameless dog's back legs lower. Its head drops and it crawls the remaining short distance to join them with its belly on the floor in total submission.

'Hello,' a voice calls through the front door. 'My name is Saabira. My husband, Aaman, and I have taken the house next door. I just wanted to introduce myself.'

She is so close. The thin plywood door provides only the illusion of a barrier. He listens. Her breathing is slow and controlled. Under the shawl she wears a long piece of material that covers her head and falls nearly to her knees at one side. The other end is loosely thrown over her shoulder. This thin scarf has a golden binding to its edge, stiffer than the silky purple material. What little sun there is causes it to shine, a halo, the brightness reflecting off her dark-peach skin. The glow of her fine features is at odds with the grey sky behind. The clouds shape-shift behind her and become frills and ruffles, only adding to her beauty.

Cyril's own breath is caught in his throat, and even swallowing does not release it. The ever sensitive Coco gives him a nudge with her wet nose, and his hand curls around her cheek and under her throat, her pulse against his fingertips. Or is it his own tempo? His heart is pounding so strongly he can feel the criss-cross of muscles expanding, stretching beyond their normal confines, threatening to either explode or stop as they contract into a knot.

'Hello?' Her voice rings like music, the middle of the word dipping, the end rising to a higher pitch, and the melody takes on colours that melt everything around him. He can feel the present receding, and the magic coming. If only she could come with him.

The sound of wheels squealing against the cobbles turns Saabira's head away from the door. A blue car grinds to a sudden halt and a woman fusses with a bag and a mobile phone, struggling to free herself as she clambers out. Her arm catches in the seat belt and her long, navy-blue, sagging cardigan flaps open. Leaving the door partly open, the seat belt hanging out, she straightens up and looks Saabira squarely in the face.

'He in?' The woman demands.

'I am sorry. To whom are you referring?' Saabira straightens her scarf, looping it tidily over her head.

'Him. Septic Cyril.' She points at the wardrobe. 'I'm from Health and Safety. It can't go on. Him and his animals, people complaining. God, how can you stand so close? Can you not smell him? Mind you, p'raps it smells much the same where you come from.'

'I beg your pardon?' Saabira wonders if she has misheard, or misunderstood.

The woman looks quickly at her phone before dropping it in her bag. 'So, is he in or not?' She doesn't bother to look Saabira in the face as she speaks.

Glancing back at the wardrobe door, Saabira thinks she sees movement inside, the glistening of an eye passing the crack in the door. The wind changes direction again.

'Oh my God, the stink!' The woman by the blue car pulls the sleeve of her cardigan over the end of her hand and stuffs it against her nose.

'Make her go away.' The words whisper through the breeze.

Saabira leans ever so slightly towards the keyhole of the wardrobe door.

'Make her go away,' the voice hisses again.

'Look, I don't know who you are but I'm Dawn Todman, Health and Safety. I've a' order here as we've been given to understand that he has a lot of rabbits, again, and if he has they've got to go, again, and we need to limit the number of dogs.' The woman, still with her sleeve over her nose, steps forward, holding out a bunch of papers towards Saabira.

'He is out,' Saabira says, making eye contact and keeping a steady gaze.

'Oh.' The woman straightens her cardigan and begins to get back into the car. At the last moment, and with renewed energy, she pushes the bundle of papers at Saabira.

'Give 'im these. Have 'im read 'em. He'll have to get rid o' all them poor animals.' She thrusts the papers at Saabira, whilst scanning the lane as if planning her exit.

'No.' Saabira uses neither strength nor aggression in her voice.

'What? Did you not understand me?'

37

'I understood and I said no.' She wonders if she can hear a quiet chuckle coming from the crack between the doors.

'Listen luv, I have authority here. I'm from Health and Safety. He needs to get rid of them animals and these papers make it so he has to. You don't want to live next to that stink. Do you?' The woman sighs out her words as if it is all too much effort. 'So you give them to him, right?' She pushes the papers at Saabira again, but without her previous conviction.

This is not Saabira's country, and she is unsure whether she should take the papers or not. Her instinct is to defy this woman who has insulted her and is now making demands as if she were a Dalit.

'You are police?' Saabira asks.

'No, I work for the government. Health.' Dawn says this word slowly, and a bit too loud. 'And. Safety. Do you understand?' She lowers her chin, staring, head to one side.

'I do not believe you have authority over me, so I give no one papers.' This time she clearly hears first a gasp and then a very small chuckle from the wardrobe porch behind her.

'Oh, for God's sake.' The woman raises and drops her arms, the papers flapping against her knees as her hands come to rest. 'It there a letterbox in that thing?'

Saabria steps to one side so the woman can see that there is no place to leave her paperwork.

'Anyway, if he's out then what're you doing standing there?' One of the woman's hands rests on her hip, and the other scrapes back through her lank blonde hair to show dark roots and a white scalp. She wears no jewellery.

This time it feels it might be safer not to answer at all: Saabira is not sure she can remain polite. The woman seems tired with the whole business and she returns to her

38

car, and backs it hesitantly down the cobbled street, narrowly missing a car parked at the bottom.

'Thank you.'

The voice behind her makes Saabira jump. The wardrobe doors are open an inch and a nose and one eye are visible.

'Hello.' She smiles the word.

Chapter 7

She called herself Saabira, and her voice was so soft he almost felt he could open the door to her. But then Coco, Zaza and Sabi – yes, Sabi, that's a good name for the new dog – would get out. The dog catchers might come. Sabi's paw is still not healed and Zaza is still thin, and they would not be able to run fast enough to get away. Sweet, trusting Coco would not even run. Better to keep the door closed.

'Hello,' Cyril replies cautiously.

'What is your name?' She sounds out every consonant as she talks, but somehow her voice still flows softly.

'Cyril.'

'Cyril. I am Saabira. Did you hear what the woman said who was here?'

'Never useful, never a plate of food, or a bag of wood.' He sounds out every syllable himself, just as she did, but his voice is not gentle. Every consonant is spat out. He is sick of people interfering in his life under the pretence of doing good or being helpful.

The bulge under Saabira's shawl moves and a breathy whine follows.

'Cyril, I am sorry, but it is her feeding time. I must go now but perhaps we can talk some other time.' She turns to leave but then stops and adds, 'It is very nice to meet you.'

With a flash of her purple shawl beyond the gap she is gone. Cyril closes the doors up tight.

'Welcome home, my husband,' Saabira greets Aaman. After her brief talk with her neighbour and Jay's

40

feed, the afternoon seemed long. She cooked, and discovered the hot and cold spots in the stove, but there was little else to do. She swept the floor twice, and kept both the fire and the stove stoked. She considered moving the table and chairs to one side of the room to make space on the floor for rugs and cushions so it would feel more like home. But the stone flags were too cold to sit on and, besides, it was perhaps better to use the table so Jay would grow up with it as if it were normal. So, leaving the furniture be, she went upstairs to make the bed, adding all the blankets she could find, and finally she cleaned the windows inside and out – but it seemed it was the clouds that were dirty and not the glass, and there was no more light to be let in. Late in the afternoon, Jay became fractious and she spent an hour rocking and cooing to no avail. It was only when Saabira found some glass beads in a jar in one of the kitchen cupboards and rolled them across the floor that her precious daughter managed to put aside her bad mood; she began to laugh and squeal until her good humour was fully restored, and exhaustion set in just in time for Aaman's return.

'How are my two princesses?' Aaman first kisses the baby who is now asleep in her mother's arms and then he kisses Saabira, gazing into her eyes. It is the same gaze he had for her when they first met, the same gaze she remembers when he returned from his life -changing adventures and the guilt sweeps over her again and she looks away.

'Please do not look away, Saabira. You must not keep condemning yourself. I chose to go,' he answers her.

'You went to please me, because I suggested it.' Saabira clasps her hands and bites her lips as she repeats her time-worn mantra, looking out into the darkening road.

'But, my moon and stars, we have been through this all before. That time has passed. Let us live in the now. Please forgive yourself.' He kisses her again and his

41

stomach rumbles so loudly that they pull away from each other laughing. Saabira passes Jay over so she can finish making the roti. She made the dough half an hour ago and it has risen but as she still cannot find a *chakla* in the otherwise well-equipped kitchen she has made do with a flat, circular marble plate with the word *cheese* printed in a semicircle around the edge. Also, the only rolling pin is very fat. Pulling off a piece of the dough, rolling it in the palm of her hand, she is transported to hotter climates and everything is familiar and easy, and she looks over to Aaman and smiles. She has kneaded the dough well and the rotis puff into balloons as they cook. They sit to eat together.

'You've had no problem with the stove, then?' Aaman asks as he scoops up the curry with his roti.

'Tomorrow I will practise with a couple of dishes. If I make too much I thought it would be a nice gesture to give it to the man next door. I believe he has no one to cook for him.'

'The one with a wardrobe for a porch?' Amman pours water into her glass and then fills his own.

'Ah, it is a wardrobe is it? Yes, him. I think he is alone.'

'I think it is his house that smells so badly.' Aaman's mouth distorts as if to accentuate how unpleasant the smell is.

'Sometimes I am glad I am spared that problem!' Saabira laughs. Most of the time she forgets that has no sense of smell. Her mother told her when she was very small that smells are similar to tastes, but experienced though the nose. She can imagine how things smell if she looks at them – flowers sweet like sugar, stale dung from the animals like burnt oil, mint just like it tastes – and she does not feel she is missing anything. Occasionally it feels like a blessing. Bad smells sound awful and she has no desire to experience them, and from people's reactions it is clear that Cyril's house smells very bad indeed.

'I think it would be a very fine gesture to make the time to feed our new neighbour,' Aaman says, a piece of roti curled around a curried potato, poised in front of his lips. Their eyes meet and she knows they are both thinking about the same thing.

Back in the village outside Sialkot, when the old man next door, Hanfi, lost his wife, he retreated inside his house and did not come out. On the occasions that the villagers saw him he kept away from them. He had nothing to say now and he became a recluse. As the days turned into months he grew thin, and with no sisters or aunts to cook for him and his daughters and daughters-in-law away in the cities his adobe stove remained cold. Even when Saabira, Aaman's mother and other women of the village left food for him he did not eat it. Not for a long time. But she persisted, taking a dish every day, collecting the food from the day before, until finally one day the dish was empty. Not long after that, Hanfi was sitting at their table. Now he is part of the family.

Aaman's look changes, as if he is proud of her, and Saabira feels her cheeks flush.

'It would be a good way to get to know him,' Saabira says.

'What about the people on the other side, have you met them yet?'

'No, I don't think they are there. They didn't leave before or after you this morning and I have not seen anyone return. How are your cousin Tariq and your colleagues at work?'

'Ah yes, they are very nice people! I feel very lucky to have been chosen for this!'

'It is not luck, Aaman – you are family and a very good programmer and you work very hard.'

'Even so...' He smiles. But Saabira catches a sadness in his voice, and she guesses from the look on his face that he is thinking of the last time he was so far from home.

Chapter 8

After they have eaten, Aaman picks up Jay, who is awake now, and rocks her in his arms, making gentle noises to soothe her.

'Is she wet?' Aaman feels and shakes his head. 'When I was knocking on Cyril's door a woman came up the street in her car. Cyril didn't open the door, and he wanted her to go away. She said something about too many dogs and rabbits. She said that they were a problem. She was most brisk and tried to order me as if I was her servant.'

'A problem, the dogs and the rabbits?' Aaman replies. 'Shall I make some tea?'

Saabira takes the baby and pulls her scarf over her. 'If rabbits and dogs are a problem can you imagine what they would say if we had our buffalo here?' Saabira says, head bent, watching the looks of bliss on her baby's face. Jay's features are small but she looks so much like Aaman.

How comforting it would be to go out to tend to the buffalo right now, shovelling the mess into a bucket, heaping the straw and filling the water pan in the blazing sun, the animals snorting their sweet stench, their tails whipping at flies. If she could open the back door to something so familiar, part of her old routine, it would feel very grounding. The heat would be a blessing. She shivers.

Why would the woman in the blue car want to rid her neighbour of his animals? Clearly there must be a horrible smell coming from his house, but smells are not from animals, her mother has told her so often, but are a result of not cleaning. Because of this, she knows, she has always been overly fastidious. With no sense of smell it is her only option.

'May be he just doesn't clean his house well enough.'

'Who?' Aaman looks sleepy.

'Cyril.'

She will definitely cook enough to feed Cyril as well tomorrow. Cooking for just her and Aaman is very strange anyway, her big pans all exchanged for little ones. Back home Aaman's mother will be the cook again, preparing the food for her husband, their aging parents, an unmarried auntie, two cousins and Hanfi, living all on his own next door.

'I am so tired.' Aaman rubs his stomach and Saabira puts Jay, who is now fast asleep, down on the corner of the sofa, surrounding her with cushions for comfort and safety. 'I have found it is very difficult to see her there whilst I cook.' She takes the dirty dishes to the sink.

No sooner has she said this than Aaman, despite his fatigue, is up off his chair and moving the sofa around. The wheels twist in the rug so he lifts one end, moving it around carefully so as not to wake his daughter. Its back is now towards the front door and Saabira will be able to see Jay when she is cooking or washing up.

After the dishes are done, in silent mutual agreement they make their way up the stairs, and, by the time Jay is settled, Aaman is asleep. For a few minutes Saabira sits and listens to her family's breathing and she promises herself for a thousandth time that she and Aaman will never be separated again.

The next morning Aaman is banking up the stove as Saabira comes down from what was a very deep and peaceful sleep. The house is surprisingly warm. Through the small window at the front of the house large grey clouds are visible, moving swiftly, banked high in big puffs that change shape as she watches. It is very dramatic, exciting. A brief gap allows the sharp sun to light the grey stone wall opposite and paint the leaves of the tree a brilliant emerald. But all the heat is that which is radiating from the Aga.

'Good morning, my love.' Aaman leaves the stove and attends her, placing kisses on her cheeks. He looks into her eyes and she can see all his love glowing strongly for her there. The promises in their depths tell her that he will do everything and anything to make her happy. It thrills her.

But this does not dilute the guilt that is still there, creating a barrier between them. Because the truth is her demands of him could have killed him. He might never have come back. How could she have ever suggested he make such a journey, such a sacrifice?

Saabira briefly glances out at the theatrical sky. It is such an opportunity to be here, this job of Aaman's, the chance Jay has to grow up and be schooled here, but she wonders if coming to England so soon after Aaman returned to Pakistan was such a good idea. It is so far from home.

Aaman has his coat on and is ready to leave for his second day but he pauses and, taking a box of matches from the kitchen table, lights the open fire which roars brightly and flickers colours onto the padded sofa. The flames break her introversion.

'I hope you have a good day.' Saabira crosses the room to take his scarf from the hook by the back door and returns to Aaman to put it around his neck.

'I hope we both do.' He strokes her cheek. 'My dream is that we find our lives here so fulfilling that we do not miss home. Then Jay will grow up speaking English with no accent and she will be highly educated.' Aaman releases his arms from around her. 'The world will be at her feet. The choices she will have we cannot imagine!' He smooths her hair, and runs his hands over her shoulders and down her arms until he is holding her hands.

Aaman was so proud of her when she suggested that they call their daughter Juliet. She might not have met her

46

daughter's namesake but that woman saved Aaman on his 'adventure'. Calling her daughter after this person was the very least reverence that was due. It was also a way to remind herself every day, by using Juliet's name, of the situation she had pushed Aaman into: a reminder of all she owes him. She is not sure who first shortened it to Jay. It might have been Aaman's mother. It might have been herself on one of the days when it all became too much.

He is staring at her, a look of concern.

'You look very smart in your coat.' She releases his hands and smooths the lapels of the winter overcoat he bought in his lunch break yesterday. 'Very English,' she adds. Aaman picks up his umbrella and tucks it under his arm, and parades stiffly around the room. She laughs and Aaman looks pleased. 'Do you know what time you will be home tonight?' Her laughter fades. He has the excitement of the job, a role to play, like-minded people to talk to. She will be sitting here alone, no auntie in the next house, no cousins opposite her. Her family are half a world away. What will they be doing right now? Coming in after a morning of work, chatting and drinking tea in the shade to avoid the direct sun.

'Do not be sad, Saabira. I will come home as soon as I can. I do not know the bus times yet, but I am sure as the week goes on both our lives will become smoother.' He puts the umbrella by the door so he does not forget it and returns to her. 'We must think of it as an adventure. We may not have family here but we will make new friends. There are more people out there like Juliet, who helped me.' And he kisses her with such tenderness that it brings tears to her eyes. As he pulls away she covers her face with her silk shawl and he smiles as if she were teasing him, and all the suffering of their lives dissolves and there is only their love.

It is his love for her that makes her feel strong, and in that moment she decides all over again that she will do everything in her power to help Aaman in this new country

47

and maybe, just maybe, she will even find a role for herself. Motherhood is paramount now, but what an intellectually rich world England is. It is all there waiting for her, for when she feels ready to spread her wings outside of the home. She has even heard that there is no discrimination here, that she would have a chance equal to a man's if she decided to take a job.

But for now, she will cook her love his favourite meals, make this house into a home and take good care of Jay. She waves from the doorstep and he walks down the road to the bus stop, his umbrella up.

Chapter 9

The cages in the backyard are all full again, the fluffy bright-eyed rabbits jostling for space. He should release a lot of them before the smaller ones' bellies begin to bulge and he is into a new cycle of pregnant females.

He picks one of the rabbits from its cage on the top row and feels its belly. 'Okay, you can go, you're big enough and strong enough now, and' – he feels another rabbit's soft white underfur – 'you're not pregnant, so go!' He lowers the startled creatures over the garden wall. Their paws scrabble in mid-air, but after Cyril has let them go they just sit there, startled by the vastness of no cage, until first one and then the other takes one small hop, and then they run in different directions, at full pelt, disappearing into the bracken. He watches the dark spaces in the undergrowth where they disappeared. He won't see them again.

'Okay. It's okay,' He tells himself. 'They are happy and well and free. So who else can go? You, and you.' He takes two more and closes the door of the hutch with his knee. As he releases them he keeps one eye on the billowing, fast-moving grey clouds that roll over the heather-covered landscape, a blanket of softness. But he is not looking at the weather. Black circling dots can arrive at any time. The kestrels haunt the area, looking for dinner. A small rabbit would be easy prey. The first rabbit he found had been mauled by their talons but was still alive. It was a kindness to take it in and care for it. The second one came from a trap, and was in a much worse state. The two shared one cage in his backyard. But then, with no warning, one of them was full in her belly before the wounds were even healed. The other must have been a daddy rabbit so he let him go. He cared for the mummy until the babies came, all thirteen of them, and he could not let her go whilst she was still feeding her young. Then another wounded rabbit came his way, looking like a dog had played with it. So he took that in and cared for it too, tended its wounds with warm water and cotton wool; he didn't think that one would recover, and despite his care it didn't. But in the meantime the first rabbit babies had grown and he had lost track of who was who, and now some of them were pregnant. These he kept back to nurse in safety whilst he released others, but there always seemed to be more pregnant females and now there is just round after round of trying to release the babies after they are strong enough but before they are pregnant.

'You can go, and you.' He releases two more. Coco comes out to see what he is doing, followed by Sabi, who makes a dart at one of the cages.

'No, Sabi, they're not for eating.' He smacks at the dog's nose, intentionally missing. 'Zaza,' he calls, and the wiry-haired hound snakes around the furniture to slink out of the back door. 'It's okay, Zaza, you come here. Go next to the cages – there, sit. Now Sabi will keep her distance.'

A black dog with short legs and a big body pokes its nose out of the back door, but on seeing the other dogs near Cyril it does what it always does – shuffles backward and disappears. 'Come on, Blackie Boo,' he calls, but he knows the dog will not come. He releases more of the rabbits and watches them tear off across the moors. He wrinkles his nose and pushes his glasses up with one finger.

'How are you doing, Flop?' He addresses a big grey rabbit that takes up most of the lower cage nearest to the back door. He has had Flop the longest now, and somehow this rabbit has become a favourite. Flop eats any leftovers that the dogs do not want. Its eyes are sunk into puffy cheeks, ears slick against its back. If it was not for the twitching nose Cyril would wonder if it was still alive, it moves so little; but then Flop is very greedy and very fat. 'Whole cage to yourself. You live like a king.' But the dull-eyed creature makes no movement; just its whiskers shiver with the twitching of its nose.

Zaza barks and this starts Coco off. Sabi growls and inside he can see all the other dogs shifting, moving, burying themselves deeper between furniture or coming forward growling, ready to fight.

'What is it?' he asks Coco. But the dog relaxes and the others follow her lead. 'Did you hear something, girl?' he asks, but she has settled down again. Cyril considers taking the few rabbits left in the top cage nearest the back gate and putting them in with Flop. He doesn't know how Flop will react but it will give him a chance to repair and clean the cage. The baking tray that makes up the back of it is coming away from one of the wooden sides.

Coco stands, nose to the moors, alert again.

'Hello,' comes a voice.

He recognises her from yesterday. In a panic he tries to push all the dogs back inside, close up the rabbit cages, go indoors before she comes any closer.

'Hello.' She steps past the tall stack of cages, on the moor path from the direction of her own backyard. 'I am Saabira. We met yesterday?'

Coco is motionless; the other dogs sink and retreat. The scuffling in the cages stops. Nothing moves besides the wind from the moor lifting and dropping the bits of ragged tar paper that cover the tops of the rabbit hutches.

Cyril turns on one foot, ready to run, but he is mesmerised. Today she is wearing mustard-coloured trousers and scarf and a green tunic top. There are sequins sewn into the hem of her trouser legs and along the scarf's edge. They twinkle at him and he wants to touch them.

'I have brought you something. I hope you do not mind. I was making experiments with the stove and now I have too much food.'

From a dish in her hands comes the most inviting smell as she lifts a corner of the silver foil. He is not going to be able to resist but he cannot invite her in.

Chapter 10

'I – er...' he begins, but words elude him. The sequins on her scarf are shining so brightly they are like captured stars, blindingly brilliant like the sun must be above the clouds, where everything is golden. He closes his eyes – the light filling his vision, the sequins expanding their prism – and tumbles along the colours and floats along paths of multicoloured rivers that run between glistening clouds and mists of gold and silver and bronze. The air begins to fill with hums and murmurs, with the sounds of wonderful tunes that are too beautiful for most people's ears, but he can hear them, and it is as if he is dancing, spinning, whirling, until he is dizzy, until the colours in his mind dissolve and he dissolves and fragments of him are in the clouds and the rivers of colour and even in the songs.

'Cyril?' Saabira's voice is musical, like the songs. She does not enter his gate. He blinks a few times, recognises where he is, braces his arm across the back door, to present a barrier. She takes a step back. 'Cyril?' she repeats, a look of concern on her face. She retracts the arm that was holding out the food towards him.

'What?' he manages as the clouds of colour beneath his feet turn back to rabbit and dog faeces.

'Perhaps if I put the dishes on the little table outside, at the back of my house, where there is a bit more room, you can come if you feel hungry?'

He looks at his hands, stained and smeared with dirt.

'The dishes can just wait for you,' she says and with these words she turns to leave. Cyril stares after her, relieved, but also disappointed that she is gone. He checks the latches on the cages and herds the dogs back inside.

53

His stomach grumbles with hunger. He has an open tin of beans somewhere in the kitchen, from yesterday.

But as he steps inside and begins to close the door, the smells of her cooking drift to him again.

'Any time!' she calls, unseen, and the sound of her own door shutting eases the tension out of his shoulders. The smells are beckoning, like the sound of her voice. He looks at his hands and with sudden and exciting spontaneity he runs them under the kitchen tap, wipes them down his tank top and hurries out to the source of the temptation.

Her backyard has nothing in it besides a table and chairs, and it seems startlingly large and very tidy and clean. Her back door is closed. There is no sign of her but on the smooth wooden table is laid one plate and a steel bowl of something that smells amazing, and next to it in a glass dish there are what appear to be a stack of pancakes, neatly folded.

He waits at the boundary between the houses for her to come out, like a mouse sniffing the cheese in a trap, and with every minute that passes the aromas pull him a step closer. He hovers, touching the very edge of the table, wondering if he can take the plates back to his house, eat sitting on his bed. But there is too much to carry and it is laid out so beautifully. A shiny ceramic plate, a knife and fork, a sparkling glass of water and a jug containing more. The food itself steams in separate dishes, the aroma of spices and herbs drifting to him until he can no longer stand it, so he sits with a heavy thump, grabs the fork and eats straight from the stainless steel dish.

The flavours cause his eyes to roll back in his head. He never imagined that food could taste so good. His hunger pushes him to fork more into his mouth than he can manage but he also wants to savour, relish each morsel. It takes great effort to slow down. His picks up the glass dish and sniffs the pancakes. They are warm but they have no smell. Tearing a tiny piece off, he samples the unknown and is pleasantly delighted to find it is like bread, but delicately flavoured. Without unfolding the pancake-bread he tears off a hunk and gnaws on it between forkfuls of the mixture from the stainless steel bowl.

Both dishes are nearly finished when he realises his plate is still clean. She will think him an animal for not using it. With a quick glance at the back of her house he scrapes what little there is left of the flavoursome food onto the plate and wipes it round with the remains of the pancake before stuffing the flavoured bread into his mouth. If he leaves his knife and fork on the plate as well, as he has been taught, the two together, neatly, she will think he used everything in the correct way, that he has manners.

His stomach groans against his trousers. Leaning back, he undoes the top button. The braces beneath his tank top will keep them from falling down.

From the window halfway up the stairs to the second floor, Saabira can just about see into the backyard. Cyril's glasses have fallen almost down to the end of his nose as he eats, but she feels certain that she has done the right thing. He was obviously hungry, and she will leave him undisturbed to eat. He seems to be a shy man, and a little lonely, certainly used to being left on his own. If she pushes her company on him he will retreat; that is something of which she feels sure. She cannot afford that. It is her job to make friends with the neighbours, become part of the community which they have chosen to live in, and which, hopefully, Jay will grow up in and become one with. This is the least she can do for Aaman.

If she stands on tiptoes she can see the tabletop, and the dishes that are almost empty. She sees him pouring what is left onto his unused plate and wonders why. It is almost as if he is dirtying the plate for no reason. She only gave him the plate because that is the custom here. With a shiver she continues downstairs, wrapping her Kashmir shawl more tightly around her. By the time she has checked on Jay and then opened the back door, Cyril is gone.

'A lonely man,' she whispers to herself. 'Maybe he is in mourning.' She thinks of Hanfi.

She dabs at the corners of her eyes with her shawl and picks up the stainless steel bowl, nodding her head in satisfaction. The dishes of food have not a morsel left on them.

Chapter 11

Cyril strides across the moors, watching the grey clouds twist and turn in billowing shapes, threatening to disgorge their contents at any moment. But he has seen such dramatic displays before. It will rain, there is no doubt about that, but he probably has a couple of hours to get home, maybe longer.

Coco runs past, followed by Sabi. They have become inseparable now, and Sabi's paw is all healed and Zaza is no longer thin. Loyal Zaza stays just a few paces behind him. Blackie Boo, the black dog with short legs, named on account of her colour and her fear of – well, everything, makes her own way, sometimes close, sometimes not to be seen at all. The others he has left at home.

The sky might be grey but there is a whiteness to the light that reveals the storm to come. The breeze is picking up and he has turned up the collar of his tweed jacket. The moths have been at it again and there are more holes around the shoulder. He pulls his flat cap down over the side of his face against the prevailing wind. The moors smell of heather and ozone, wet earth and, occasionally, woodsmoke drifting up from the village.

He has been right over the tops this morning and could see Heckman-on-Thirstle in the distance. On his way back, where the cairn marks the way, he found a rucksack. It wasn't big, and one of the fasteners was missing and another was broken, but there were no holes in it. He carried it over one shoulder and put the other things he'd picked up inside it: a hanky with the initial 'J' embroidered in one corner, and a comb with no teeth missing. He discovered them trodden into a puddle by the triangulation station. 'Triangulation station.' He rolls his tongue over the words. 'The highest point, marked with a small pillar.' Archie taught him that. 'Triangulation station,' he says again.

He also found a blunt pencil and a shoe. He quite often finds single shoes, usually trainers, and it always worries him to picture the owner hopping home with only one foot protected from the stones and wet.

Today he has also found a baby's dummy. Maybe he could give it to Saabira.

'Coco, leave it!' Up ahead Coco is sniffing at the remains of a bird, the wing feathers wet and spread, most of the body gone. Coco does as she is told, turns and waits for Cyril, and then walks close to him, pushing her nose into his hand. He pats her and she runs off again, full of joy, chasing Sabi who bounces as she runs, jumping high over the bracken.

'Maybe Saabira will make me lunch today,' he muses, following Coco's wake. 'Maybe she will? Triangulation station.'

Blackie Boo is back by his side.

'Blackie Boo, how are you?' He laughs at his rhyme. 'Triangulation station.' Then a new thought comes to mind. 'The family next door are so quiet,' he says to the dog. 'We might disturb them.' He looks down to see Blackie Boo's response but she is off across the heather.

He hadn't tried to be quiet in the first few weeks. Quite the opposite; he had wanted them to leave and was as noisy as he could be. He had thought that they might start knocking on his door, or leave spiteful notes on top of his rabbit hutches like Mr Brocklethwaite on the other side.

Other letters have come in the last few weeks but he has left them under the stone on the doorstep where the postman put them; they became soggy with the rains, slowly disintegrating, until, in the last downpour, and with a nudge from the toe of his boot, they washed out into the road and he didn't think about them any more.

Turning his nose to the sky, he looks for the sun to judge the time, but the clouds are too dense. He has been walking for hours and is hungry, and they said he must not be late for work again or he will be sacked.

'I hate it!' he tells the nearest dog. 'I hate everything about it.' The only relief is that work starts at five, when everyone else has finished. But it is a small consolation, with the whole place stinking of death and shit and fear. It still makes him cry, every day.

He has tried imagining that everything he sees and smells and feels is unreal, that it is all a game, that none of it is true, but his heart knows, his soul cries and his eyes water.

Coco is at his ankles, and he stops and kneels down to cuddle her. She licks his face.

'What do you feed your dogs, then?' one of the men at Hogdykes goaded him when he first started. At the time he had only been out of Highroyds for a week and the world felt alien, threatening, oppressive and confusing. He had just moved in with Archie and his care worker said he must work, as he was an 'independent man now'. She said it as if it was something of which he should be proud, and he imagined it would be work like he did in the hospital, helping in the gardens. But the place that they sent him made him cry. He missed the doctors and some of the nursing staff, and he had real trouble working out his money and what he could buy with it. In the beginning, if it had not been for Archie and Archie's dogs, he might have walked across the moors and not stopped until the cold or hunger had taken him.

'Dog food,' he had replied, confused. All the men in their overalls and wellingtons had laughed.

'Dog food, he says.' The man had looked around at his co-workers. 'Where you think dog food comes from if not dead animals?'

He made sure after that day that he always arrived a bit late so the men would have left before he came in to clean. But a few of them stayed behind to smoke cigarettes by the back gates and there was often some quip, some laugh at his expense. But that was not as bad as the smell of fear that hung in the air when he went inside. Did they not smell it? He could almost feel it, it was almost tangible. The terror those animals must feel watching the animal in front, smelling the fear and not being able to follow their instincts and run. The red was everywhere – running in the gutters, splashed on the walls, on every surface. Even with the hose on full, some areas had to be scrubbed and, as he worked, unidentifiable morsels would get under his fingernails, flick up onto his glass, hang in his hair.

'Maybe she will have cooked.' He distracts himself from his own thoughts. She never puts meat before him, only exotic mixes of vegetables and spices and always the folded bread which she calls roti. She does not cook for him every day, but rather when she has made too much. It is often enough, though, for him to no longer find a cold tin of beans appetising, regardless of how hungry he is, and he has been without any food at all on more than one day.

Usually she cooks mid-afternoon, which means he can eat before work. Work is only two hours each day, and on his walk back he will sometimes see Saabira's husband, from a distance. Aaman. He always looks tired as the bus pulls away but his steps take on a bounce as he turns into their cobbled street.

The telephone box is a good place to remain hidden as Aaman makes his way to his door. It is not that he dislikes Aaman; he is probably a nice man since he is married to Saabira. But his stomach turns and his mouth goes dry when he tries to think of something he could say if they met and so, as yet, he has not even said hello.

'Triangulation station,' he mutters to himself.

The first spot of rain hits his glasses, sooner than he expected, but he is on the home straight now. He can see the back of the row of houses, can make out his own. There are curls of smoke snaking from several of the other chimneys. The other dogs will all be hungry when he gets in, and so will the rabbits.

He hopes Saabira has made too much food.

Chapter 12

The scraps he brought from work are torn and chewed and swallowed within minutes. Several of the dogs take the bones and disappear under the furniture, into the dark. The rabbits are equally keen to be fed and as he opens doors and shovels in feed he finds one of the animals lying on its side, eyes glazed over, and the other rabbits huddled in the corner, creating as much space as they can between them and their lifeless brother. Cyril puts down the feed scoop and with both hands flat he lifts the animal from the cage.

'Oh, you poor little thing.' He raises the rabbit and puts its nose near his cheek to see if he can feel even the slightest breath, but there is no doubt it is dead. There is a small area of bare earth just up the slope behind his house, and here he digs a hole with a trowel and buries the small animal, covering it gently and picking some heather for a memorial. The tears run down his cheeks, and as he closes his eyes he can still picture it lying in the cage. The cage warps and becomes a chair, the rabbit's hair turns white, its face becomes bald and it has on trousers and a shirt. It is Archie, just as he was when he found him.

'Cyril.' Saabira's call releases him.

He turns, hurriedly drying his eyes. Saabira has her purple outfit on, the gold of the scarf haloing her face.

'I have food.' She holds up the dishes to him before putting them down on the table in her yard, and returns indoors.

Cyril bounds back down on energetic legs, trowel forgotten. He does not hesitate to enter her backyard and he eagerly sits down and lifts the foil lids to see what she has prepared.

Her back door opens.

'Ah, you are here.' She comes out with small steps, another dish in her hand. As she puts this down next to his plate, Cyril's chest contracts. His hands are filthy, covered with mud from burying the rabbit. He puts them in his lap, under the table, and hopes she has not seen.

'The tap is just there.' Bangles on her wrist jangle as she points to the sink inside her back door. If he accepts he has to go inside, into her home, but if he does not he must eat with dirty hands. The choice twists in his stomach.

'Juliet, my baby, is sleeping upstairs. I am just going to check on her.' She leaves behind her perfume of flowers and musky warmth. It is a smell that brings comfort and the feeling that someone cares. It reminds him of Matron Jan, whose perfume was so strong it filled her small room.

'Come in, Cyril, come in, and how are you today?'

But even with only Jan in the room his tongue was not immediately freed.

'Today Steven is on duty, James, Peter, Teresa and Andrea.' She would reel off the list from the ledger on her desk, ticking boxes. 'Do you have a meeting with Dr Shilling today? Yes, at – let me see… one, just after lunch.' And she would talk on, checking her day's diary, telling him what paperwork she must do as she did it, the calls that she must make before going on to make them, and generally including him so much in everything she was doing in her office that he felt it was alright to stay, and the longer he stayed the more relaxed he became, and sometimes he would even talk to her.

It wasn't a physically comfortable office. The desk was jammed into the far corner with just enough space to fit a chair behind it. Six other chairs lined the walls between this and the door, which were used for the daily staff meetings. On the wall opposite the window, on the left, was a big whiteboard, and the writing on this changed daily.

63

When he first started going into the office he would choose the chair nearest the door, but as the years passed he sat closer and closer to Jan.

She is dead now as well. Everyone he has ever loved is dead. His mother, his brother who never had a name, his teacher, Matron Jan, Archie. He loves them, and they die. Now he loves no one. Just the animals, and they die at an alarming pace.

'Do you need to dry them?' Saabira holds out a towel and Cyril finds he is washing his hands in her kitchen. He cannot look at her, let alone take the offered towel. With a quick movement he wipes his hands down his tank top and steps back outside, sits. All feelings of hunger melt away as she follows him out with a second plate and sits down opposite him. He looks at the gate.

'Please, help yourself.' Like bells and trees in the wind, soft and melodic. He is almost not afraid but he rechecks his hands and sees his nails are still dirty. It will be better if she serves herself first then she will be occupied with eating and will not see his fingers, but she is waiting. Carefully, trying to hide his nails, he scoops up some of the food with the serving spoon and moves his plate to the dish so as not to spill anything in the transfer. Saabira offers him a second dish covered with a cloth. He is not sure whether to take it or lift the cloth, so he does neither, and she lifts the cloth for him. His hand trembles as he takes a roti-pancake.

She serves herself, each movement precise, gentle and flowing. Animals would not be scared of her, but even so when she settles to eat the backyard feels smaller and Cyril looks out to the moors.

'I feel I have been a very bad neighbour,' she begins, and Cyril pauses mid-mouthful and briefly looks away from the moors to see her face. She does not look back but keeps her gaze on her plate. She is so close. He finishes his mouthful and takes another. He will eat quickly and leave.

'We have been here a little while now and not once have we sat and talked. I feel very bad.' Still she does not look up. It seems a strange thing to say. She is not obliged to talk to him. Most people avoid making any contact with him, unless it is to tease and laugh, or complain, so why would she feel bad?

'Aaman, my husband, sends his apologies too. After work and the long journey home he is so very tired. But he says it is getting easier as he gets to know his job, and so maybe we will all eat together soon.'

Cyril stares and her eyes flick up to meet his just for a second. She is waiting for him to say something. The silence continues. She eats, he does not.

'Did that woman in the blue car come back?' she asks, but does not wait for a reply. 'At home, my home in Pakistan, I have two buffalos. They have a bed at the back of my house, and every day I would feed them and give them water. Most of the village have buffalos, for the farm work, and a goat for milk, so I am finding it very strange that this woman considered a few dogs and some rabbits to be a problem.'

'The old couple complain.' His words surprise him. He had not planned to say them and they just came out.

'Old couple?'

'The house next to mine.' There! It happened again. It had sometimes happened with Jan, and quite a lot in the year before she was dead.

Saabira smiles at him. It is heartening to see Cyril relaxing enough to talk.

'Treat him like you treated Hanfi,' Aaman suggested one morning as he was putting on his overcoat. He picked up his work bag and Saabira handed him his lunch and pointed to the umbrella by the door. 'Patience and kindness,' he advised, kissing her on the forehead.

'Like you showed me,' Saabira responded, and Aaman put his bag down again and pulled her in close to him.

After he left she willed the evening to come quickly, for him to be home again. The days were becoming colder and, now, every evening, they lit a blazing fire and curled up on the soft sofa, and when he was home it was not so bad. But she was beginning to feel she needed more to do than taking care of Jay. She loved her like she could never have imagined love to feel, but it did not seem unreasonable that she should also need some intellectual stimulation. Her time at Murray College in Sialkot, with her prized bursary grant, had not sated her appetite for learning; rather, it had stimulated her to want to learn more. It needn't be English Literature again – it could be something else, anything, everything. It is the process of studying that is so engrossing, so satisfying.

Chapter 13

'Ah, so the old couple complain?' she says, bringing her attention back to Cyril.

'Yes.'

She watches his hesitation.

'They complain about the animals. They say they smell.'

The last word is spoken so quietly that Saabira cannot be sure she heard correctly.

'They smell?' Cyril sinks into his chair and colour rises up his neck, covers his cheeks and spreads all the way up to his hairline.

'I have no sense of smell.' She releases him; his shoulders drop and his colour grows more natural, but his eyes widen and he is staring at her. 'Really?' he asks. She assures him it is true.

'I was born with no sense of smell. I can taste, but they tell me it is not like most people can taste. The smell is part of the taste too, they say. So when I cook I am extra careful how I spice the food. It is easy for me to give it too much flavour.'

She pauses to eat a little.

'I can imagine smells though. My mother taught me this. She explained which smells were like which tastes, so I have an idea. So if someone tells me something smells like a flower, for example, and they say it is sweet, I almost imagine I am smelling it.'

Cyril looks away again as she finished speaking.

'They say the animals smell bad. Not horrible bad, like death and fear. Just bad.'

'I see. How many do you have?'

He would like to give her a number, to be part of what feels like a normal conversation.

'Fifty dogs and a hundred rabbits.' They sound like good numbers.

'Fifty dogs...' Saabira smiles, but the corners of her mouth immediately pull down and he is not sure if she is going to laugh at him or not. 'I saw you had a number of rabbits.'

'The rabbits are the problem.' He quite likes these words that just come with no thought. She does not seem to think him strange for saying them, and does not frown or tease him.

'They make small rabbits quickly, I understand.'

'Yes. Yes!' He is amazed that she knows what the problem is without being told. 'Yes. This is the problem.'

'Why do you keep them?'

He tells her the tale, and a part of him observes himself talking to her and it feels amazing. She does not laugh. She looks him in the eye and she does not seem to fear him and he finds he does not fear her. Not once does she yawn.

'So you need to take out all the boys as soon as they have finished drinking from their mothers.'

'Yes.' He cannot believe how she knows so much.

'If you like, when you have finished eating, we could try to do that.'

'I have to work.'

'Oh! Where?' Now she sounds surprised.

'At the place they kill animals so people can eat them.'

'That seems a strange place for someone who loves animals to work.' There is no accusation in her tone, just curiosity.

'They make me work there.'

'Who?' She seems genuinely concerned.

'They do.'

'Who?'

68

'I don't know, the people who tell me what to do.'

She frowns.

'Can you explain?'

Cyril has never really thought until now who it is that was tells him what to do. It is just *them*. They just always have done. How does he explain that? Where should he start?

'My mum used to tell me what to do but she is dead. Then the home for children told me what to do. They said I was unwell. So I went to live in Highroyds Hospital, but no one there was sick. Just some of them were unhappy and some used to shout a lot.' He watches himself talk and likes it. 'No one really told me what to do there. I had to eat when they said and I had to take the medication they gave me. But that was all. I helped in the garden.' His collar seems to tighten. He pulls at it, loosening his knitted tie, and the words become stuck again. 'But then the wards started closing. And no one would tell me what was happening.' He can feel little beads of sweat forming on his brow. 'I kept hearing people saying, "Care in the Community helps us instigate."'

'Do you mean integrate?' Saabira asks. She doesn't laugh because he got the word wrong and still seems interested in what he has to say.

'Aye. Care in the Community helps us integrate, they said. It was the new big idea.'

People started disappearing from Highroyds. First they were gone and then their beds gone; the doors to the wards were closed, no lights, no nurses, no explanation, nothing. Whole sections of the hospital just lay empty and unused as Cyril continued to cut the grass and weed the flowers in the beautiful grounds. He was not concerned about the disappearance of anyone in particular, and he was quite glad about some of the people who were leaving, but it did make him wonder if he too might disappear one day, and he didn't like that. Highroyds felt safe, and some

69

of the nurses were very kind, and he liked to work in the gardens, and to be trusted with caring for the plants.

Saabira's eyes are wide. Her lashes are wet, her kohl running. She sweeps a finger under her eye, wiping away some of the bleed. She is waiting to hear more.

'Then one day Matron Jan gave me a plastic bag and told me to pack. I put my toothbrush in the bag because I saw Bernie do that but I didn't know what else to do so I waited. Then they took me to a hospital bus.' His bottom lip begins to quiver. There was a mouse with a bad leg in a cage behind the rose bushes. He didn't even have a chance to let it out. It will have died because of him.

'Are you alright?' Like the landing of a moth, the ends of her fingers touch his forearm. He stares at her nails, rounded at the ends, the half-moons so white against her tanned skin.

'They brought me here. Put me in Archie's house. Care in the Community. They told me to work where they kill animals because I would need money to give to Archie for food. They said Archie would take care of me, but Archie got ill and then Archie slept all the time and then Archie was dead and I have to make money to buy beans and to get scraps for the dogs.' He cannot stop his tears. He tries. He tries really hard but his eyes won't obey him.

'Oh my goodness.' Saabira's fingers lift away as if the moth took wing. She offers him a paper napkin from the holder on the table.

Cyril's tale of hardship draws her thoughts to Aaman, and the tales he told her when he returned from his 'adventures', as he so optimistically called them. It makes her think of the misery she inflicted on him, and how he made light of it on his return, assuring her that it had been his choice to go. But she knew she had encouraged him, assured him, spun a web of words to make him believe that it would be a simple journey – a heroic one, even – all along knowing that it was a lie that she was telling him and, to be honest, herself as well.

Her fingers twist on each other but it does nothing to ease the weight in her chest. Her shoulders tense, stiffening the muscles all down her back.

Chapter 14

She hadn't planned for Aaman to go away. It just came about. But when it did she gave him all the encouragement he needed to make the decision. He would not have gone of his own accord. It was she who had presented an argument strong enough to convince him.

Their village was dying. Everyone saw it, everyone knew it. Their family's way of life had always been hand to mouth. That was how it had always been. But for the younger generations, the generation after her, this was no longer enough. As a result, in recent years, every family in the village had a son, even a daughter, in the city, working, trying to improve their lot in life and sending money back home.

But with sons and daughters gone it was necessary to employ casual labour, especially at harvest time. The sons and daughters in the cities would send extra money, but Saabira knew that this was not the answer; she saw it was a trap. The more young people who left the village, the more casual workers must be hired, and paid for, at harvest time, and this put a strain on everyone. It was a cycle that only made the village unhappy, with families forced apart.

So it was she who first suggested, quietly, gently, privately, that the village buy a harvesting machine and Aaman, with her encouragement, brought up the idea at the *chopal* one evening. It was a practical solution that would lower the costs at harvest time, and it would bring the crops in more quickly from the fields, giving them time to get the produce to the marketplace before their neighbours. It could be a partial solution to their poverty and, at that point, she had no ulterior motives. The idea was met with a positive response by the other farmers and the subject was much discussed over the following weeks at the meetings and in the fields. Aaman, as the initiator of the idea, grew in stature. He walked taller, and she was proud.

After much deliberation the village agreed that a brand-new machine could never be bought, as they cost many, many thousands of rupees. But there was, however, a big trade in second-hand machines whose working life had expired – officially, at least. They were bought at scrap value by the importers, who sold them on to the farmers, who had the time and ingenuity to bring them back to life. These farmers sold them on to other farmers when they could afford an upgrade.

The villagers agreed that the fairest way forward was to divide the price of a machine by the amount of land each of them owned. They worked out how much time each would spend harvesting. This showed how much time would remain, when the machine would sit idle, and they invited a nearby village, where there were many cousins, to become part-owners too, to use up all the machine's idle time. In this way, the divided price became ever smaller, making it possible for all but the poorest families to contribute and reap the benefits.

Although Aaman had become a respected man in the village because of this idea, he quietly pointed out to her one evening that they were one of the poorest families and could not afford to contribute their fair share. He spoke with delicacy, but as his words came out it was as if all the recent status she had enjoyed as Aaman's wife was torn from her, leaving her disappointed and frustrated. She knew that her recent loss was making her extremely sensitive, but not contributing was an impossible option.

The simple fact was that the farm was not bringing in enough money to pay for their share of the machine, and nor was Aaman qualified to do anything but menial work. Even if he were to get a job in the nearby town, he would

73

not make any more money, and the farm would be neglected.

'They pay much more abroad,' she said to Aaman one night. A man from a neighbouring village had just returned from a trip to Europe. Although he did not quite make it all the way, he brought tales of great wealth to be obtained, and he planned to try again – soon. Aaman replied with a smile that he would pray to grow wings so he could fly there.

Saabira began to research how the plan could be realised. Much of her initial information was from a man who came to the village offering to escort people for a fee. But Aaman did not need an escort; he just needed to know how, and he could make this journey by himself. Once she started talking about it to neighbours, friends and cousins, she found there were plenty of rumours and gossip. Then she took the bus and went into her old university in Sialkot to use the library computers. There she even met someone else with the same idea, and together they ventured into a part of Sialkot she had never been to before in order to put questions directly to a smooth-talking man who claimed to help people get across borders, and to another who had tried to make the journey and had failed. Her research filled her mind and, to her relief, her heart. It distracted her from her recent overwhelming loss and helped her bury the bottled-up emotions that threatened to consume her. She planned and plotted until she felt sure she had found a way Aaman could have safe passage, earning as he travelled, until he reached Spain, from where he could, possibly, fly back.

But she did not admit, even to herself, that she felt an element of relief because this journey would take Aaman far away.

The information she discovered gave her words authority and she assured Aaman that he could use each country's authorities to aid his journey. There was a man in the next village who would soon travel to visit relatives near the Iranian border. He already had two passengers, distant cousins, and he said Aaman could join them. 'Yes,' she said to the man, 'Aaman will go with you.'

That evening she told him about the man's offer, and explained the route he would take. She explained how the three of them could cross the border at night, and then walk to Kerman, as if it were a game. She did not tell him how long that walk would be, and he did not ask. Instead, he looked terrified and she assured him his feet would be light and the excitement of his journey would carry him. He trusted her, trusted every word and wanted to go willingly for her, but there was fear in his eyes.

'If you can make it beyond Kerman it will be a victory!' she said, 'Because there you are sure to be picked up by the authorities, who will take you to the capital, Tehran. But you really need to get past Kerman before being picked up, or they will bring you back to the Pakistani border.' She spoke as if she was directing him to a shop to pick up a sack of flour. But she knew from those she had spoken to that the Iranian authorities were not particularly friendly, and they might hold Aaman and the others in very unsavoury places until they could confirm that they were illegal. However, as soon as that happened they would assist him out of the country. The nearest country was Iraq but, as the authorities knew that taking illegal immigrants there would only result in their return, they took them instead to the Turkish border, to help them on their journey to Europe.

Her research had been thorough and she felt she knew what she was talking about.

'Once in Turkey, you will head for Ankara. The authorities there will probably give you a lift to the capital.' All the authorities knew the direction of travel, and if they took them back to Iran they would simply be brought by the Iranian authorities back to the Turkish border. So the Turkish authorities would take them to Ankara. There they could be held in warehouses with many other illegals. They could be held for up to two years before being deported.

'But this is nothing to worry about,' she enthused, 'because the government uses illegal immigrants as underpaid labour in tourism and local industry. You will already be earning money, and that is the whole point.'

Saabira spoke to a man who had actually made it as far as Ankara. He said that if Aaman did the same it would be good to bribe the police, to get one of these jobs sooner rather than later. When out labouring, he said, it would be easy for Aaman to make contacts and escape the authorities, and make his way to the border with Greece. But he himself had not done this, and Saabira did not ask why. He had a scar from his ear to the corner of his mouth.

She did not mention any of the possible dangers to Aaman. No – she pressed on, explaining how he would need to bribe the border authorities, or get into Bulgaria and then down to Greece where the border was not even marked in some places. From Greece, everyone knew, it was possible to make money and go to Italy. In Italy it would be possible to make even more money and go on to Spain. In Spain, it would be better of course to get papers to work legally and then fly home triumphant. It was generally accepted that papers were easier to get in Spain, but she had not actually met anyone who had done it.

Later, after he left, she wondered to what degree she had perpetuated this rumour, and perhaps others, because she wanted so much to believe they were true. But it was too late by then.

How simple and yet heroic she had made the journey sound. How she had promised that Aaman would return tall and wealthy and save the village and help the elders buy the machine. How she had lied to herself and to him about the real reason she was eager he should go away.

She had treated the plan so frivolously; she had been unrealistically optimistic, and counted away months and years of Aaman's life as if he had a surplus to play with. She had estimated that the journey to the first country where he could make money would take maybe four months if he was lucky, which, she felt sure, he would be. He would then need another ten months, travelling and earning, to make the money they needed back in the village, and a bit more to aid his journey home. So he would be back within two years, just in time for when the village planned to buy the machine. How proud she had promised him she would be.

Saabira draws her scarf over her mouth, the corners quivering.

Cyril is looking over the moors, lost in his own world, at the clouds that are being pushed up over the horizon. Diagonal lines of sun spear the purple heather. The backyard is well sheltered from the fresh breeze that has picked up. If Cyril would say something it would release her from her own thoughts, but he does not and Aaman's struggles continue to torment her.

He made the journey to Greece in five months. He said he was very lucky compared to others he met. The longest part of the journey was the walk through the hills in Iran and he has never really told her of his time in Ankara, or what the authorities were like. When he arrived in Greece, he managed to telephone her, and she can remember her neighbours running to her excitedly, holding out a mobile phone. And did she delight in his achievement? Did she delight in him even still being alive, did she praise him for his efforts? No – she acted as if she had expected his great achievement, as if it was natural that he should have got so far, so quickly. He didn't talk over the phone of the horrors he had seen and the hardship he had suffered, until he returned and the nightmares started. He didn't mention that the way into Greece was patrolled very tightly, or tell of his skirmish with patrol dogs or explain that he had been beaten and robbed in Bulgaria – not until he awoke one night, when he was safely back home, sweating in fear and hiding in the corner of the room fearing the dogs in his dreams.

'I think I hear my daughter.' Saabira stands before the tears escape her thick lashes and she hurries indoors.

If he blamed her, or shouted at her – beat her, even – it would be easier. But he is gentle and forgiving, and this makes it worse. He has forgiven her, and never blamed her in the first place. It is she who cannot forgive herself.

Chapter 15

Baby Juliet sleeps on, nestled into the corner of the sofa, cushions all around her, blanket tucked in over the top. She will not wake for another half hour at least. Her tiny lips pulse at her dreams of suckling. Saabira washes her face in the kitchen sink, the cold water stemming her tears, cooling her cheeks. She smooths her hair, loosely throws the end of her scarf over her shoulder and takes a deep breath, and only then does she feel ready to return to Cyril.

Before she can make a move, there is banging on the front door, so loud it makes her jump. With a glance at Jay she hurries to open it before the noise is repeated.

'Yes?' She swings the door open.

'Is he there?' The old man on her doorstep has a strong regional accent, which, although it is becoming familiar to Saabira, she still struggles to understand. This man has a flat cap firmly pulled down on his head; the sleeves of his collarless shirt are rolled up. Small eyes are set close to a thin nose in his weather-beaten face, and he has not shaved for a few days, the white stubble contouring the creases around his mouth.

'Excuse me, who is it that you are seeking?' Does he want to speak to Aaman?

'Tell him to come out. The woman from Health is going to be here soon and I've also put in an official complaint to Housing, so they might turn up too. It's not right that he rents somewhere right next to normal folk.'

'Do you want Aaman?'

'Ah – who? No, I want that Septic Cyril. I know you're all pally with him. I banged at his door and he's not there so I'm guessing he's with you?'

'He is eating.'

'Well, tell him it's time to face the music.'

'May I enquire who is calling?' Saabira cannot remember which novel she has read this sentence in, but to be using it in this context makes her smile.

'This is no laughing matter! I intend to get his animals and himself evicted. Go tell him. He knows who I am, I live at the top here.' The man nods his head to indicate the house above Cyril's and then shoves his hands deep into his front pockets and looks down the street.

'One moment, please.' She pushes the front door closed, but gently, so as not to be considered rude. With a quick glance over the sofa to satisfy herself that the talking has not disturbed Jay, she quietly opens the back door. Cyril is paused, eyes wide open, like a hare caught in a bright light.

'Cyril, there's a man at the door who is talking about evicting you?'

His hands start to shake and he puts down his fork.

She wants to ask what 'facing the music' means, but somehow it does not feel like an appropriate time.

'He said he lives at the top,' she adds instead.

'Mr Brocklethwaite.' The colour drains from Cyril's face.

'He says the woman from Health is coming, and that he has put in a complaint to Housing. He said something about you and your animals being evicted.' It sounds serious to Saabira but she waits to see how Cyril will react. It seems a little extreme that someone has the authority to take away Cyril's animals and remove him from his own home.

'Is he waiting?'

'He said the woman from Health was going to be here soon and maybe someone from Housing.'

'Mr Brocklethwaite will let that woman from Health through his house to the back, show her the rabbits over the wall.' He nods to the low wall that separates the yard from the open moorland behind. She'll take them and kill them.' Tears are filling the space behind his glasses, against his cheek.

'Has this happened before, Cyril?' He does not meet her eye and this is her answer. 'Maybe it is best not to save any more rabbits, not if it means the woman from Health will kill them.' Cyril nods his head gravely. 'Perhaps it is even better to let them go, yourself, now?'

He is on his feet before she has finished her sentence, and jumps the low wall. She follows, through her gate, to his yard next door. He pulls out a rabbit from the first cage but then hesitates. The tears behind his glasses escape and flow, down the side of his nose, following the line to his mouth and on down to his chin where they gather and drip. His nose is running too, but he does nothing to stem either flow.

'I don't know if she's pregnant. She might even be a boy.' He falters, looking at the animal that is hanging in his grasp.

'Why can you not let it go if it is pregnant?'

'She won't be safe, will she?' The question seems genuine.

'Of course. She will be fine. She will dig a hole or find a hole. That's what rabbits do, is it not?'

Cyril's eyebrows lift and he puts the rabbit gently on the ground over the low wall. The animal sniffs and they both watch as its nose quivers, and it sits there not moving. They wait, but it still does not move. Saabira reaches to stroke its long ears and at the first touch it leaps away, its speed increasing with the distance until it is a blur and is gone.

Cyril has taken out two more, one in each hand.

'So I can release all the ones that do not have babies right now and they'll be fine?' He asks. He uses his forearm to wipe the wet under his chin now.

'I cannot see why not. They are wild creatures.'

The next two that he releases do not immediately bound away either.

'Go, go.' He pushes the rabbit nearest him and it takes one trial leap before scurrying away at great speed. Two by two he empties the cages, his tears never stopping, little childlike groans escaping him as if the event is causing him real pain. He shudders in deep breaths, as if he is holding in any louder noises his crying might make. Saabira has not seen many grown men cry. Aaman cries on occasion, but then he is more sensitive than most. Cyril is older than Aaman, physically bigger, and it seems odd.

'He's letting the evidence go.' Mr Brocklethwaite is the first to arrive, puffing, out of breath, from the direction of his house. The woman from Health, Dawn Todman, is behind him, wrapping her cardigan around her, one hand over her mouth.

'Hello, again,' she says to Saabira. 'Got yourself involved, have you? Typical.'

'I do not know what you mean by that?' Saabira feels she has been insulted again by this woman but she is not quite sure how.

'Mrs Todman, he's let 'em go. Look, half the cages are empty,' Mr Brocklethwaite complains.

'Why is this a problem?' Saabira asks. 'You yourself said that you wanted to get his animals out. What was that word you used? Evicted. Well, they are evicted. Time to be happy.' She smiles at the man but it seems getting the animals evicted may not be what he wants after all. It certainly does not seem to make him happy.

'Look!' Mr Brocklethwaite demands of Mrs Todman. 'Look, a rabbit with young 'uns, and look at the size of that one. It's too big to even turn around in its cage. Is that not enough?'

'I don't think two rabbits and some babies is going to be enough to get an eviction order.' Mrs Todman pulls her cardigan more tightly around her. Saabira does not find the wind off the moors as cold as she did when she first arrived. In fact, these days she considers the breeze refreshing, invigorating. Today, with the sun out, there is warmth to it and she wonders if there is an aroma to the purple flowers that cover so much of the common ground.

'What about the smell, then?' Mr Brocklethwaite persists.

'Well, I for one am grateful the wind is blowing the way it is right now,' says Dawn Todman. 'But yes, we can look into that. But it will take longer. Perhaps the best option is to get in touch directly with the landlord. Do we know who that is?'

'You are talking as if Cyril isn't right here!' Saabira's voice comes out high-pitched.

Mr Brocklethwaite looks first at Saabira, then at Mrs Todman, who is looking at the ground, and then at Cyril who is scanning the open moor, no doubt for signs of white tails and long ears.

Mr Brocklethwaite begins to say something but then starts to cough. The wind is changing again and Mrs Todman is inching away from the back of the house towards the moor path, back the way she came. Saabira watches the woman pull the sleeve of her cardigan over her nose.

Mr Brocklethwaite's coughing continues with no one coming to his aid until Cyril, eyes still on the open ground, slaps him hard on his back. Mr Brocklethwaite nearly falls forward with the force, his flat cap shifting over his forehead.

'I – I could have you done for assault,' he stammers, putting his hat straight. His face is red, blood vessels showing in his eyes as he regains his breath.

'Oh, come on,' Mrs Todman says through her bunched-up sleeve. 'Let's not get ridiculous.' The pair step through the gate and head towards the back of Mr Brocklethwaite's house. Saabira wonders if she should be concerned to be breathing in whatever it is that they are both so keen to get away from. After all, every smell is particulate.

'You're right. We should get in touch with the landlord. But you know what, I've just realised summat.' Mr Brocklethwaite seems very pleased with himself suddenly. As he steps out of view into his own backyard his voice can still be heard behind the stack of cages. 'He was renting off Archie and Archie died – what? Nearly two year back.'

'So what are you saying?' Mrs Todman follows him.

'I'm saying he might not be a legal tenant, that's all. Who's he paying rent to? I can't think why I didn't think of this sooner.' He sounds excited.

'Well, if that's the case he cannot stay.' The words are stated very seriously by Mrs Todman, but Mr Brocklethwaite titters.

'You'll take a sherry with me and t' wife before you head back then, Mrs Todman?' he asks.

'Dawn, me name's Dawn,' she replies. The back door closes and no more can be heard.

Chapter 16

Aaman is back later than usual, and Jay has been fed and bathed and is now sleepy.

'Hello, my love. I am sorry I am so late, but the bus did not come for nearly an hour and then two came at once.'

'And you were waiting outside in the cold?' Saabira helps him off with his big English coat and he takes his shoes off with a deep sigh.

'Never mind, I am home now.' His shoulders drop.

She moves in, her arms around his waist, her head against his chest. The days seem long without him. Aaman hesitates for only a second and then his arms are around her too and he is kissing her hair, enjoying the moment, his tiredness forgotten, or at least pushed to one side.

'Did you go to the phone box? Did you talk to anyone back in the village?' His voice is slightly muffled as his lips kiss her under her ears and then move down into her neck.

Last night she shed a few tears for her loneliness and the lack of familiar faces around her. It is a feeling that comes and goes these days and is not as bad the insistent nagging ache in her chest that she had felt soon after they moved in, once the new house was in order and Aaman going to work every day had become a routine. It is just that her days seem so long and, except for the care of Jay, without purpose. There is too much time to think. She misses her family, her neighbours, the buffalo, the chickens, even the dust that she used to spend so much time sweeping from the house. Last night she missed her old life so much it was a relief to curl up in Aaman's arms and cry, just for a little while, just to release the feelings rather than bottle them up.

'No, I did not go to the phone box. Today I did not feel the need to spend all that money phoning home.'

'I think that perhaps it would be a good idea for you to come into Bradford with me one morning. We can meet for lunch and later come home together. Bradford has many shops and so many of the owners of the smaller shops speak Urdu, and there are interesting places to visit.'

'But what about Jay? She still needs her naps?'

'She would be fine, would she not? She can sleep resting against you, or we can get a...' He pauses, and a frown passes across his brow, 'Ha! I am not sure what they are called. Like a pram, but for older children. I see a lot of those being pushed through the town on my way to work. Talking of which, how is my beautiful daughter?'

Jay is on the rug by the fireplace. Saabira lit the fire half an hour ago to make the room cheerful for her husband's return. Their daughter's face is illuminated by the flames, the orange dancing on her brown skin. The doll she was holding is abandoned and she makes an attempt to stand as Aaman approaches her. Yesterday she walked three steps from the sofa to his outstretched hands.

Taking a cloth from the kitchen sink, Saabira opens the oven door and steam permeates the room. She stirs the vegetables and closes the door again.

'That smells wonderful, my love.' Aaman has Jay in his arms now, and she turns and reaches for the doll. With the fire behind them it is the perfect picture. It may not be home but, with the curtains drawn, and the sound of the wind creating a background hum, there is something very seductive about the English autumn.

'And how was your day?' Saabira asks.

'It was good. Every day I get quicker at programming and I am always learning something new. It is very exciting.'

'The other programmers, are they all very experienced?'

'Some are, but some know less than me. How was your day?' He sits down with Jay leaning against his shoulder, her eyes closing.

'She tried to eat by herself but she made such a mess.' Saabira moves towards them both, strokes the curve of her daughter's back. 'She was using a spoon but she kept using it with the bowl of the spoon upside down and she could not understand why it worked when I used it and not when she did, but I think she got it in the end.'

'Ah, my clever girl,' Aaman replies.

'I had a strange day.' She lays the table. 'I invited Cyril for lunch and I sat with him.'

'You are a good neighbour.' Aaman slowly lowers himself into one of the seats at the table with his daughter still resting against him. Saabira takes out the aloo gobi from the oven and puts it down on the table, and then gently takes Jay and lays her back in her nest of cushions on the sofa. Saabira leaves a bracelet with her; she twists and turns it in her small hand, feels it in her mouth.

'Mr Brocklethwaite is the man who lives above Cyril and he came with a woman to try to remove both Cyril and his animals. Mr Brocklethwaite was very harsh in the way he spoke, and he had no time for Cyril at all. He reminded me of old Barkat, do you remember? Aswab's cousin, who had only one eye and was always quarreling with the neighbours? Do you remember, once your daadi tried to reason with him, and he tried to push her into the buffalo dung pile!'

Aaman shakes his head in memory of such disrespect to his grandmother.

'Not everyone has your view of the world, Saabira.' Aaman holds his plate out to her.

'But also, the woman that was here the other day came again. I suppose she is just doing her job, trying to keep the peace, but she has a way of making me feel as if she has insulted me.'

'Perhaps it is just the different culture. What is rude in one place is acceptable in another. But is all this fuss just over a few rabbits? Why does Cyril not just get rid of the lot?'

'How can you say that?' Saabira smiles as she speaks. 'You, who told me how you cried as a boy when your goat was taken for the village feast?'

'Ah, yes, well, she was different, we were friends.' Aaman selects a roti and starts on the potatoes and cauliflower in a thick spicy sauce that Saabira has placed before him.

'Anyway, I do not think it is just the rabbits. It is also the smell, judging by the way they were reacting.'

'I am just glad the wind tends to blow up the street. It is a pretty invasive smell.' Aaman takes a mouthful of food, chews, closes his eyes, breathes through his nose and swallows. 'This is really good, my love. it is taking me straight back to my mother's house.'

'I think perhaps he just needs some help. No doubt he is not very good at cleaning, and maybe it has all got too much for him. Your mother, she taught me this dish.'

'The ginger is perfect.'

'I was going to say something, you know. Offer to help, but I wonder how he would take such an offer from me?'

'You are very kind, Saabira. Can you pass me the jug of water, please?'

'It might be better if a man was to offer help. You know, so as not to show him up.'

'Yes, perhaps you are right. This is so good, I hadn't realised quite how hungry I was.'

'So will you talk to him?'

'Me?'

'You are very sensitive in the way you talk to people. You would never offend anyone. But if it is the smell that is causing the problem for our neighbour then I am sure we can help him with that. Can't we? Then maybe they won't be so keen to make him move. Also, if the smell bothers you, it will be an opportunity to remedy the situation.'

Aaman chews thoughtfully.

'But I am bombarding you, my love. I am so sorry. You have been working all day and I am certain you do not want to be bothered with all this.' The potato she picks up with her roti falls apart as she pinches it and she wonders if she has overcooked it.

'Sorry?' Aaman seems to pull himself out of a daze; he faces her but his eyes flicker left and right. He has not heard what she said.

'I was just apologising for bombarding you, my love,' she repeats.

'No, Saabira, no. You are not bombarding me. I am a little tired, that is all. But your life is my life and I will deny you nothing. If you want me to talk to him, I will. He is lucky to have a neighbour such as you.' He puts down his knife and reaches for her hand. 'Anything, Saabira,' he adds, more breath than words, and the familiar feeling of tightness in her chest raises the memory of what she put him though. She does not deserve him.

Chapter 17

It is a Saturday and Cyril relishes the fact that he does not need to go into work today. The first birds begin to sing and the sun is shining through the curtains. His legs are pinned to the bed, as usual, by Coco, who is fast asleep, and Blackie Boo is on the floor by his bedside table. He does not need to open his eyes to know she is there as her snoring makes it all too clear.

'Coco?' he whispers. The morning feels too unbroken to speak out loud. Coco lifts her head. But he cannot say what he is thinking. If he says it, it might become real. His hands tremble ever so slightly and he feels a little bit sick. What if they make him move?

'Coco,' he starts again. Coco does not lift her head this time. They will try to make him move if he does not get rid of the smell. That means he must tidy. He clenches his fists.

After his mum was dead he was moved into the big house with too many rooms. At first he shared a room with four other children but after a few weeks the grown-ups put him in a room of his own. He was glad to be on his own. In the shared room the boy on the next bed spat at him as he slept and it clung in his hair, and the boy in the opposite bed would take his blankets off him after last check because it was so cold. All of them were very noisy, laughing and making jokes about him long after lights out.

But when he had his own room it was soon the adults who picked on him. They said his room was a mess, that he must tidy it. He tried, but he wasn't sure how to do it. How does anyone know what they will need in the future? You can't throw things away unless you know.

90

Also, his things filled the spaces. Staring at blank walls, uncluttered surfaces, made pictures come into his head: Mum's bloated face, her arm hanging over the edge of the bed all grey, her shoe on the floor, the painted nail of her big toe poking out through a hole in her stockinged foot.

'You need to get this room tidied *now*. This is your final warning. Don't come for dinner until it's done.' Mr Richards was the staff-in-charge, and he closed the door more loudly than was necessary.

Cyril gathered a handful of orange peel from the windowsill and put it in the bin. The smell of oranges filled his nose.

'A nice smell,' he declared to himself, and he took the peel out of the bin and put it on the radiator to perfume the room.

He took an unfinished drawing from his desk. It was no good. But the back of the paper was not used, so he put it back, upside down.

Yesterday's shirt was on the bed and it looked messy, so he hung it on a wire hanger, but it smelt so he took it off again and threw it behind the door ready to be washed.

He made the bed, which made the room look much better but then he found a pen without a lid, and he hunted for the lid and in the process the bed became a mess again.

'Oh for goodness' sake, you've done nothing.' Mr Richards stood in the doorway. 'You've got another half an hour then your dinner's going in the bin.' He slammed the door this time, and it stayed shut. Cyril went to bed hungry.

The next day Mr Richards and the other staff came. They put him in the television room and locked the door and would not let him help. The other children chanted Septic Cyril, and pulled faces at him through the television room door, which had sections of glass in it with squares made of wire. Whilst he was trapped there the adults took everything that was his away in black bin liners. They cleared the walls and the desktop and tidied his wardrobe before he was allowed back. His pencil with the dinosaurs on it was gone, and his ruler with the picture of the Thunderbirds and the end missing. His book of knots was gone too, and so was the bootlace that he had found and was saving to practise tying the knots.

'Coco.' He kicks his legs about a little, and she gets up, yawning, pushing her tail into the air with her nose and lowering her chest to stretch. 'We need to tidy.' There, he has said it. But the image of the house downstairs fills his head. He cannot throw it all away. He rescued everything from being smashed up and dumped in a hole that scars the earth. He saw them on the television at Highroyds. Someone must want a bureau, a chest of drawers, a bookcase, surely? He just has to find them. He hasn't thought how to do this yet.

Now Coco is awake, Blackie Boo stands and the two of them whimper for breakfast. The yard – he will start with the yard. If he does as Saabira says the cages will empty. Even now, only two of the six are occupied. He can chop the cages up, stack the wood ready to burn and not rescue any more rabbits.

Eager to put this plan into action, he jumps out of bed, pulls on his clothes, and dashes down the stairs. The dogs get biscuits for breakfast and he goes into the yard. The day has not really begun yet but he is chopping wood, and he grins as he chops. He could make his yard like Saabira's – get a table, or use one from inside.

Soon the unused cages are smashed and the debris is scattered over the yard floor. The creak of the hinges tells him Saabira has opened her back door. She will be pleased to see what he has done. She understands.

'Good morning.'

Cyril tightens the grip on his axe as Saabira's husband comes out into his own yard. There is no privacy now the cages have gone.

'My name is Aaman. I don't think we've met. You are Cyril, isn't that right?' Saabira's husband extends a hand over the low wall between them. Cyril looks down at his palms. They are dirty from the axe and a blister has burst at the base of his first finger. It will hurt if it is squeezed. It hurts anyway, now he has stopped.

'Are you alright? Have you hurt your hand?' Saabira's husband, Aaman, asks, taking a step closer to see. 'I found it was best to wear gloves when I was a gardener,' he says. 'I think we have some plasters, do you want one?'

'No.' Cyril finds his voice but the one short word is all he can say. Aaman is like Saabira in the way he speaks: gentle, concerned, non-judgmental. But he is not Saabira and he does not know him. Cyril takes a step backward.

'Shall I help you to stack all this?' Aaman changes the subject and points to all the smashed cages. 'Come, it will be quicker with two people.' And, uninvited, he steps over the wall and takes a pair of seam-split leather gloves from his back pocket. Cyril feels rooted to the spot. 'These are my old gardening gloves,' Aaman says as he puts them on. 'I kept them as a memento but today we shall make them work, shall we not?' He starts to gather the wood and stack it by the two remaining rabbit cages. Cyril watches.

'Here is a good place, yes?' Aaman asks. Cyril nods and then without a word picks up some pieces and hands them to Aaman.

They continue in this fashion until all the wood is cleared. The patches where the cages once stood are surprisingly clear, thanks to the wooden bases they sat on, but the animal faeces covering the stone flags in the centre of his yard remain.

'Ah! I have an idea.' And with a hop Aaman is over the wall and back again, bringing with him the hose that is attached to a tap outside his back door. He puts his finger over the end and the trickling water suddenly comes out

93

with force. Cyril wants to giggle. He would like to try, and he reaches for the hose.

'Oh yes, here you go.' Aaman relinquishes the pipe but as he does so the spray of water turns back into a dribble. Cyril fiddles with the end but he cannot get it to squirt.

'Put your finger there, like that – there you go!' Aaman's hands meet Cyril's as he shows him what to do but Cyril does not mind his touch. 'The water is going to spray! Now hold it low and watch the water force the dirt away – yes, like that, make it go through the gate – yes, that's it!' Aaman encourages him and Cyril begins to think that he likes Saabira's husband. A rainbow forms in the water's mist and Cyril tries to make more. But then a big piece of dirt peels off one of the flags and he remembers what he is meant to be doing.

Watching the years of boot-impressed dung peel off the flags and skitter on the surface of the water out of the gate is a great game. He forgets Aaman is there until the yard is clean and clear, and then the water stops running and Cyril looks up to see Aaman in his own yard turning off the tap.

'Do you need it some more?' he asks. Cyril thinks about making rainbows again but his mouth will not open to say so. With an easy movement, Saabira's husband winds the hose around his arm and then hangs it on a purpose-built rack on the wall of his house. When all is neat he takes off his gloves and puts then back in his pocket. His hair, which was all neatly combed back when he first came outside, now flops over his eyes, shiny and dark.

'Saabira wonders if you need any help inside?' He stands with his hands on his hips, admiring the clean flags over the low dividing wall. He is wearing jeans and a shirt under a V-necked jumper. He does not wear foreign clothes like Saabira.

'I don't want to interfere, but perhaps some help would be useful?' As he speaks he leans over the wall even further and looks through the open door into Cyril's darkened house. Cyril's instinct is to jump to the back door and shut it, to stop Aaman's prying eyes, but something stops him. If he doesn't tidy, the woman from Health might come back with more people and put all his things in black dustbin bags and take it all away.

He screws up his eyes; his upper lip curls towards his glasses. Sometimes this helps him think but today he does not think. Instead, he finds himself nodding in agreement.

Chapter 18

'I have to go the phone box at the end of the lane,' Aaman tells Saabira. 'Cyril would like some help, but his downstairs room is full from floor to ceiling. In Bradford, I have seen, when there is much to be got rid of, they hire something called a skip, like a big bin.'

'How big?' Saabira is playing with Jay. They are on the fluffy rug in front of the open fire and they have a tray across which they are rolling the beads to each other. Jay is giggling wildly.

'Really big. They leave it on the road, you fill it up and then they come and take it away.

'How civilised. But do you really think he has so much to throw away?'

'It's hard to say, but I got the impression that anything small wouldn't be very useful perhaps? Maybe they do half-size ones.'

'You have a number?' Jay is trying to open her hand for a bead and Saabira is teasing her by making it difficult.

'No.' He smiles. 'But I have learnt the number you dial to get other numbers.' He puts on his coat, leaving his faded and torn gardening gloves on the table.

He is back in only five minutes.

'Didn't you manage it?' Saabira asks.

'Not only did I manage, but I found someone who does it in the next village. They used a new expression that I have not heard. They said they were geared up to do a lot of deliveries today, with it being a Saturday.'

'Geared up,' Saabira repeats.

'One customer has just cancelled so he said the skip could come to us instead. They will come in an hour.'

'Really! The British, they are so organised. If it was our village everything unwanted would be left by the road.'

'Yes, but at home someone with as much as Cyril has would be a rich man!' He looks away from her to the rug, his focus gone. 'But why would a man make his home so unusable?' He shakes his head but he does not say it unkindly.

'We are run by emotion. The only trouble is we sometimes think the things we do are helping us when in fact they are not.' Saabira cannot look him in the eye as she says this. He shrugs off his coat and Saabira allows Jay the prize of the bead.

'Anyway, I said we would help him.' Aaman puts his hand against the teapot on the table, to test the temperature.

Whilst they wait for the skip, Aaman and Saabira hide the bead in their hands and Jay tries to guess. She taps their fists with her tiny perfect fingers and shrieks with delight when she gets it right. When she is wrong she shrieks even louder, her eyebrows dropping as she grabs at their fingers, trying to pull them open.

Presently there is the deep purring of an engine outside their front window.

'I will go out and show them which house.' Amman jumps up and leaves without his coat. Saabira can hear the sound of chains jangling and metal scraping on stone. A moment's silence, the engine stopping and then voices.

'Oh my godfathers, what on earth is that smell!' the truck driver exclaims as he climbs down from his cab. 'Here's the paperwork. God, that is bad.' He dumps the skip in the road, thrusts a crumpled sheet of paper at Aaman and wastes no time climbing back into the truck.

'I am not sure what to do with the bill,' Aaman says. 'Cyril did not order the skip. Perhaps I should have asked him first.'

'Is it very much?'

'No, not so very much,' Aaman concedes and shows her the bill. Saabira glances at it and notes the darkness that passes across her husband's eyes. At one time this sum would have been a fortune to him, to them, but now, in theory, he has a substantial wage, although he has not received his first paycheck yet. She is not sure whether to comfort him for all he has been through or congratulate him on how far he has come. She does neither.

'Then we will say nothing about it, unless Cyril does or it arises naturally.' She returns to marking out shapes on the rug with the beads. She reshapes a circle into a triangle, giving Jay the last few beads to finish the pattern.

'Will you come?' Aaman picks his gloves up off the table.

'We might come and watch in a minute.' She hands Jay more beads.

Cyril watches the van from inside his porch. He wonders why his neighbours have put their skip in front of his house. It also seems strange that they should need a skip after only having been here such a short time, but it is none of his business and the truck has gone now, so he returns to tidying the room. He puts three cork-lidded jars in a carrier bag. Someone will want those. He puts the bag with the jars inside a crib that is balanced on top of a large table in the front room.

Coco growls in response to a knock on the back door. It could be Mr Brocklethwaite, in which case he will not answer. But it could be Saabira with some food, which would be most welcome. He puts his ear against the door, listening for Mr Brocklethwaite's wheezing. After a minute or two he opens it a crack.

It is Saabira's husband, Aaman. He is holding his gloves in one hand, and he looks friendly, but Cyril still feels a little nervous. 'The skip has arrived,' he says. 'I don't know how much you need to get rid of but it seems like the easiest way to go about this. No matter if we do not fill it.' Aaman is not wearing his jumper and the sleeves of his shirt are rolled up, and he looks ready for work.

Cyril does not open the door any wider. Despite the sudden tightening of the muscles around his neck his voice carries through the gap as he hisses.

'Get rid of? Skip?'

Saabira can hear shouting from next door. It sounds like Mr Brocklethwaite. Poor Cyril. But Aaman is there and he will be able to manage the situation. But as she listens it becomes clear that it is Aaman's voice, and Cyril's in reply. Why would either of them be raising their voices? Aaman never raises his voice, and Cyril hardly even speaks.

After scooping Jay into her arms, she heads out of the back door and runs round to Cyril's.

'But I am trying to help you.' Aaman is just inside Cyril's back door, with one hand over his mouth and nose, and he sounds exasperated. 'Please to tell me what I have done wrong and I will make it right.' Saabira can hear the emotion in his voice.

'What right have you to throw away my ruler just because the end is missing!' Cyril shouts. He is further inside the back door than Aaman, and has his arms out, either side of him, his palms facing behind him as if he is protecting the whole room. As he repeats this sentence his eyes are half rolled towards the ceiling and have no focus.

'Cyril, Cyril.' Saabira passes the now-screaming Jay to Aaman. She puts her free hands on her neighbour's forearm. 'Cyril, no one is taking your ruler.' She looks over to Aaman to check that what she is saying it true, but he just shrugs and shakes his head. 'I haven't touched a thing. I just told him it was alright if we did not fill the skip.'

'No!' Cyril shouts. He is rocking now from one foot to the other. 'No,' he says again but it is more of a moan. He repeats himself but the word has become a grunt.

'Aaman, perhaps it is better if you take Jay home. I will talk to Cyril.'

'I was only trying to help,' Aaman says. She can see how upset he is; moisture is gathering on the lower rims of his eyes. Jay continues to cry, loudly.

'I know, but please take her. I will come soon.' Saabira tries to sound soothing. Aaman looks at Jay but then looks warily at Cyril.

'Will you be alright here alone with him?' he asks her quietly, in Urdu.

'I will be fine,' she replies, smiling reassuringly. 'Go.' Saabira turns back to Cyril whose head is nodding in time to his rocking.

'Cyril?' she says clearly and firmly. He does not respond. She waits and calls his name again, but still he does not respond. Maybe she should just go home, leave him to it, but she and Aaman started this so, somehow, she should find a way to get Cyril out of this state in which he is stuck.

Gingerly she touches his shoulder, but he is oblivious. Standing beside him, she tries to halt his rocking with a firmer grip but he continues to stare and rock. She does not have the strength to force him and she is not sure what else to do. Then an idea comes to her and, slowly, tentatively, she starts to join in. Not too obviously – she does not wish to cause offence. But once she starts rocking as well, it feels as if they are doing something together, and she makes her movements bigger, rocks as much as he does, keeping time. She keeps up for some minutes and it becomes unclear who is leading and who following. Then, ever so slightly, ever so slowly, Saabira begins to slow the speed she is rocking at and Cyril follows her lead. They adjust to this new, slower speed until it is not clear who is leading and who is following again; then Saabira slows her movement again, makes each rocking a smaller action, and Cyril follows. After some time, they are standing side by side, neither of them moving. Cyril has stopped groaning but he is still staring at the ceiling.

'Cyril, we are friends, are we not?' She waits. She waits a long time but he does not move or speak.

'Cyril. Are we friends?' She makes the question easier to answer and then waits again. His lowers his gaze from the ceiling and stares straight ahead.

'I think we are friends. Are we friends?' She asks.

'Yes.' The answer almost makes her jump.

'Oh, I am glad to hear that. I was worried that we were not. As friends, can you tell me about your ruler?' He might start rocking again, he might start shouting. But to Saabira's relief he does neither.

'They took it.'

'They? The same "they" that tell you where to work?'

'Yes.'

'Ah, I see.' She leaves a gap of silence. Her eyes are beginning to adjust now to the grey light coming in through the back door. All around her, it seems, there are piles of dilapidated furniture. The table in the middle of the room has one leg shorter than the rest, and a brick is wedged under it to keep it level. On its top is a child's crib with one of the rockers missing. Around the room are armchairs with torn upholstery and an old sofa pinned under a pile of varnished wooden pieces. Everything else is such a jumble in the dark she cannot make out individual items. The floor beneath her feet is uneven. One foot is on hard but sticky flooring and the other is on a soft and slippery kind of carpet.

'So why did they take your ruler?'

'They said I had to tidy my room.'

'I see...' In the gloom she can make out things moving about in the shadows, animal eyes reflecting light.

She panics and is about to scream and run until one of them comes into the light to reveal itself as a dog.

'But what if you need things later and you've thrown them away?' He sounds like a child.

'That is a problem. I suppose you can make some sort of rule up for yourself. Perhaps, if you have not used something for the last month or so, it means you don't need it.'

He glances at her briefly but then stares back out across the moors.

'But they make holes in the earth.'

'Who do?'

'The people who take the rubbish.'

'Ah, yes, this too is a problem,' Saabira admits. 'But in the next village there is a shop that is selling things to make money for animals. We could start with everything that someone might want.'

'Yes,' Cyril says. He looks at her now, and almost smiles.

'Then we can look and see what can be recycled.'

'Recycled?'

'Yes. Some things can be used again.'

'Yes' he says, with a little more energy in his voice, and she sees his shoulder drop.

'Then we are left with things that no one wants. My guess is some of that might be wood – we could chop these to burn. After that I don't suppose that there will be much left.'

'It will be tidy?'

'The room will be tidy.'

'Like before Archie died?'

Saabira looks at him. Cyril looks back. It feels to Cyril like he has made an agreement and there is a bubbling feeling in his chest.

'So, shall we start?'

'Tomorrow.' The bubbles in his chest pop and a tight band has replaced them.

'Tomorrow?' Saabira reiterates. She contrives to looks him in the eye for a minute, as if she is searching for something there. He does not know if she has found what she is looking for, and he begins to feel nervous, but then she stops searching and says 'Tomorrow,' again, and she stands and leaves.

Chapter 19

After she is gone, Cyril looks around at his gloomy room. There is a lot of stuff, and he doesn't use any of it. He doesn't know what most of it is. A book of wild flowers, which he found up by the triangulation station one day when it rained so hard Gorilla Head ran home on her own, rests on the arm of the sofa. The pages have dried crinkly and stuck to each other, and one falls out as he tries to flick through the book, arcing its way to the floor, the last curve taking it under the sofa. He hasn't used the book yet, but who knows when he might come across a new plant on the moors and need to identify it? That's the thing about throwing stuff away. You never know if you might need it the next day. He rests the book on the only free corner of the table. The crib that covers most of the tabletop is also in poor shape. The missing rocker makes it useless but someone might want to repair it. Maybe Saabira could use it. He lifts it from the table and puts it on the floor. The tabletop looks sparse now, open. His breathing quickens and it reminds him of the days after Archie was first gone. The whole house felt empty then, after the hospice nurses came and washed his stiffening body to prepare him for the funeral men who they said would come, still talking to him like he was alive. Then the men took him away, impersonal and cold; Archie's body was all covered up, rigidly half-sitting on a stretcher that they rammed through the front door and out again, clattering into the back of the Volvo estate they arrived in. That was the last he saw of Archie.

Then there was just him and Archie's dog and a few sticks of furniture, and the sitting room and the open kitchen felt huge. The dog died not long after. It never settled after Archie was gone. The poor animal would sit whining at Archie's bedroom door for Cyril to open it, and once inside would circle the empty room and crawl under the bed, still whining. Cyril watched it grow thinner and thinner upstairs, poor thing. No matter how hard he tried to encourage it, the animal refused to eat, and then one day it came downstairs. Cyril thought it was a moment to rejoice, but the animal whined by the back door and when he opened it the dog went out on weak, shaking legs, through the back gate and up onto the moors. It never came back. After that the house echoed to the sound of Cyril's own footsteps, his breathing, his heartbeat, his loneliness.

Thank goodness for Coco showing up a few days later, sniffing round Hogdykes Abattoir, thin and hungry. Beautiful Coco filled some of the empty space. He made her a kennel and put it in the backyard but when it started to snow he brought both the kennel and Coco indoors and there they stayed. Blackie Boo came next, and with her arrival the emptiness subsided a little more.

He did a lot of thinking after that, walking for hours on the moors, first with Coco and then with the other strays that came his way – walking and thinking to avoid the emptiness of the house. People left rubbish behind on the beautiful, wild, open moorland. Some of it wasn't even rubbish; some things he found just needed repairing, like the rucksack with a broken buckle, and the thin waterproof coat that needed a new zip. Taking them home with the intention of repairing them meant that the moors looked nicer and also they were saved from the dustbin men who would throw them in big holes in the ground. Matron Jan once watched a television programme with him that showed how beautiful places were turned into horrible places that smelt and burnt with the rubbish that was thrown away. The more things he brought into the house, the less he noticed Archie was not there. The things broke up the large room downstairs into smaller spaces that felt containing, comforting somehow. When he put the bookcase, the one that Mr Dent from number five threw out, against his front window, the room also became dark. Instead of finding it impractical he felt it made the room more comforting.

A collection of single shoes is arranged neatly on a board resting on top of the radiator, and he turns one of these over in his hands. The lace is still good and it has an inner sole that could be taken out and used again. Also, one day, he might find the other one, and it is his size. So perhaps he won't throw that one out. Not yet, anyway. He picks up another one. Blackie Boo found this one and chewed it, and sometimes he lets her take it on walks. She always brings it home. No, he cannot get rid of that either. The shoe collection is difficult. He will start with something easier.

The two old pillows on the hearth – they could go. One is sweat-stained from the really hot summer two years ago, and he cannot remember why the other is there. It looks alright, apart from a small tear where the fluff is pushing out. He could keep it for when the one he is using gets old. The stained one could go, although it is always good to have an extra of something. Best to keep them both just for the moment.

On the sofa, under the boards and varnished wood of the dismantled bunk bed, is a pile of magazines. He doesn't need those. He could put them in a bag and show Saabira how he has started without her. She will smile and be pleased. The pile is heavy; there must be hundreds and hundreds. The top one looks so smooth and glossy, as if it has never been read. The angry man at number three was throwing them out one morning when Cyril was on his way to work, and there were too many to carry but he thought that they might still be there on his way home, and he could take them then. Just as he was thinking this, the man came out of the house and dumped even more magazines on top of those by the bin, their covers equally new and shiny.

106

He can remember this man moving in, not even six months before. He had a woman with him that looked like she could be his daughter, but someone in Greater Lotherton bakery said he was a pottery teacher at a nearby school and the young woman was his wife.

'You throwing those out?' Cyril mumbled, taking a step backward, looking down at his feet.

'Yes, I bloody well am,' the man snapped, and Cyril put his hand back in his pocket and took a step back, ready to walk on. 'No, go on,' the man continued, 'you want them, you can have them.'

Cyril stepped forward again.

'Sorry mate. It's just that the wife left me and it's me who's having to clear up after her. It's one thing her buggering off to Greece to make a new life, but it's quite another leaving me to clear all her stuff out. That's not right.'

Cyril didn't know what to say to that so he said nothing; putting his hands back in his pockets, he walked on, and went back after work to get the magazines when the man's door was firmly shut.

Sometime after that, he saw the man come out of a house in Greater Lotherton, down the hill, by the train station. Another time he saw him walking on the moors with a man and they were holding hands, but when they saw him they moved apart.

He puts the pile of magazines on a three-legged stool. It's a seat that the farmer who farmed the land behind Old Mill House had thrown away; he said the old ways of milking had gone, or something. Useless in this modern age, the farmer said. But to Cyril it is a piece of history, then. Better not throw that away.

The cover of the top magazine shows a picture of a mug with a donkey painted on it, and the animal's tail comes out of the side of the mug to form the handle. He would like one of those. There must be a plastic bag that he can put the magazines in. But as he searches it occurs to him that when the room is tidy he will be able to get to the fire. Then he could roll and twist the pages of the magazines into slow-burning firelighters, the way Archie used to. He takes them off the stool and balances them on the mantelpiece, but as he turns away they slide off and skid over one another, filling what little space there is on the floor.

Blowing air out through narrowed lips, he surveys the mess and wonders if he has the energy right now to pick them all up. They are very colourful, like the clothes in his mother's suitcase. He bends to pick one up. The colours begin to swirl into the paisley patterns of her blouses, and he rocks forward onto his knees. Before he knows what he is doing he is curled up on the colours, pulling some of them over him. Coco joins him and the heat against his body makes him feel sleepy. He will deal with the tidying tomorrow. It will be easier with Saabira's help.

Chapter 20

The next day Saabira is later than he expected. He has been up since the sun stole over the horizon, the chill of the night still in the air. Coco was joined by Zaza and Sabi and with three dogs nestled around him on the mess of colourful magazines he woke sweating despite the early morning cool.

He has gathered the magazines and taken the dogs for their first walk of the day before she arrives.

'I think we need some tea,' she says almost as soon as they are inside and she has had a brief look around. The sink is full of empty baked bean and dog food cans, forks and spoons thrown in on top, mugs with furry mould inside and burnt pans that look like they have been there so long they have adhered to the sink. The drainer, to one side of the sink, seems to be where Cyril keeps rope and string. One coiled piece of rope is thicker in places, where it is covered in what looks to Saabira like buffalo dung. Below the drainer is a cupboard with no door, only the hinges remaining, which is full of crockery. Much of it appears broken. There is bound to be a teapot somewhere – there is everything else – but there might not be a suitable item from which to drink.

'So, you find two chairs and I will bring tea,' she says and Cyril immediately breaks his stare and looks around himself, presumably for seats.

At home Aaman is soothing Jay, whose face is all red as if she has been crying.

'Everything alright?' he asks, eyes wide, that familiar look of concern on his face, which makes him look like he is worried he has done something wrong.

'Fine,' she answers, putting on the kettle.

'Was it me that upset him yesterday?'

Saabira pauses with a spoonful of tea over the teapot to look at him as she says, 'No, my love, it was not you.'

'What, then? What has so upset him?'

'I am going to drink some tea with him, and maybe he will tell me.'

By the time she gets back, the teapot in one hand, two mugs in the other, Cyril is sitting down, and the empty seat next to him looks odd amongst all the clutter. The stool he has found for her is three-legged and so does not rock on the uneven floor. She pulls it away from the table a little. It is like satin to the touch, so worn and smooth is its surface – with age and use, probably. She puts the teapot on the table and pours tea into the two mugs. She has put milk in the bottom of his, but hers is black. The milk in the shops here does not taste like buffalo milk and she cannot get used to the difference.

'I brought you sugar. Look, little packets! Aaman is given them at work with his tea but he does not take sugar.' At first, Aaman brought them home every day as he did not want to make a fuss about how he took his tea, but now he has got to know his colleagues it is he who sometimes makes the tea. But whoever makes it they all know now that he does not take sugar and the little packets no longer make it back to their kitchen. She still finds the sugar in packets funny and, as a consequence, she smiles as she offers them to Cyril. He must think they are funny too, as he smiles in return.

'So, you were telling me about Archie?' She sits down on the three-legged stool.

The lights behind his eyes flash and spin; he blinks hard, he wants to stay here, with her.

'Archie.' He says the word to stop the present receding. It seems to work. 'He's dead.'

'That is sad.'

'They all die.'

'All?' Her tone is soft. 'Who else died, Cyril?'

'My brother, the puppy, my mum, Matron Jan, the mouse, Archie, Archie's dog, the rabbit.'

'Oh my goodness! That is a long list of sadness.'

The way she says this makes him look up from the floor instantly, but she doesn't meet his eye; she looks away down into her tea.

'Heartbreak is a funny thing, Cyril. It makes us do things we would not normally do.' As she says this she looks up again and this time they hold eye contact. But then he feels too exposed and this time it is he who looks away, towards Blackie Boo who has come to sit at his feet. But the way she said that heartache makes people do funny things sounds like she was talking about herself, and Cyril finds he wants to know more. What has she done out of sadness? It is hard to imagine her in any state of sorrow. It's hard to imagine her anything but... He searches for a word that suits her. Peaceful, that is the word. He doesn't want to disturb that peace.

'I didn't do anything,' he assures her.

'I did.' She says it with such simplicity and openness he is not sure what to say in return. But somehow these two words make it feel safe to be with her. She has things inside her, memories, sadnesses, that disturb her just like he has. She is not perfect. He would like to ask her what it is she has done but he is not sure if he is allowed.

'Who died first?' she asks, which catches him off guard as he was thinking about her.

'My brother,' he says and drinks some tea to wet his dry mouth.

'I am very sorry to hear that. Aaman had a brother who died. It made him sad for a long time. How old was your brother when he died?'

'My twin.' The word sounds so alien. He never says this word, not even quietly to himself. His mum didn't like him saying it, not even about other identical siblings.

He feels nothing for this brother. But as soon as he considers this, he realises it is not true. His feelings are strong; he feels anger at this brother, this twin that he has never known. This brother took all his mum's energy and happiness and love. All of it, every last bit. There was none left for him. She only wanted his brother. She would lounge on her bed, drinking and drinking because she missed his twin, pushing Cyril away. She wouldn't even touch him because she said he reminded her of the child she did not have. But he doesn't want Saabira to know that his brother was better than Cyril, that he was the lovable one and that Cyril is nothing in comparison. He doesn't want Saabira seeing him as his mum saw him, so he simply says, 'He died when I was born.'

'Oh my goodness.' The words come out of her in a strange voice, high-pitched, breaking halfway through into a sob. He watches her swallow hard as if something is stuck in her throat and tears well over the dark rims of her eyes. All the structure in her face is lost and she leans over to put her cup on the floor and remains with her face on her knees, her arms wrapped over her head.

He stares.

What is he supposed to do?

Chapter 21

He waits for a while, trying not to make any noise, but aware of his own breathing, and aware that his feet make tiny scuffing sounds on the floor. After what feels like a long time he says her name as tenderly as he can.

Maybe he should go and get her husband. Or maybe he should lift her so she is sitting straight. She is curled up like a butterfly when it has just come out of its chrysalis. You are not supposed to move them. You are supposed to let them unfold their wings by themselves. Geoff at Highroyds told him that in the greenhouse. Geoff knew a lot about plants, and animals, and he was sure to have been right about the butterflies.

So Cyril waits and finishes his tea as quietly as he can. But she is still curled up over her knees, the end of her scarf trailing on the floor as her upper body shudders. He cannot help it. He reaches out to touch the fine crimson material of her tunic where it is stretched across the nodules of her spine.

With his touch she sighs and uncurls. His arm is still outstretched. Trying to lift it off as she moves, he slides his hand up her back and onto her shoulder as she sits up straight.

'Thank you,' she says, but he is not sure what she is thanking him for. He takes his hand away. 'I lost a baby.' As she dabs at her eyes with the corner of her scarf, she looks like a child. He is not sure if he is meant to say something now. He never knew what to do when his mum was sad about his brother. The day before his fifth birthday, the fifth anniversary of his brother's death, she went on and on about her sadness, his brother not being there, her loss, and he gave up trying to say anything. The

113

next day, on his actual birthday, she did not come out of her bedroom. That was when she had a painted toe sticking through a hole in her tights, her face all swollen.

'Losing a baby can make you sad for a long time,' Saabira says. 'Even when you have another one there is still a void, and that place where you love them from never dies.'

'Five years?' he asks.

'Five years, six, ten... As long as it takes.' She seems to be recovering, her voice growing lighter.

'My mum died five years later, on my birthday. On my twin's birthday, but he didn't have a birthday because he was dead.' Saying this out loud brings a strange feeling in his chest, a bit like when he watches a hawk hover over the rabbit warrens.

'Your mother?' is all she says but it feels exactly right.

'She didn't come out of her bedroom. I waited all day. I sat with my back to her door to be closer to her but she didn't come out.' He expects the darkness to come and the present to recede but it doesn't. Instead, he is aware he is sitting next to Saabira, and he can recall every detail without actually being there.

He woke up so excited on his fifth birthday. Two days before, his mum had promised an iced bun and maybe, just maybe, they would take a bus to the zoo, and see the hippos. Yesterday she had been sad but today was his birthday. He got dressed and then he waited on his bed, his knees under his chin. He waited for ages and ages but she did not come out. The door stayed shut and he didn't go in. He dared not go in – the last time he did, she had been play-wrestling with a man with no hair on his head, or something like that, and she had shouted and shouted at him and made him promise he would never go in her room ever again.

As the day turned into the afternoon the hope that they would make it to the zoo faded, but there was still the promise of the iced bun. By late afternoon the temperature had dropped but he dared not turn on the electric bars that were set into the wall. She had told him many times not to touch them, so he didn't. Instead, he took the sheets from his bed and pulled them to the door, wrapped them around himself and leaned against the wood. He thought if she was sad again him being close might help. He wasn't sure how but he hoped it was true.

But then, for no reason, he began to be scared and lonely.

'I knocked on her door but she didn't answer.' He can remember how much his stomach hurt but at the time he was not sure if it was hunger or the fear of what he might find if he opened her door. 'So I opened the door. Not to disobey her,' he added quickly. 'I just thought she had forgotten about me.' He looked briefly at Saabira to make sure she understood that he had not been disobeying her.

Saabira nodded her understanding whilst dabbing at her tears.

'As I opened the door I knew something was wrong. It smelt different. It smelt like Mum, but in a bad way.'

He opened the door slowly so as not to disturb her but before it was even wide enough for his head to go through he knew all her sadness had overpowered her.

'There were lots of empty pill bottles by her bed and a piece of unfolded paper with nothing on it, just some white powder in the creases.' He is still in the present, still with Saabira. It is still horrible to recall, but not as bad and revisiting.

'Her eyelids were all swollen, her cheeks big, her face fat and her lips red but without lipstick. She didn't open her eyes.'

'And this was your fifth birthday?'

'She had promised me an iced bun with a candle. I told her that she had to get up because it was my birthday, but she didn't move.'

'Mum', he said, leaning over, speaking right into her ear. 'It's okay that you didn't get me an iced bun.' But then he started to cry. He tried to make the tears stop. She didn't like him crying but the tears just kept coming, silently, flowing down his cheeks, dripping off his chin onto her bedspread.

The fear came up into his throat and blocked his airways until he spluttered and shouted, 'Mum!' at the very top of his voice and he put his hand on her arm and shook her hard. 'Mum,' he repeated, but more quietly this time, sinking onto the bed next to her. He put his hand on her bloated cheek, which was still warm.

'She was lying on the bed, with her legs sort of curled up a bit, her top arm in front of her, hanging off the edge of the bed. She was holding my ruler. The space between her arm and her knees and her chest was just big enough.'

He watched her for several minutes, and then he crawled under her arm and snuggled up to her, his back against her still-warm body, the back of his legs against her knees so she was spooning him like she had done, long ago when they lived in a place that was just one room, one single bed. Pulling her arm over himself, he imagined that it was her choice to cuddle like that. He imagined her arm had life and that her holding him tight was her choice and not him pulling on her sleeve. But as day became night she became first stiff and then cold, and in the morning he crawled from under her arm and stood by the bed and looked at the corpse that was no longer his mum. Still in her hand was his ruler. The one she had given him one day for no reason. It had the Thunderbirds printed on it and the end was snapped off so it had lost the first quarter of the first inch. As he took it from fingers that were no longer hers he saw it had lipstick imprints all over it. He wiped it on the bedspread and then padded out of her bedroom, out of the flat and along to the only other place in the world that he knew and could go into, the fish and chip shop on the corner. He knew the pub on the opposite corner too, but he wasn't allowed to go in there.

Chapter 22

'I understand her sadness,' Saabira says. 'I did a terrible thing because I lost my child.' Her voice sounds far away, even to herself. Poor Cyril. He did not deserve the life his mother had given him, but then how much of the life Aaman lived did he deserve? The damage that Cyril's history has done to him is apparent. At four he was already starved of the love and affection that every child needs to grow and learn. She wants to hear more about his life but the weight of her own deeds are sitting heavily inside her, struggling to get out.

'I didn't mean to.' Her words gush out before she is ready. And they are untrue. 'Actually, I did mean to, but I was so sad.' She corrects herself but feels compelled to add the justification. 'I was distracting myself trying to make other things feel important...' She listens to herself recounting her own tale of the village dying, the need of the harvester, their lack of money and, as the story rushes out, her tears flow, because what she hears most clearly are her manipulations and excuses to try to justify what she did. So she stops talking. She sits still and reflects, and then, demanding the truth from herself, she starts again, speaking slowly.

'When they told me my baby was dead it was as if the ground had been opened beneath my feet and I felt like I was falling. I fell and fell and everyone and everything around me became unimportant because nothing matched the death of my baby and there was no bringing him back.' She takes a breath. 'When you fall you expect at some point to hit the bottom and I willed this to happen. I wanted whatever the bottom was to come quickly. If it was death or madness it was better than the feeling of falling.

118

The chest-emptying, gut-wrenching, sadness in which I was lost. But the bottom never came, I just seemed to keep falling and in that black hole I was so alone.'

Her hands are intertwined on her knee and very gently Cyril puts his fingers on her forearm. His nails are black with dirt and split and torn, but it is such a tender, respectful touch that it gives her comfort and courage.

'Aaman was too real. His tenderness touched me so deeply that when our baby died I pushed him away.' The truth was she had not wanted to feel anything at all. Nor did she want anything to do with her life. Most of all she wanted nothing to do with the man who helped her create the life that was gone. If not for him it would never have happened. The life would never have been there in the first place and she would not have felt the sorrow. She blamed him. It was his fault.

Also, as time went on, there was the fear. If she allowed her sorrow to find refuge in Aaman's arms, which, after a while, she really wanted to do, then of course they would become close again. If that happened they might create another life which might die too and she would spiral down the dark wasteland again. There might be no recovery the second time.

With a stiff back she compels herself to go on.

'I sent him abroad. I told him it was to raise money for the machinery the village needed, but really I wanted him gone so I could be alone with my misery and to ensure that we would not create another small life that might die.'

'Where did you send him?' Cyril asks. The innocence in his voice makes her snort but to assure him that she is not laughing at him she lifts her head and gives him a small smile.

'I sent him overland to Greece. From there he was meant to go to Italy, and from Italy to Spain where it is easy to work and get papers, and then he would fly back. But...'

'But what?' Cyril asks. Coco's nails click across the sticky lino floor. She sniffs first Cyril and then Saabira, and then gently pushes her muzzle into Saabira's hand. Saabira strokes the dog's fur, which is surprisingly soft. It is very soothing.

'But the world can be an unkind place and he was locked in prison in Turkey and he was beaten and robbed in Bulgaria.'

'Oh.'

'Then he got stuck in Greece. He could not make money to move on or to come home.'

'Oh.'

The first time she had woken in the night to find Aaman sweating and crying and hunched in a corner of their Sialkot home after his return she had been terrified. He wouldn't speak about what was troubling him and she could not guess. But slowly, as the weeks turned into months, he tried to explain to her how he had become a faceless, worthless illegal immigrant and how that had stripped him first of dignity and then of hope. He thought he would never see her or his mother and father, or his grandparents again. That he would die before he could return home; it was just a matter of when and how. The world around him considered him less than human, a problem to be moved on to another location. Every morning before the village was awake he would be up and ready in the square to try for work, but on so many days he was not chosen by the farmers seeking casual labour because he was so small. On the days he did not work he often did not eat. He had seen others starve to death and there was no one there to care.

'But the world is not a bad place.' Saabira recovers herself a little, enough to realise that Cyril knows only too well how hard life can be.

'He got home?'

'Yes.' This knowledge still gives her relief. Aaman got home, he is safe.

120

'He got help from a lady. Her name was Juliet, and we named our daughter after her.' She says all this in one breath and tries to keep her voice, light, breezy. 'She was English like you, but she was living in Greece. She gave Aaman back his pride and his dignity. In fact, it is because of her that it is now possible for us to be here in England.' How she feels about Juliet shames her. So far she has kept these feelings to herself, shared them with no one, and she is not about to share them now.

Suddenly she feels the need to be active and declares that it is a good time to do something other than sit. Coco is still pushing her nose into her hand.

'Shall we see if there is anything that you would not mind being taken somewhere else?' she asks as Cyril stands too. He takes a plastic bag from the broken crib on the table and hands it to her.

Chapter 23

'Shall we start with these?' Saabira picks up a pair of jars. 'They could be of use to someone, and we could give them to the charity shop in Greater Lotherton. If someone buys them, the money will help sick animals.' She pauses to let Cyril consider. He takes one of the jars and turns it around in his hands, and gives it back to her. He is grinning now. Saabira smiles. 'So we are agreed, yes?' Cyril nods, and the grin grows wider. 'Good!' exclaims Saabira. 'That was not difficult. I believe we are going to be successful.' The jars are deposited by the cooker, which is as good a place as any to start a pile for charity, and she turns her attention to the crib.

'I don't think that this can be mended. A spring is missing along with a rocker, and three of the uprights around the handrail have also gone,' she says, and Cyril looks sad. 'But I think it will burn well,' she adds; Cyril puts it in the backyard and with two strokes of the axe it is in pieces, which he stacks. Back inside, Saabira is looking at the bookshelf. The dark rims around her eyes have spread because she has been crying but Cyril thinks she looks just as nice. He would never have guessed that she had all those emotions inside her. It is messy, like his insides. Maybe other people are like that too?

'This bookcase.' It lies on its back; one leg is missing and it will not stand. She touches it gently. Everything she does is flowing and soft. 'It has only half a back and two of the shelves are missing. I don't think anyone will want it.' She speaks slowly. He knows she is trying to be gentle. Not even Matron Jan tried to be gentle. Archie did a bit, especially at the end.

'So we can recycle it?'

'It is plastic. I don't think it will recycle and, also, we cannot chop it because plastic is not good to burn.'

He knows plastic does not burn. Or rather, it does, but the fumes are bad.

'So it will fill a big hole in the ground?'

'I think if we put it in the skip the people who take the skip will crush it until it is very small.'

'How small?'

Saabira makes a guess, showing him with her hands. He nods sagely, picks it up without her help and, with a push and a shove, manoeuvres it out of the front door through the wardrobe porch and into the waiting container.

They continue like this for some time and the chaos in the room reduces until all of the ceiling is visible and in some places the collection of things is only shoulder-high. The top of the table is clear, and Saabira declares that she needs to take a break and check on her family.

'Is he alright, did I upset him?' Aaman asks as she comes in through the back door.

'He is fine, it wasn't you. And I think we are making progress. We are talking as we work so it is slow. Almost every item we have thrown away or chopped up has required a discussion, why he needs it, why he doesn't.' She puts the teapot and the mugs by the sink. 'Do you know, they put him in a mental asylum because he did not get on with the children in the children's home?' She puts the kettle on and washes out the teapot and the mugs. It's a relief to be home. The morning has been exhausting, and Cyril seemed relieved too when she suggested they have a break. He went out onto the moors with the dogs, some of which had started to whine.

'He was in a children's home?' Aaman is sitting cross-legged on the rug in front of the fire with Jay. Between them are a selection of pans and lids. Aaman is holding a wooden spoon which he passes to his daughter. She immediately starts bashing away at the pots and then, with her left hand, she picks up a lid and uses this to hit the biggest casserole dish. Aaman leans back and laughs heartily, which makes Jay bash even harder.

'Yes!' Saabira shouts over the noise, knowing her answer is useless. Aaman has probably forgotten his own question, and they cannot have a conversation with Jay in full swing on her improvised drum kit. But Saabira's shouting gets Jay's attention and her fingers uncurl, the lid falls forgotten and her arms stretch out before her for a cuddle from Mummy. 'Ahh, come here my little love.' Saabira joins them on the rug and Jay squirms onto her lap.

'So do you think he has been in homes and hospital most of his life then?'

'He said he didn't fit in at the home and he had trouble sleeping, which is not surprising really. His mum killed herself and he found her.'

'Oh my goodness, the poor man. I think that is enough to confuse anyone. Why did she kill herself?'

Saabira opens her mouth to answer him but shuts it again. If she says it is because her baby died in childbirth they will spend the rest of the evening talking about their own unknown child. She will stay mostly silent so that she does not have to talk about the black place she went to, in which case it will be almost inevitable that the darkness of their loss will turn the conversation to Aaman's trials and all he has suffered. It will make a very miserable evening. Better to say nothing.

'She was sad.' Saabira dismisses the poor woman's anguish and feels like a traitor. She is grateful when the kettle sings and gives her an excuse to put Jay on the rug and give herself some physical distance from Aaman.

'So, does he want to continue tomorrow with his house clearance, and if so can I be of any help?' Aaman asks.

'Yes and no in that order.' Saabira brings the teapot and mugs over. 'I am going to see if I can persuade him to accept your help though. He is having to do most of the heavy lifting himself. I am not strong enough for the bigger things.'

'So you chucked some stuff out then?'

'Yes, quite a lot. It seems that he has an issue with clear surfaces. He feels like they are canvases or drawing boards and his mind fills them with horrible images he has seen in his life. His mother's suicide, the children at the home laughing, a boy at the hospital who had something called ECT, which is a form of electric shock treatment for the depressed. But I think he may have imagined that. I cannot imagine such a thing in this day and age. Anyway, the boy had a seizure and Cyril witnessed this. Ah, so many unpleasant things.' And as she says it she wishes she could take the words back. She will have thrown Aaman right into his own store of memories of unpleasant things. She stops pouring the tea to look at him. But he is smiling at Jay as he stacks up the pots and pans to put away. 'You know, it has been a few years since my return from Greece. I have said this to you before but I will say it again. There were bad things, yes. But the good things were so much more than the bad. Without Juliet and her kindness I would not have even been offered a job here. The past cannot be changed, but we can turn negative experience to positive by the way we handle them in the present and how we let them affect our future.'

The familiar thumping of her heart starts at the mention of Juliet's name. She knows that it is very wrong of her to feel the way she does. Juliet's kindness changed their life for the better and yet all she can feel at the mention of her name is a petty jealousy.

'I think I will feed Jay before I put the food on. Tonight we are going to try something very English. Fish fingers. But it is not the fingers of fish because, of course, fish do not have fingers.' She hides behind her role of mother and cook. Taking a jar from one of the cupboards over the sink and grabbing Jay's bib and a tea towel from

125

the rack over the Aga, she pulls out a chair and puts out her hand to invite Jay to walk to her and sit on her knee. Steadying herself by clasping Aaman's little finger, Jay makes it all the way from the rug to the table on unsteady legs. Aaman lifts Jay onto Saabira's knee and returns to flop on the sofa. Sometimes he behaves as if he is very English.

She can feel him watching her and Jay as she goes through the routine of trying to feed their daughter. After a mouthful or two, Jay tries to take the spoon. Saabira allows this but still endeavours to guide her so she does not make too much mess – to no avail.

'You must count your fortune,' Aaman says. 'My mother would never have let you get away with letting Jay make so much mess.' He laughs. 'Shall I get a damp cloth?'

Saabira looks at Jay to see what Aaman sees. She has food all around her mouth, right up onto her cheeks as if she has painted on a big smile. She laughs at the sight and all the tension leaves her.

Aaman baths Jay after she has eaten, whilst Saabira starts to cook. Halfway through she goes to the bottom of the stairs and calls up, 'Aaman, you must count your fortune too,' she says. 'Your mother would never have let you bath Jay back at home. That is women's work.'

Aaman laughs but he does not reply and the splashing continues.

Chapter 24

The morning sky, pale blue, empty of clouds, stretches over the moors, lightening towards the horizon. Cotton grass dots the heather, white pinpoints in a sea of purple and green. There is a hawk, a black spot high in the sky, but too high to be hunting. Cyril scoops grain from a large sack and pours half of it into Flop's cage. The big rabbit's nose twitches but the animal is otherwise motionless. The rest goes into the nursing mother's cage. That's it! He is done! Two cages, two lots of breakfast, no fuss, and he has finished. How much easier it is with fewer rabbits. He reaches for the sky, his fingers splayed, and allows all the noises that make a good stretch even better to escape him.

The creak of her back door tells him that Saabira is coming and he lowers his arms and darts back inside his own door, and then wonders why he did. He likes to be with Saabira. She makes him feel good. No one has ever done that before. Not his mum, not Matron Jan, really. Apart from the dogs, and Archie, maybe. He goes out to feed the rabbits several times that evening hoping that she might return but he doesn't see her again until the next morning.

'Hello. Did you sleep well?' Saabira is smiling and her teeth look very white. Today she has her mustard tunic and trousers on, with the dark-pink cuff around the ankles. Her bracelets jangle as she opens her gate and steps onto the moorland path. He expects his tongue to get wrapped around itself as he tries to articulate his answer, but instead the words flow easily as he listens to his answer.

'I had sweet dreams. Big empty spaces, like the moors but flat and smooth and no horrible pictures. It felt like clouds.'

'That sounds very nice. Do you feel like doing some more to your home today?' Her hand is on his back gate.

If he says no she will probably leave, and if he says yes she will come in and they will spend more time together.

'Yes,' he says enthusiastically.

He stands to one side of his open door to let her in and he hopes she notices the teapot he has put on show on the table. He looked really hard after he got back from walking the dogs and found it amongst his blankets. He also discovered that the woollen blankets had mostly been eaten by moths.

The teapot is not new but the mould inside came away with a bit of poking with a stick. He couldn't wash the teapot up, or any cups, because the sink is full and he doesn't know how to get the pans clean to make it less full. When he got to this point he did do something right. He put all the dog food tins and the baked bean tins in plastic bags. As Saabira steps over the threshold she kicks one of these bags.

'Tins?' she asks, surveying the sink and the table. She smiles when she sees the teapot. 'Tins can be recycled,' she assures him. 'And what a fine teapot! It has a picture of the queen on the side! Shall I make some tea, and we can drink it whilst we work?'

He bites his bottom lip; he does not have tea. Nor does he have a kettle. What should he say?

She saves him from the mild panic that is starting in his chest. 'I won't be a minute,' she says, and picks up the teapot and mugs and leaves.

Maybe he can do something nice for her whilst she is gone? He looks around. There is nothing but mess and dirt. But outside the blue sky beckons. The drizzle of dawn has gone, the heather sways and small birds are singing, hidden in the bracken maybe. Their song is so full of life he is tempted to shut his eyes and let himself drift, let the pictures come, fly with the birds, but Saabira will not be long so he will not indulge himself.

Coco whines when he does not let her out of the back gate with him. Up the hill at the back of the houses, just by the stream that only flows in winter, is where the heather is at its best, marked by a line of cotton grass. He picks several stiff stalks of the flower. It cuts into the creases of his bent fingers as he pulls. One sprig comes out whole, its earth-encrusted roots dancing. He twists them off, bunches what he has picked and returns to the house where it only takes a second to locate an egg cup under the sink for a vase.

The heather is too heavy and falls sideways out of the egg cup as he lets go. After tearing off the label from a half-eaten can of dog food on the side of the sink, he scrunches it up and uses it to jam the stalks of heather into the egg cup. It works; it stays upright. He is surveying his handiwork when Saabira returns with the tea.

'Oh, how lovely.' She notices the heather immediately. Cyril thinks he will tell her that it is for her, but then finds he doesn't.

Over a mug of tea each they look at all that there is to be sorted out.

'What is this?' Saabira points to the jumble of planks and varnished wooden pieces that are piled over the sofa.

'Beds, bunk beds.'

'Oh, really? It is all there?'

'Yes.'

'Okay, so, if you are happy to let this go there is a colleague of my husband who is looking for big beds for his twins. He might find bunk beds acceptable, and if he does he may even pay you something. How much would you want for it?' Saabira is lifting up one end of the top piece to look at all the underneath pieces.

What should he say? Is it fair to take money for it when he got it for free? Nev and Helen, who live at one of the houses built at right angles across the top of the road, were just throwing it away, taking it to the rubbish dump. He rescued it for nothing, to save it being dumped in a hole in the earth. No, he doesn't want money, but maybe he could swap it?

'A tin of dog food,' he says.

'Oh, I think they would manage a sack of dog biscuits at the least.' She laughs but it does not feel like she is laughing at him. 'Shall we put it outside our house and then Aaman can arrange for the man to come and look at it without us disturbing you?'

Saabira takes two pieces and Cyril piles as many as he can in his arms, mostly to make her think that he is big and strong but also because he is quite enjoying the idea of the room becoming emptier. He can imagine sitting at the table, maybe even with the fire lit, drinking tea with Saabira, maybe even eating there, together. In his thoughts Aaman is also there but he isn't sure why, as he doesn't know him.

Saabira fluffs up the cushions on the sofa and dust fogs the air.

'Oh, dear me!' she says and takes them outside where she bangs them against the low wall, and the breeze from the moors blows the dust towards Mr Brocklethwaite's house. Cyril chuckles.

When she comes back in they start to look through other piles of things. The blankets are declared unsalvageable but Saabira assures him that as they are wool they will rot to nothing if they put them in the skip. 'Tell me about Archie,' she says.

The sudden mention of Archie's name makes his head spin. Archie's waxy skin and staring eyes fill the blank back of the bureau he is trying to move. Rubbing his eyes makes colours swirl on the inside of his eyelids but when he opens then the image of Archie is gone and Saabira is handing him his tea.

'Matron Jan in the hospital, she said I should not have been there. She said I was fine, just in grief and shock. All I needed was stability and love, she said. But there was nowhere else that would take me.' That was odd – the question he answered wasn't the one Saabira had asked. His mouth opens again. 'I overheard her one day when there was an argument in her office. Matron Jan was shouting at a man in a dark suit.'

She looked so angry that he felt scared. But he also wanted to tell the man to go away, so he stayed outside the door listening, in case he was needed.

'If you lock a young boy in a place like this, and this is all he knows for twelve years, then what do you expect?'

'We're not a charity. He's eighteen now.' The man in the suit said, with no emotion.

'So you want to just kick him out onto the street?'

Cyril's blood ran cold. Tears stung at his eyes and he slithered down the wall to sit on the floor.

'It isn't quite like that,' the man said, not sounding quite so cross now.

'He is put into a children's home with no one-on-one support, having suffered the trauma of his mother's suicide when he was five. He doesn't get on in the children's home because of this trauma so they focus on his shortcomings and label them mental disorders so they can dump him in here. He stays here for twelve years surrounded by people who are not functioning well out in the real world and these are his peers, these are the people he learns to interact with as he grows, and then aged eighteen you want to kick him out into the real world!'

Matron Jan sounded really angry now, and the man must have thought so too, because he didn't answer that.

'Look, he needs sleep medication, he is still having sessions with the psychologist every week, he comes in and sits and talks to me every day. He's just not ready for the outside world. He's had very little exposure to it. He's just not ready.' She stopped shouting then, her voice calm, explanatory. 'We can start a programme, he can go out with a nurse, to the shops in the towns, a visit to the cinema, that sort of thing, but it has to be done gradually. If we overexpose him it could well push him back. It certainly won't help him to move forward.'

'Go on,' Saabira encourages.

'Well… I knew her for years and then she was dead. No one would tell me where she was and then one day a new nurse told me. She got in trouble for telling me but I don't know why. Matron Jan had a heart attack. She said her job was very stressful. It wasn't the patients that were the problem, she said, it was the nurses and doctors. So many of them where not interested, she said.'

'I don't know why they start their training,' Matron Jan said to him one day when he went into her office to sit with her. 'They know that psychiatric nursing is one of the modules that they have to do, yet when they get here they are just so unengaged. I have to motivate them, encourage them, sort out their bickering, keep track of medicines, and you just would not believe the way the doctors carry on. They're just as bad – worse probably. Especially Dr Scalebor – what an arrogant sod he is.'

He didn't understood what she meant, but as usual the whole of her speech had lodged in his head. It was useful to remember things this way because as he got older he could understand more and more of the things he didn't understand at the time.

'I think they were not meant to tell me because they thought my mum dying was too difficult for me. Matron Jan was my friend.'

'And Archie?'

Chapter 25

Oh yes, she had asked him about Archie.

'Archie was my friend too. He died too but there was no one to hide that from me. I think it was bad of them to hide Matron Jan being dead from me, because if you don't know where someone is you worry about them but if you know they are dead that sort of works through your head, comes out of your eyes like water for ages, then it's sad and then it's not so bad.'

It is his anger that makes him grab a box of things without looking through it. He takes it out through the wardrobe porch and throws it over the low wall into the skip. The box bursts, spilling colour in the form of broken toys he saved from the house next door before the family moved out and Saabira came. The children would break their toys and the mother would throw them away. When she saw him picking them out of her rubbish one day she started putting any new broken toys on top of the dividing wall between the houses. Later, she moved to the house further down the road, which used to be two houses but the builders came and made it into one. She had to move because she kept having more children and they needed more space. She is still there but he doesn't see her very often now. He has seen her in the bakery shop in Greater Lotherton wearing a white apron and blue plastic gloves and a white paper hat, and sometimes she waves to him but that is all. He used to repair the toys and leave them on the wall for the children to take back. What is left, now in the skip, is all the parts that could not be used or repaired. They will be crushed to the size of a marble and the earth will swallow them up. Is the clearing out of his house more important than the earth? He uses his finger and thumb to measure a space the size of a marble, then frowns and turns to go back into the house.

Back inside, Saabira continues the conversation as if there has been no break.

'When Aaman was away I did nothing but worry all the time. Sometimes I even used to say to myself, if I knew he was dead at least I could stop worrying.' Saabira sounds sad.

'I worried about Archie when he started to cough so hard he was in pain. Then he didn't get out of his chair.' Cyril turns around and looks at the unlit fireplace.

'Where did he used to sit?' Saabira asks.

'On that chair, but the chair was over there then.'

'Does that chair remind you of him in a good way?'

'No.' A lump has filled his throat. His eyes are stinging. He hates the chair. Every time he looks at the chair Archie is there and it makes him sad.

'Perhaps it would be good to get rid of it?'

'Yes.' The chair is one thing he would be very glad was gone. But his limbs will not move.

'Shall I get Aaman to do it?'

He cannot speak so he nods. Saabira touches him on the shoulder as she leaves and is not gone a minute before she is back, with her baby in her arms, and Aaman following.

His silent, gloomy, cramped room is suddenly full of life. His initial reaction is to get them to leave, to maintain what he has known for so long, but as this thought forms so does another one – an image of a clear and tidy room into which he can invite them with no shame.

'Hello, my friend.' Aaman says. He is wearing a T-shirt and not a shirt today, and he probably has no work because it is a bank holiday. No one has ever explained why everyone gets a holiday on a bank holiday or why it is always on a Monday. Aaman is also wearing one of Saabira's scarves. He has wound it across his nose and mouth. The lump in Cyril's throat grows and his cheeks burn. The scarf is because of the smell of his house, the smell that keeps everyone else away. He can barely meet Aaman's eye. How on earth has he let his house, his life, get to this point?

'How can I help you?' Aaman asks, his voice slightly muffled by the bandaging.

Tears threaten to spill, and Cyril tries to rub his hand nonchalantly over his eyes in a way that he hopes looks like he is thinking. The embarrassment he feels because Aaman needs the scarf is mixed with his gratitude that Aaman is pretending nothing is wrong and not mentioning it.

He kicks at the table leg. He thinks that it might help the mix of emotions that are filling him, but it doesn't. In a way, it is Saabira's fault. Ever since he first met her he has noticed that he is getting cross with all the things inside his home. So if Aaman really wants to help he could just make his house nicer inside. Just make everything disappear so he doesn't have to deal with this, the smell, the humiliation. He should have thrown away the first carpet after all the accidents Coco had when she first arrived, but where would he have thrown it? A second carpet over the top seemed like a good solution at the time, and at first it didn't really smell bad, and it got worse slowly, so that he pretended to himself that it wasn't really that bad and somehow got used to it. Somehow it is as if that quick decision, to lay a second carpet on top, has defined how he has lived ever since.

Saabira jumps as Mr Perfect comes out from under the sofa. Cyril loves his dogs but he is concerned that they make her jump every time one of them comes out of their nest. Maybe he does have too many dogs, like he had too many rabbits. But he cannot put them over the wall like he did with the rabbits.

Aaman is waiting for an answer but Cyril is not sure what to say. Asking him to do something might sound like he is ordering him about, as if he is a child. How do people ask other people to do things for them without it sounding rude?

'Hello, Mr Aaman.' He tries to sound respectful.

'It is just Aaman.' Saabira's husband replies. 'What can I do?'

'We were going to throw away Archie's chair,' Saabira says, and Cyril feels grateful that she has saved him the embarassment and taken the focus away from him. 'Archie does not need it any more, and it is a sad reminder.'

'Which is the chair?' Aaman asks. He sounds jolly.

Both Cyril and Saabira point. Aaman looks at the chair and the path it has to travel to go out of the front door. Cyril would like to help but he has not touched the chair since that day.

'He didn't go up to bed in the last weeks,' he says to Saabira. Her baby has fallen asleep over her shoulder, and a thin line of dribble is making a dark-orange river in the mustard sea of her tunic.

'He stayed in the chair?' she asks, stroking the baby's back.

'I rang the number he gave me on a piece of paper but the person at the other end said they did not do house calls any more. When I told Archie he said, 'Bloody civilised country.' He looks at Saabira quickly to make sure she is not upset that he used a bad word.

'So he knew he was ill.'

'He was coughing a lot, and he'd been in hospital before I moved here but he said it wasn't nice and he would never go again. I said I had just come from a hospital and it was very nice, but he said that was different.' He has never talked about Archie, and it feels odd. After Archie died there was no one to talk to, so who would he talk to about Archie? 'The day he died there was a woodpecker in the tree opposite. It was tapping away. I saw it. Spike was on the wall, all flat, thinking that he couldn't be seen. I thought he was going to get the bird so

137

I called Archie. He always knew what to do. But Archie didn't answer. I banged on the window but Spike just kept creeping up to the woodpecker. Then the woodpecker stopped pecking and was still. Then Spike wiggled his bottom, you know, ready to pounce, and the bird just flew away. I never saw the woodpecker again.' He blows air out through his lips and pushes his glasses up with one finger.

'And Archie?' Saabira is watching Aaman, who is now struggling by the front door with the chair.

'I came down happy for the bird and I wanted to tell Archie all about it. I told Archie about everything. He even knew where the hawk's nest was that I found. He was sitting there.' He points to an empty space and then looks around for the chair. It is beside the bookcase that blocks the light from the window. Aaman is inside the wardrobe porch looking at the opening.

'He was sitting in the chair and his blankets had fallen from his knees to the floor. The moths have eaten them now...' He looks at the empty place where the blankets used to be before continuing. 'So I picked them up and I was telling him off. He sometimes let me do that. Not seriously, just for fun. I was never very good at telling Archie off but when I tried it made him laugh. This time he didn't laugh. He was staring straight ahead at the wall.' His gaze wanders to the line of single shoes on a board over the radiator on the wall.

'His face was all waxy and slightly shiny and he smelt like he had made a bad mess in his trousers.' He looks Saabira in the eye. 'He was dead, you see, and I knew he was dead because I remember my mother.'

'Yes, he is dead, so is she,' Saabira says.

With no warning at all the tears spring to his eyes and he loses control of his lips. They are quivering out of his control and the shuddering in his chest makes everything worse, and then he cries like he does not remember crying since seeing his mum's bloated face. He cries for his mum and for Matron Jan, and for the little mouse in the cage behind the bushes at the hospital. He cries for Archie and for Archie's dog, and for the rabbits and his whole sorry-looking house. Saabira, still holding her daughter, puts her free arm around his shoulder. Then strong arms are round him, leading him to a chair. The arms do not release him. They are firm and sure, and his head is tucked against Aaman's chest and he can smell his aftershave and he cries even more. The arms do not hurry him, they do not pull away, they hold him and it feels so safe.

His sobbing quietens, the tears flow less quickly, and it is he who pulls away first, the strong arms releasing him.

'Everything is fine,' Aaman says. It is a simple thing to say but it feels like the words are exactly right. 'Although, I think we might have to take your porch off to get the chair out.'

Cyril draws in his chin and looks up sharply to see Aaman smiling. He is not laughing at him; he is suggesting that Cyril should laugh with him. Through all the sadness, this invitation carries such an attractive promise that it makes him want to laugh to see what it would feel like to do so through his tears, and so he does. It starts in his chest like an excitement and then it builds as his stomach tightens; his mouth opens and he laughs so loud and so strongly he has to hold on to the table edge for fear of rocking off the stool. Aaman is still laughing and Saabira, who is rocking the baby, chuckles along with them, her eyes shining as she looks at them both.

Chapter 26

Aaman does not dismantle the porch. He examines it and shows Saabira where it is screwed to the wall, and how it is altogether sturdier than it looks. Cyril's laughter, which seemed to be endless, eventually fades and when he faces the room he looks lifeless. Saabira suddenly realises how tired she is; Cyril must be tired too.

'I think the next step is for another day,' she announces. Cyril looks relieved.

'I must walk the dogs,' he says and looks around for his jacket. It cannot be found and, for an awful moment, Saabira fears that she – or, worse, Aaman – has thrown it in the skip. It is with relief that she remembers she hung it up on a peg on the wall outside to keep such a thing from happening.

Once he has it on he seems keen to be gone. The light has turned pink and the purple heather looks soft and inviting. Coco and Zaza come out from their hiding places behind the furniture. Blackie Boo joins them, and Sabi, behind Coco. Cyril calls, 'Gorilla Head, Mr Perfect, Teddy Tail!' and three more dogs appear, one from the cupboard under the stairs and two from the floor above, their nails tapping on the bare wooden treads.

As Saabira closes her back door she turns to see a rush of dogs heading onto the moors, bouncing, chasing and happy. It seems that Cyril is taking them out all together.

'It was very kind of you to give up your day off to help,' she says to Aaman.

'If I am truthful, Saabira, the sooner that place is cleared and clean the happier I will be. You are lucky that you have no sense of smell, but it is really quite unbearable. I am a little concerned that we took Jay in there.' This last sentence is said very quietly. He pauses to light the fire. 'You know, I am really not surprised that his neighbours are not enjoying living next door to him on the other side. I am sorry for them but grateful that the wind is favourable to us.' The fire is alight now and he turns his head to face her. 'I think your way of dealing with this is very kind, and much more productive than being aggressive and getting all these official people involved.'

'I worry it might not turn out very well for Cyril. If Archie died two years ago, who is Cyril paying his rent to? It might be that he is illegal there. Mr Brocklethwaite could use that to make him leave.'

'Well, I know how it feels to be Illegal,' Aaman says. Saabira sits on the sofa and reaches out her free hand to him.

'You know, it was not as I would have imagined,' he says. 'Mostly it is shock, that such a thing has happened to you. You feel that the world has turned against you and you cannot understand why. You are still you, and have not changed. You are still the caring, law-abiding citizen you always were. My heart had not changed. I still loved as I always have, had feelings just as I had always had feelings, and yet I was being treated as if I was something else. Something inhuman. Everything I believed was safe about society and the world was gone because I was suddenly on the other side of this invisible wall. The world turns its back on you.' Aaman rocks back as the fire catches, and he sits on the floor, leaning against the sofa. Saabira strokes his hair with her unencumbered hand as she feeds Jay. 'Yes, I think the first thing is shock, then disbelief,' Aaman continues, 'Then horror and panic and then loneliness.' He is silent for a moment.

'I began to judge myself by how I was treated. I began to wonder if they were right, if I was this thing that they made me out to be. I treated myself as if, indeed, I do not have any value. I even caught myself behaving as I thought they all expected me to behave once or twice, lowering my standards.'

He sighs.

'I am not sure if I have told you this, but when I first met Juliet in Greece and she had given me work in her garden – this was before we became friends – I asked her if she had any clothes that would fit me.'

Saabira cannot help her intake of breath. She has heard so much about his adventures but she has not really considered the day-to-day practical side of his life whilst he was away. Where did he get his clothes, his shoes, his soap, when he didn't even have money to feed himself?

'She offered me a carrier bag full of clothes. But do you know what I did?' Saabira shakes her head. 'Instead of thanking her and taking them graciously, I was angry. I was angry that I had to ask and angry that I had to accept. I was angry that she thought that, because she could offer me a bag of her old clothes, she was better than me. I was angry that she thought she was better than me because I spent my days cleaning up the mess in her garden, cleaning up after her. It made me lash out like a heathen, like the illegal immigrant they had labelled me. I wanted to hurt her. So I looked through these clothes as if I had a choice of what I would wear. I showed her where the trousers she offered had a hole, I dismissed the shoes as being too big or too small, I forget which, and then, as a final insult, I left all that she had offered just strewn over her verandah so she would have to clear up after me, so she would spend her time clearing up the mess I had made. The dirty, messy, ungrateful, illegal immigrant.'

Saabira knows from his tone that he will not want her sympathy. He is analysing his own behaviour, telling the events out loud to allow him to see them more clearly, trying to find his peace with them.

'Did Juliet understand?' Saabira asks.

'I think that is why it has stuck with me. I have never explained it to her. Whilst I was still there I was too embarrassed to mention it. Now we are apart, our emails are more matter of fact. We do not mention the past, just our present and future plans. But that is how it has always been since we became friends, just looking forward.'

Even though she knows they stay in touch by email, this reminder of it tightens her chest. But she keeps stroking his hair as if there is nothing wrong. Does he expect her to make some sort of response, offer a reply?

Chapter 27

Jay continues to suckle. Saabira tries to remain relaxed, so as not to pass on her agitation.

Aaman looks tired.

She is still considering her reply. It is forming – something about explaining his actions to Juliet when the time is right. She is checking over what she is going to say to ensure that it betrays no signs of her jealousy when she says it.

'I think I might take a bath,' says Aaman, yawning. He leans his head back against her knee. His fringe, which she has been smoothing flat against his head, bounces as she takes her hand away.

'Yes, I feel dirty, too, after being in Cyril's house, even if I touch nothing.' Saabira agrees.

'You want a bath too?' Aaman speaks in his teasing tone, a spark in his eyes.

'Ah, so now, suddenly, you are not so tired?' she teases back, the relief of the change of subject apparent in her voice, to her if not to him.

'Maybe I am. Maybe I am so tired that it will be you who has to wash *my* back.' With his hand on her knee for leverage, he pushes off and stands.

She picks up the nearest cushion and gently bashes him on the back of the legs.

'Okay, I am going now – I know when I am not wanted.' He scissor-jumps to avoid the second swipe of the cushion, all tiredness gone.

His bare feet slap up the stairs, water whines through the pipes, and the sounds of splashing and singing can soon be heard: the song is an Urdu song he sometimes hums to Jay.

Saabira sits staring into the fire as her daughter falls asleep on her knee. How does she resolve this whole thing with Juliet? She is jealous of a woman she has never met. Jealous of a relationship that she has never witnessed. It is impossible to put it in perspective because it is all in her mind. Nothing Aaman has said has led her to believe that anything happened between them, but somehow it is difficult to understand why someone would be so generous for no reason. Employing him to help with the garden is just a straight transaction, but offering him the use of her laptop, finding an online course for him to do in order to learn basic programming, getting him customers so he could gain experience. Why would anyone do all that? Unless...

With Monday being a bank holiday the working week is only four days and then Aaman is home all day again.

Saabira is pleased with the progress she has made with Cyril on his house, and the skip on the road is becoming fuller as the rooms are emptied. The magazines add a colourful layer to the top of the rubbish as their pages flutter in the breeze. The greatest triumph as far as Saabira is concerned came when Cyril himself suggested that they dispose of the bookcase up against the window. It seemed too heavy for them to move, but then Cyril remembered that Mr Dent had told him it came apart, and they spent the rest of the time until Jay woke up breaking it down into pieces. With this item gone, what light could get through the grubby front window illuminated all that was left in the room. It did make the work a little more cheerful and it was certainly easier to see what they were doing, but it also showed the level of grime everywhere.

'It's such a waste,' Cyril says as he stacks pieces of the bookcase outside his back door. The plan is to chop it into pieces later and use it as firewood. 'Everything is plastic or that pretend wood now.'

145

'But do you have books to fill it?' she asks. Cyril's cheeks mottle and the colour extends all the way down his neck. It seems an odd reaction. He looks away from her and with a little frown of her own it occurs to her that he might not be able to read. She accepts this without question but as the moment passes it also occurs to her that she, who is supposedly from a poor country, a tiny village, has a degree, and this man, a white man, born and bred in Great Britain cannot even read? Maybe?

'What about this, Cyril?' Saabira asks, holding up a coal scuttle with a large hole in the bottom. She has his attention for a second but then, with no warning, he dives into his wardrobe porch and peeks through the crack in the door. The sound of a car stopping tells Saabira what he is doing.

'It's a man,' Cyril inform her. 'He's getting out.' He pauses. 'He's going to your house.' Pause. 'He's knocking.'

'My house? Who could that be?' She leaves by the back door to go round to her house. Jay is still sleeping. It is the only time Saabira feels she can help Cyril. Aaman has bought her this wonderful thing that plugs into the electricity next to Jay so she can hear every one of her sighs on another device that she has hung on a piece of cord around her neck. She stops to press a kiss lightly on her sleeping daughter's forehead as she heads for the front door.

The knock is repeated and she opens it to a man with a smiling face, his teeth glinting. Behind him the sky is still bright, so she cannot make out the details of the rest of his features.

'Hello.' He holds out his hand for her to shake. 'Gavin – I work with Aaman. Did he tell you? The twins have just outgrown their cots and he said you had a pair of beds.' He sounds nervous.

'Oh yes. Beds.' She opens the door for him to come in and leads him through to the backyard.

146

Over the moors the skies are a blue-grey, darker than the sky out of the front door, and slightly threatening in a romantic way. This country is so changeable, so dramatic. The blue-grey sky is such a wonderful colour it draws her in, and for a second she stands there staring at the purple of the heather, the green of the ferns and the deep hues of the sky. Deep, rich, hues.

The man coughs politely and Saabira recovers herself.

'It is a bunk bed, one bed on top of the other.' She points to the stack of wooden pieces.

'Even better.' He is young, with red hair and glasses. He touches the pieces of bunk bed with the air of someone who has no idea what he is looking at.

'I am afraid we have no mattresses,' Saabira adds.

'Aaman wasn't clear on the price but he said it would be reasonable.' He clears his throat and pushes his fringe to one side with the flat of his hand, stroking his forehead. 'It's amazing how two such little kids can use up so much income.' He laughs but there is a tension in his voice as if what he has said is more of a worry than a joke.

'The man who is selling the beds says he would like a bag of dog biscuits, or the equivalent in money, I suppose,' Saabira says.

'A bag of dog biscuits?' The words come out with a great deal of air, as if he allows all the tightness he is holding to escape. He takes some money from his back pocket and carries on talking. 'There you go, a bit more than a bag of dog biscuits.' He offers her the note, quickly sealing the deal. 'I don't suppose you have anything else you're selling, have you?' The price is presumably the attraction.

'No, sorry.' She watches him take an armful of the pieces to his car and come back for more. He is on his last journey when she says.

'Oh, actually, do you need a bookcase? Solid wood. Tall?'

147

'Oh my God – what is that smell?' The wind has changed and he puts the end of his suit jacket over his nose and mouth.

'That is why next door is being cleared out. That is where the bookcase was,' Saabira explains.

'Would I have to go in to get the bookcase?' The man's eyes widen. The wind changes again.

'It is just here.' She points over the low wall.

'Oh, thank goodness for that,' he says.

The young man inspects the bookcase briefly, before taking the pieces out to the road and strapping them to the roof of his car. When the pile is gone, Saabira goes out to see him off. He tries to closes the door of his car. The pieces of bunk bed are laid from the back window all the way into the footwell of the passenger seat. He rearranges them, pushing at them so the door will shut. A knee against the door encourages the latch to click.

He fumbles in his pocket again.

'Here – for the bookcase,' he says, a gruff giggle escaping him. He sounds pleased with himself. 'Get another bag of dog biscuits.' He is just about to speak again when the breeze switches direction and the man puts his nose into the crease of his elbow and hurries to get into the car.

Saabira flattens the two notes out, one on top of the other, and goes back to Cyril's.

'Here,' she says, offering the bills. 'For the beds, and the bookcase.'

Cyril looks but does not touch.

'So much?'

'Two bags of dog food.' Saabira nods encouragingly.

His hand lifts from his side, his fingers twitching towards the money.

'The skip,' he says, and looks away from the money and into her eyes.

'What about it?' Saabira asks, her attention slightly caught by the sounds of Jay's stirring coming through her monitor. She will have to go back soon. Also, she needs to think about cooking... She loves Jay dearly and Aaman is her life, but there must be more to her life than cooking and feeding, she thinks. Something a little more intellectually demanding, perhaps?

'How much?'

'How much what?' Saabira has lost the thread of what they were saying.

'The skip. It must have cost something. How much?' He points to the money in her hand.

'Oh yes, about this much.' The cost was double the value of the notes in her hand. It is not that she wants to undermine Cyril's independence but, judging by his clothes and his house, he barely makes enough to keeps his life together on what he earns.

'Good.' He turns his back to pick up the coal scuttle. He puts his finger up through the hole and wiggles it. 'Can this be mended?'

'No, but it can be recycled,' Saabira says. Jay is definitely stirring, and seeing as Cyril is now sorting things without her help it seems like a good time to leave.

Chapter 28

Cyril doesn't even notice Saabira leave. A bent metal lamp base clangs as it hits the skip. Cyril punches the air with one hand, then looks up and down the street. There is no one watching. A tattered wicker basket is squeezed in a tight embrace and then put underfoot, stamped on until it is flat and put out with the wood. It will make great kindling.

A chipped vase is next, and it will shatter marvellously if he throws it into the skip from any distance. He starts to take aim but then stops. Glass is recyclable; the lamp is placed gently in a line with six old milk bottles and two beer bottles by the front gate.

He is getting good at this tidying. If he had known he was capable of doing such a thing he would have done it years ago. He looks around for Saabira, to share this feeling with her, and realises she has gone. The light feeling in his chest that, until that second, he had not noticed deflates a little, but not much. The growing space in the house keeps him buoyant. He will continue, make real progress so when she next comes she is amazed.

The radio alarm up in his bedroom rings, muffled by joists and floorboards. His head rolls back and he screws up his face, closes his eyes tightly and moans out load. It is so unfair that he has to go to work.

His boots drag on the moor path that leads to the road down to the abattoir. It is an old stone building, which would have been built for the wool trade, and which sat derelict for decades until a group of local farmers used an EU directive to take on the building at a very low rent – the directive said it was an offence to cause or permit an animal to suffer avoidable excitement, pain or suffering, and the farmers used it to manipulate local government so they could have it, along with a sizeable grant to convert its use. That was what Archie had said. He had been to the library in Bradford, looked it all up. That was not long after the hospital had moved him into Archie's house and Cyril had been told to start work. They didn't know each other then.

'Truth is, those greedy sods just wanted to cut down their transport costs. Easier to move lumps of meat than live animals,' Archie said, tottering across the room from his easy chair to the table.

'Look here, I got this today.' He picked up a printed sheet and began to read.

'"John Cartwright, a long-time worker, told the *Bradford Post* that he frequently has to cut the legs off completely conscious sheep. "They blink. They make noises," he says. "The head moves, the eyes are wide and looking around... They die piece by piece. Because they are unloaded from trucks so quickly and the lines move so quickly and many workers are so poorly trained, the technique of stunning the animals often fails to render the animals insensible to pain."'"

He hated Archie for reading him this. As he physically reacted to the words, the back of his head bumped against the wall. The pain was better than the thoughts of the animals suffering so he jarred his head back again... and again, and again.

'Hey, hey.' Archie dropped his printed sheet and rushed over to him, pulling Cyril by the shoulders and putting a hand behind his head to soften the impact. 'Hey, fella – hey, my friend, hey Cyril, it's okay.' Then he muttered to himself, 'Oh shit.'

'Come on, Cyril, sit down, I'll make some tea.' Back then Archie was stronger than him and he used brute force to manipulate him into a chair.

'Hadn't realised you was so sensitive,' he said and filled the kettle. 'Sorry, mate.' He put tea in the pot. 'I know now.' The teaspoon rang as he threw it in the sink.

The abattoir rests in a gully, by a stream that would have once powered a waterwheel. A beech tree and a couple of hawthorn bushes soften the building's edges.

Coming to work this way is quicker than taking the road, but means he has to scramble down the steep, dry stream bed. The water has been diverted and flows through a nearby farm now.

Grabbing ferns and holding on to them stops his feet skidding down the soft mud. In the winter it is like a slide and he cannot come this way at all. He grabs at a root as the ground gives, but it pulls free of the earth and his balance is disturbed. One leg buckles under him and he falls forward. Twinkling reflected light, his glasses fly off – his hand is being skinned on the pebble-impacted stream bed, but he cannot stop. Down below, by the building, he can hear laughing.

Crouching to lower his centre of gravity, he makes the quick decision to forgo the seat of his trousers. If he slides the rest of the way on his bottom he will be muddy but unhurt. As this thought flies through his mind his foot catches in a tangle of brambles and he is catapulted forward, his legs flying over his head and, as one foot lands, he badly jars his ankle. The laughing stops. Someone shouts, he rolls the last few feet, and it occurs to him that he is safe, but he had not counted on how hard the tarmac at the bottom would feel. His shoulder takes the hit and then everything goes dark.

'Cyril?' The voice is unfamiliar.

'Tell him not to move,' another voice says.

His eyes open, blinking; the light seems strong but as he gets used to it everything is still out of focus.

'Where are his glasses, don't he wear glasses?'

'Could be anywhere. He fell all of thirty foot from up by the small oak tree.'

'There,' a new voice joins in. 'Ain't that them, shining over there?' His voice fades as he says this, as if he is moving further away.

'Where's that blasted ambulance. I wanna be off.'

'Here you go.' Someone fiddles with his ears; there is the familiar sensation of his glasses across his nose. 'I'm afraid one of the lenses is bust but at least t'other one's alright.'

Things come into focus through his right eye, but the left eye sees a thousand prisms. Through his good eye he can see that he is surrounded by the men that smoke. His heels kick against the floor to back away.

'Nay, you're alright lad. Sit still, the ambulance is on its way.'

Ambulance? Hospital? He relaxes.

'They're here.' And the men part as a white van with alternate yellow and green boxes along its side crawls to a stop. A man in a green shirt and trousers gets out of one side, and a woman wearing the same colour from the other. The green is the same as the hawthorn bushes behind them.

'Hello, what's your name?' The man crouches beside him.

'This is Cyril,' one of the smokers says. 'Fell down that bank, might of cracked his head. You won't be able to tell though 'cause he's not all there anyway.' This comment draws a few sniggers from the remaining smokers. 'You alright here now, 'cause I have to get off?' the lead smoker says.

But the paramedic ignores the speaker and then all the men who work there make a move to leave.

'Cyril, don't move. We have to make sure you haven't injured your head or neck.' The woman in green says this, and she gently takes off his glasses. She shines a light in his eyes. He winces and feels the strain in the back of his sockets as his eyes roll.

'Is he having a fit?' a voice asks and then everything is silent.

Chapter 29

'But he was not there yesterday either.'

'Saabira, we do not know him well. Maybe he goes off to see friends. Perhaps he leaves very early and comes back very late, or maybe – well, maybe anything. We have no idea.' Aaman says over their evening meal on Thursday night.

'I think he would have told me. Also I am worried about the dogs. When is he walking them, and feeding them? He would never leave his dogs.'

'You cannot know that. Also, why should he tell you if he had something that he needed to do that filled his days?'

'Because we are clearing his house. He sees it as something we are doing together. I just cannot imagine that he would not tell me if he was going somewhere. He is polite, is he not?'

'Yes. That is true, but what if he has a sick aunt, for example, who needs him, or something like that?'

'He has no one and I do not believe he would leave his dogs. So if something has happened to him then who is there to care?'

'You are a good woman, Saabira. But you would be an even better one if you were to pass me more of that moong daal. The chilli garlic combination is perfect.' He flashes a flirty smile and she purses her lips as she passes the dish. Aaman eats without speaking. When the food has taken the edge off their hunger he speaks again.

'So, this is what I suggest. If he is not around tomorrow morning, go to the place he works and ask if he is there. They will know.'

'Ah, why did I not think of that? That's the answer.' And she serves him more daal without his asking.

'Steady on.' He laughs. 'You want me to get a little round belly?'

Saabira leans towards him, squeezes his knee under the table. 'It might be quite nice,' she says. Aaman puts down his fork and his hand slides under the table; the hem of her kurti is lifted, and he looks into her eyes. She knows what will happen next and a thrill turns her stomach and then, as if on cue, Jay starts to cry and they both withdraw their hands.

Aaman leaves for work next morning and Saabira does not wait for Jay to have her morning nap. Instead, she adds another layer of clothes to her daughter's outfit and steps out into a fresh morning breeze from the moors. The purple of the heather is darkening into a rich reddish-brown as the days pass. The cold is not something she relishes but she is curious to see what the winter will bring; perhaps the moors will be piled high with snow.

There is a scrabbling noise and Coco's distinctive whine can be heard in response to her tapping on Cyril's back door. She shifts Jay up more comfortably onto her hip.

'Cyril?' But there is no answer, just more whining from the dogs and the sound of nails scratching frantically against the door. If he is not there and has not been there since she last saw him that means the dogs have been without food and water since Tuesday. She leans against the door with all her weight and tries the handle. Maybe the lock will give.

The door gives with such ease it is clear it was never locked. The force that she applied causes her to stagger forward, and her instinct is to protect Jay so she twists and loses balance. The corner of the table digs firmly into the back of her legs. She will have a big bruise there tomorrow.

The dogs, instead of running out into the freedom of the fresh air, cluster around her. There is nowhere that looks clean enough to put Jay down so with one hand she ladles biscuits, and meal for the rabbits. Jay points at the dogs, her little finger choosing one after the other. 'Dog,' she says.

After she has filled several bowls of water, a horrible thought occurs to Saabira. Perhaps Cyril is not out at all. He could be sick, upstairs in bed.

'Cyril?' she calls as she starts up the uncarpeted stairs. 'Cyril!' The first door she comes to swings open at her touch. Nothing about this room is in harmony with Cyril. Next to the neatly made bed there is a sepia-toned photograph of a woman in a high-necked white blouse. She is standing by a cloth-covered table, her hand gently resting on a book. Her hair is wavy and thick, piled on top of her head, and her gaze looks out at nothing, the spectator unseen. The picture is preserved in an ornate silver frame. Next to the window is a spindly chair on which is folded a pair of stripy pajamas. On a shelf by the bed are five books and another that lies open, a pen in the crease.

It is as if someone has just walked out of the room, but at the same time the air hangs heavily as if it is never disturbed. The floor is clean, with no dog hairs or any signs of the dogs at all.

Jay wriggles. Saabira soothes her as she tentatively steps over to the bedside table. The book with a pen in the crease is handwritten. Very gently, with just the tips of her fingers, she lifts the leaves to see the inscription on the first page. It is as she suspected.

'This is the Diary of Archie Sugden.' It is dated just over two years ago.

As she lets go, the pages fall quickly; it is as if she has never touched it. She backs out of the room, closing the door carefully. The landing is laid out the same as hers, so the other room, at the front of the house, will be the larger. The door to this is closed too.

'Cyril.' She knocks. It opens with a turn of the handle and a gentle push. The sun is shining through the thin curtains, which do not have enough hooks to hold the material evenly, and they sag near one end, framing an eye of sky. The bed is made and, apart from a bedside table, a mat by the bed and an open suitcase on the floor, the room is empty. Clothes are heaped in both halves of the suitcase: knitted tank tops in earthy colours, small checked greeny-brown brushed cotton shirts, grey socks. Everything is old, faded and worn, and similar to the clothes she has seen Cyril wear. There is no doubt this is his room, and he is definitely not here. She feels very much like she is trespassing and makes a quick retreat.

Downstairs, she checks again that the dogs have enough water, and leaves. She will put on her warmer shawl and find her way to where he works. He walks there over the moors each day, so it cannot be far. There is bound to be a way by road. It is better to go that way in case the darkening clouds spill their contents and the peat becomes boggy.

Chapter 30

Saabira turns left at the end of the cobbled road, out of Little Lotherton and away from the next village, Greater Lotherton, past the red telephone box and on into open countryside. Drystone walls flank the road on either side, guarding the moors beyond. A bird calls, a trill and a whistle, a trill and a whistle – a lonely echoing call. A flash of white belly, black wings and a necklace to match swoop over the road. It lands on the other side of the wall and turns its head rapidly, one way and then the other, making the crest of feathers on its head bob vigorously. It calls again.

'Jay, this is a very lovely country,' says Saabira. 'It may be cold and a little bit wet but with it comes the green of the trees and the passion of the weather.' Jay is looking out over the walls, watching the birds. A sheep's head appears above the tops of the ferns, alert; the animal spots them both and relaxes, disappears again.

The road seems to twist and turn for no reason, the drystone walls following every curve. Here and there the top curved stones are missing and the walls beneath are not held as firmly, and some of the large jagged stones below have slipped off.

The skies overhead gather dark and stormy blue-grey clouds that rumble from deep within. Saabira makes a mental note to buy an umbrella. Aaman takes his huge black one with him every day to work and, so far, she has rarely left the house on a weekday. At the weekends they go into Greater Lotherton to shop, and on these occasions when it has rained they huddle together under the one. But it is time for her to venture out into the world – explore Bradford, maybe, find out if there is more to Greater

159

Lotherton than the corner shop, the supermarket and the train station where they first arrived.

A white lorry with a picture of a bull's head on the side forces her onto the grassy verge. It drives slowly up the narrow road and turns right onto a steep lane up ahead.

At the turning there is a small sign by the road, half obscured by the long grass, that points the way to Hogdykes Abattoir. Outside the abattoir a group of men stand smoking, in white aprons stained red, and they stare at her as she comes up the hill. Others are loading the truck, and they stop and stare too. None of them offer her help or ask what her business is.

'I'm looking for Cyril. I–' she begins, but one of the men cuts her off and points to a side door. It leads to an office where a man who is talking on the phone looks her up and down. Saabira waits whilst he finishes the call.

'Right, love, what can I do for you?' he says finally, wiping a grimy hand across his stubbly chin.

'Do you know Cyril?'

'Course I know Cyril, and if you're a friend of his you can tell him he'll need a letter from his doctor for the paperwork.' The man arranges the papers on his desk, makes a note of something and looks up as if surprised to see her still there.

'His doctor? Has something happened?'

'You not a friend of his then?'

'I live next door. I haven't seen him for two days, and I was worried.' Saabira tries not to look at the calender behind the man's head, which displays a photograph of a half-naked woman.

'No, you wouldn't have.' He leans back in his chair, glancing briefly at Saabira before looking back at his paperwork. He traces his pen along a line of print and his lips move. When he gets to the end of the line he remarks, 'Fell down the bank out there. Ambulance took him, my guess is he'll still be in hospital.'

Leaning against Saabira's shoulder, legs around her mother's waist, Jay begins to wake up from her snooze. The man frowns as if he had not noticed her before.

'Which hospital, please?'

'Airedale, I expect – that'll be the nearest.' He looks at Jay again and returns to his paperwork.

The way back seems quicker, but it is close to Jay's dinner-time and she is becoming grizzly.

'This is your stop, love,' the driver shouts back to Saabira as the bus pulls up outside the hospital grounds. She stands, but hesitates. 'Just follow the path.' He points.

Jay is awake and wriggling to be let down but this is not a good time for her to practise her walking. The path the driver indicated cuts through a hedge and across a neatly trimmed lawn. On the other side of the grass the path widens and joins a maze of roads that lead to a large car park. It takes Saabira some time to find the main entrance. Inside, the floor is smooth, the walls are painted and there is a sense of busy organisation. There are chairs for those that are waiting, and the staff, in their uniforms, give off an air of quiet competence. The unity causes a small thrill to run through Saabira.

She waits her turn to talk to the woman on reception, who checks her computer.

'Follow the blue one,' she says, pointing at a series of coloured lines on the floor that lead off down various corridors. Jay is quiet, turning this way and that, trying to take everything in.

Apart from the coloured lines, the floor is smooth and green, curving up a little way around the edges where it meets the walls, which are a paler green. There are people everywhere: some on crutches, some in wheelchairs, one wheeled along still in his bed. Even with so many people, it is relatively quiet.

The blue line continues through a set of double doors where it is quieter now, with fewer patients and more white coats. Through the next set of doors the corridor is empty and the mood seems to change. Now there are windows along either side that look out over courtyards, which are flanked on every side by further corridors. The courtyards are well tended and planted with bushes and flowering plants, and, in each, neat paths lead to a central wooden bench. No one is in either garden.

The blue line turns right and then sharply through solid double doors, into one of the wards. Beds line either side of the room, some with green curtains pulled around them. It seems spacious, clean and not overcrowded, and very quiet.

No one asks her her business, and she wanders along the ward trying to spot Cyril's face.

Without his glasses on he doesn't look like himself, and his hair is fluffy, as if it has been recently washed. He is dressed in a green garment and the bed sheets are pulled tight across his chest. His eyes are closed.

Chapter 31

'Are you a relative?' A nurse in a blue-and-white uniform appears from behind a green fabric screen. 'Or friend?' she adds, eyeing Saabira's kurti, trousers and gold sandals.

'I am his next-door neighbour.'

'Ah.' The nurse sounds disappointed and settles the clipboard she is holding in against her waist.

Over each bed is a name card displaying the name and surname of each patient, but the one over Cyril's bed simply reads *Cyril*.

'Do you know if he has any relatives?' the nurse asks.

'I don't think so.' There is a jug of water by his bed, and on the windowsill that is shared with the next bed is a bunch of wilting flowers in greenish water. Saabira notices that the tables by some of the other beds in the ward are loaded with greeting cards and colourful vases of flowers, and the end of one bed even has balloons tied to it.

'No, no one has been in,' the nurse says, checking her watch. She makes a mark on the clipboard she is holding and pockets her pen. 'Such a shame when they get like this and no one cares.' She folds her arms across the clipboard and looks at the sleeping Cyril, shaking her head.

'I care!' Saabira protests.

'Oh.' She unfolds her arms. 'Well, that's great. If there's someone to care for him he can go home. To be honest, he has to go home, we need the bed. I'm afraid it's been this way since the Tories. But let's not talk politics. What he really needs is some good care for a while.'

'What sort of care?' Jay is squirming again, trying to stand. Saabira shifts her to the other hip. The nurse does not even look at her.

'Well, he should rest. He's lucky, sometimes it can be very difficult to reduce the uneven ends of the bone so that they can be immobilised and fixed – or the other complication is if the bone fragments lacerate blood vessels and muscles. That's quite common, but Cyril's been very lucky.

Saabira tries not to visualise all the nurse is saying as she continues.

'It's rare that a spiral fracture is so clean, especially in adults. He's had a local anaesthetic, it was immobilized, cast put on it. Done!' She makes it sound quick and simple. Maybe it is. Saabira finds herself oddly interested, and makes a noise to indicate this, which encourages the nurse, who is happy to go on.

'Yes,' she says, 'it'll be about four to six weeks to heal. Then I suggest swimming would be a good aid to his cardiovascular fitness, or running in chest-deep water. After that he'll need a weight-bearing programme in the physio department.' She takes a breath. 'But that's down the line a way. First thing is to get him home, make him feel comfortable, good nutrition.' She seems friendlier now, and beams at Saabira.

'I can cook for him.' Saabira grabs at the familiar ground, which acts as an anchor in this huge, unfamiliar clinical environment, full of medical terminology and procedures she does not understand. It gives her some stability.

'Well, there we go then. So we can discharge him. Have you a car or do you need an ambulance to get him home?' The nurse seems very pleased.

'I have no car,' Saabira says wondering what taking care of Cyril really involves. The nurse marches off. Has she just become responsible for his welfare? But then, why not? She and Aaman's mother saved Hanfi's life, he has said so often. He said so just about every time they ate.

'Badla.' Hanfi would address Aaman's mother by her given name. 'You and Saabira saved my life. I would have starved to death!' he would say, laughing as he dipped his roti into the spicy dishes.

'It is true,' Aaman's grandmother would agree, the skin hanging from her tricep quivering as she reached for a naan. 'He was as skinny as a forgotten goat.' Her familiarity with Hanfi was born of their mothers growing up together, of them playing together, growing side by side, attending each other's weddings and living next door for a lifetime.

The brief memory is chased away as the nurse returns.

'Right, the ambulance has been ordered and will be here in half an hour, by the side door there.' She points. 'We'll need your address.' She crosses to his bed. 'Cyril. Cyril. Come on. Wake up. Your clothes are all there. The ambulance is booked to take you home and your friend is here to help you.' The nurse is very efficient as she pulls curtains around the bed.

'Archie?' Cyril asks, blinking.

The nurse comes out from behind the curtain. 'I'll start the discharge papers,' she says and walks briskly out of the ward.

'Hello. How was your day?' Aaman asks Saabira, stepping into the house and pulling the front door shut behind him. He kisses her briefly on the mouth.

'I found Cyril.' Saabira makes a conscious effort to keep emotion from her voice.

'Oh good. What is the amazing smell? You have made your aloo gobi again?'

'Yes, I found fresh coriander when I was…' But she does not complete her sentence. 'About Cyril.'

'Yes, he is well I hope?' Aaman puts an envelope down on the table and takes off his woollen scarf and Saabira helps him off with his big winter coat.

'He is not well.' She looks over to Jay who is on the sofa playing with Cyril's identification tag from the hospital.

'Oh dear?' He follows Saabira's gaze, and then goes over to kiss his daughter. 'What have you got there?' He takes the plastic name tag from her. 'What is this?' he asks Saabira, but he looks at Jay and does not seem to be able to resist kissing her again. She giggles and grabs for the name tag.

'It's Cyril's identification tag,' Saabira says. 'From the hospital.'

'Hospital!' He straightens. 'He is so unwell?'

'He's had a fall, and broken his leg. He cannot get up for a while, maybe.'

'So why do we have his hospital tag? Is he still in the hospital or is he home?'

'Neither. Aaman, I have taken the liberty of providing our neighbour with the care he needs. I hope I will have your approval.'

'I don't understand.'

A thump of something falling upstairs creates a tiny cloud of dust that falls like wedding confetti on their hair. They both look up.

Chapter 32

Cyril has been holding his breath, straining to hear the conversation between Saabira and Aaman. Using just his arms he tries to ease himself to the side of the bed to pull open the door so he can hear more clearly. In his struggle his wrist gives, his elbow shoots out at an angle and he knocks the lamp off the bedside table.

'Oh, no, no, no,' he says to himself and leans over further to pick it up. If he bends to one side from his waist, without moving his legs, he might just be able to grasp it. But his judgement is off, the ends of his fingers make contact and the lamp rolls away. The sheets slip against the mattress under him and, knowing it is going to happen and knowing it is going hurt, he slides from the bed and falls heavily on the floor.

'Awwwwwwww.' He cannot hold back his yowl of pain. Then someone is taking the stairs two at a time, the footsteps thumping on the wood. They are coming. With the pain still coursing up his leg he pulls the sheet off the bed to cover the pajamas they gave him at the hospital.

'Oh goodness gracious me!' It is Aaman. 'Saabira!' he calls, but she is just behind him.

'Oh Cyril. Oh my.' She is crouching beside him, trying to work out what is to be done. His cheeks burn but the throbbing in his legs is more urgent. Saabira's face is so close to his, Aaman is also squatting now, on his other side. They both seem distraught at his predicament. The concern is too much, he is unused to such consideration and tears threaten to fall. He wants to be home in his own bed, with no broken leg and his dogs around him.

'My dogs.' He says it out loud.

'Your dogs are fine. You didn't lock the back door, and I have fed them.'

'Saabira, put your arm under.' Aaman grips Cyril under his left arm. 'And we can lift together.'

Cyril closes his eyes. He cannot bear to see their faces strain as they struggle to put him back on the bed. He has never caused such a fuss in his life. His cheeks are flushed and he would like the window open. He is burning up but at least the throbbing in his legs is subsiding. The tears that roll down his cheeks feel cooling.

'Ah, there you go.' Saabira pulls the sheets over him, and Aaman lets go and picks up the light. Once the lamp is on the bedside table he draws up a stool from behind the door and sits next to the bed. 'So, my friend,' he says as if nothing has just happened. 'You have had a bad accident, I hear.' He indicates Cyril's leg. 'Well, if anything is going to get you better it is Saabira's cooking.' Aaman pats him on the shoulder. 'Oh, and before I forget, I found a letter out on the street addressed to you. I think the wind must have blown it from your door. I will bring it.' The letter is crisp and white. Letters seem very official when they are like that. If they are left out a few days in the drizzle, they become old and soggy and it does not take much to tread them into the ground or toe-flick them out into the gutter. They look like nothing then. Just debris. But when they are still crisp they command his attention even though he will not read them.

Saabira intervenes.

'You will not be able to read it with your broken glasses. Would you like me to?' Her bangles slide down her arm as she takes it from Aaman.

He would like to say no. The few letters Archie read for him brought only bad news. But the way she offers is so kind, to say no might sound like he is not grateful. He is grateful, he is very, very grateful. He nods without meaning it and immediately wishes he hadn't.

168

Aaman is looking at the boxes of painkillers on the bedside table as Saabira carefully splits the envelope open.

'Dear Mr Cyril,' she begins. 'I wonder why they don't address you by your surname?' Cyril shrugs. This is one of those questions that has come up before but he has never known what his surname is and, as no one has been able to tell him what it is, it has become another area in his life that has just been left, leaving him feeling abnormal and sometimes uncomfortable. Like the time Archie took him into town, telling him that he needed to open a bank account, for example – that had felt so humiliating. The girl helping them looked at him as if he was stupid.

'How can you not know your own name?' she asked, pencilled-on eyebrows rising so high that little fine lines creased her tight, smooth skin. Archie stepped in then and called him Cyril Sugden, using his own surname. Cyril liked that. It was as if they were brothers. But the girl said that they couldn't just make up a surname and Archie said that he would see about that and the thrill of feeling like he was Archie's brother faded.

Saabira takes a breath and continues. Cyril just knows it is going to be bad news. 'Following numerous complaints, the Yorkshire branch of the Health and Safety Department have conducted investigations into the alleged health hazards present in and around the house you are currently occupying ...'

He cannot help it, it is the way it is written, the official way it is put, that makes his ears seal over. He doesn't understand it and it makes him feel a little shaky. He would like to hide under the covers for a bit but feels he cannot do this with Saabira and Aaman in the room.

Even Saabira sounds like she is drowning as she struggles with the long words. Aaman's expression tells him that it is bad news and, as she comes to the end – 'Regards, Dawn Todman' – his hearing seems to return. Saabira lowers the letter from in front of her eyes.

'That is Monday,' she says.

169

'What is?' he asks before he can stop himself.

'The date they say your house must be cleared out and cleaned by. For the inspection.'

There, Cyril thought – the proof : letters are always bad news. Archie got a letter after the visit to the bank that made him swear, and he spent several days writing and receiving letters until that last one. That one brought a smug look into his eyes, and he announced 'Ha!' as if he had won something but Cyril had never found out what.

'That is quite unrealistic, can they do that? Surely they have to give more notice than that?' Aaman says.

'Maybe, but where did you find this letter?' Saabira asks.

'It was just luck. I found it blowing down the street.'

'It is dated a week ago, but maybe we could contact them and tell them the letter has only just arrived.'

'Do you think it would make any difference if we called whoever wrote the letter and explained that Cyril has broken his leg?' Aaman is straightening the arms that hold the lampshade on the bedside light. They must have bent when it fell. He switches it on and off, but the light doesn't work. 'We need a new bulb here – can you remind me?' He is speaking to no one in particular.

'It is from Dawn Todman,' Saabira says as if she has a bad taste in her mouth. Cyril can understand why she says it like this.

'Who is she?'

'She is someone who will not care if my leg is broken.' Cyril says.

The room is silent. For a moment he thinks he might have said the wrong thing. Saabira and Aaman are both looking at the floor.

'Right.' Aaman is the first to speak. 'Well, if you would feel comfortable with us doing it for you Cyril, I have the weekend. We could get a lot done on the house in that time.' Cyril notices the look Saabira gives her husband, her eyes all soft, her pupils growing large. It is

170

the way Coco looks at him when he returns from work and she wants to lick his face but he won't let her.

'I am not physically strong but I can clean,' Saabira says.

'And we can take it in turns looking after Jay!' Aaman sounds excited, as if he has just invented a game. Saabira smiles.

'You see, it is no problem,' Saabira says, confidence growing in her voice. 'If you would feel comfortable with us doing it for you, of course. If there is anything that is not recyclable or suitable for burning in the fireplace, or we think it is personal, we will ask you what we should do with it.'

He wants to say yes. He wants the house as it was when Archie was there, with swept floors, hoovered carpets, and clean curtains, and the fire burning in the evening and Archie in his chair.

His head starts to nod backward and forward, tapping at the back against the headboard. Saabira puts a pillow behind his head, taking care of him. His head cannot rock now.

The images in his head are of his front room, one minute clean and tidy and Archie there, and then no Archie and all the things he has collected, the dark and the mess. The clean version is more like the hospital, the one he just stayed in as well as the one he lived in with Matron Jan. The dirty version is like the flats he and his mum called home when he was a child: dark, damp, and cramped. Out of nothing, a ball of emotions in his chest gathers and solidifies, and expands rapidly, surging into his veins as adrenaline. How dare she leave him! Her suicide shouted out that he was not worth living for. What a cow!

His breathing comes rapidly. Is it okay to call her a cow? She is his mum. It is wrong to say bad things about her. But is it? He was desperate for her love. Yearningly, head-bangingly desperate. She never gave him it – never!

171

She saved it all for his dead brother and then she took it to him with her own death.

Yet here is Saabira, someone he has known only such a short time, a neighbour, a woman from another land, a faraway place, who has had her own losses and sadness, and she is showing love to him, showing him kindness and concern.

He looks up at her.

All that sadness she had when she lost her baby — she was so sad she sent her husband away to make sure it didn't happen again, to stop herself having another child. If she could have her thinking so twisted by the sadness, maybe his mum did too. Maybe his mum was not to blame. Maybe the untidy, dark, miserable rooms they lived in suited the sadness, and she had no choice. Maybe she never had a choice of whether to live or not. Maybe she didn't kill herself; maybe it was the sadness that killed her.

He looks over at Aaman.

Saabira's husband knows him even less than Saabira. Yet he has been nothing but kind and gentle. He was the one Saabira took her sadness out on. She did to Aaman what his mother did to him and yet Aaman has forgiven Saabira, and understands it was the sadness.

'I would be very grateful if you would clear out the house.' His voice speaks before he feels ready. But he agrees with himself. He would be very grateful.

Chapter 33

Saabira can hear Aaman through the wall, whistling as he works. She has just been up to give Cyril a cup of tea and promised that his dogs would get a walk. She might take them out with Jay but wonders if they will follow her. If they need to be on a lead she will not be strong enough.

Jay is enthralled with their latest game. They started taking dried beans out of a storage jar and then putting them back in, but at some point the game changed and now they are making sounds in the jar, listening to how their voices change, and Jay is laughing away at the echoes.

'Eeee!' Jay sings into the jar.

Aaman appears through the back door, his hair white with dust. 'Do we know if Cyril is happy for us to take the porch off? It is going to be tricky taking out some of the larger stuff.'

'If you stay with Jay I'll ask him.'

With the teapot in one hand she heads up the stairs and pours more tea for Cyril, who thanks her again and again for her kindness and says Aaman can do just as he pleases.

Aaman does not stay for tea. He has on his old trousers, an out-of-shape T-shirt and the gloves he came back from Greece with. He is full of energy and wants to expend it, so no sooner is she back down the stairs than he is out the back door.

Now the whistling is replaced with banging and the sound of creaking wood. The rubbish in the skip is nearly up to the top.

Mid-afternoon, Aaman is still singing and clattering next door. She takes a bowl of kadhi and rice up to Cyril but he is asleep so she leaves it on the bedside table. Aaman comes round half an hour later and he washes as she readies the table.

Jay is now hiding beans under a cushion and then pushing the cushion off and finding them again. Saabira wonders for how many days she will be finding escaped beans.

'How is it going?' she asks Aaman.

'Sitting at a desk programming all day is very interesting but it is nice to be active. But I think it must be my fate to be always cleaning up other people's messes.' He does not refer to his time in Greece, when he helped clear Juliet's garden, with sadness. Jay totters over to him and then squeals as he swings her around. 'But I am now down to just carpets.' He stops swinging their daughter and cuddles her.

'What do you mean?' 'She serves him and he sits with Jay on his knee.

'Well, I was getting rid of stuff that was broken and irreparable without thinking of the whole room, just the individual pieces – but when I stopped to look around there was nothing left. There is only a three-legged chair and a small highly polished table. Apart from those two things it is just carpets.'

'Carpet,' Saabira corrects him.

'No, carpets.'

'Now what do you mean?' She sits to eat with him.

'The carpets are the source of the smell. At some time in the past the dogs have made their dirt where they please. The amount that is fresh is probably since Cyril had his fall, but the rest looks very old, dried, encrusted.'

'Stop! This is not helping my digestion!' Saabira pauses with the kadhi on a piece of roti halfway to her mouth. Aaman is helping Jay dip a piece of roti into the flavours on his plate.

'No, listen, there is more. It seems that, at some point, before all the furniture was put on top, the solution

174

to this problem has been not to throw out the carpet that was soiled but to lay another one on top.'

'Oh no.' Saabira pulls a face. Jay watches and tries to copy.

'I rolled up the top carpet and took it out to the skip and then, looking closely at the floor, I saw it was another carpet, and under the edge of that one I saw another. Five layers of carpet I have rolled up and thrown out!'

'Was the smell not unbearable?' Saabira asks.

'It is amazing what you don't notice once you have been in it long enough.'

'So all the carpets are gone?' She should have put a little more salt in the kadhi, for her taste, but then perhaps not. It will taste different to Aaman.

'Does it have enough salt?'

'Yes, it is perfect.'

'Enough ginger?'

'Give me another bowlful and I will tell you.' He smiles and looks in her eyes as he passes his dish. Jay tries to take a roti from the plate between them.

'Yes, the carpets are all gone but it is the same in the kitchen. The oven, which is very old, I am thinking, is leaning back because there are also several layers of floor covering there.'

'Oh, so much work for you.' Saabira tears off a little bit of roti and gives it to Jay.

'I am happy to do it. First, I am active, and secondly, it is better that the problem and the smell are gone.'

'So under the carpets is clean?' Saabira wonders if Aaman has been upstairs. The mess does not extend up there, and there is a different feel to the upper floor. That "The Diary of the Final Days of Archie Sugden" is lying there after eleven years, frozen in time, is slightly eerie, and also sad somehow.

'It is stones like in here.' He looks at the floor. 'I think with a stiff brush and some hot water it will clean easily.'

'Well, that is good to know.'

'Has Cyril eaten, how's he?' Aaman looks from the floor to the ceiling.

'I put a bowl by his bed, he is sleeping.'

'Ah, the best healer.' They continue to eat. Aaman's appetite seems to be exaggerated by his work. She leaves the last roti for him. When he has finished eating he sits back, his free hand on his stomach, the other around Jay who is perched on his knee, and Saabira tries to remember when she last saw him look so happy.

'Cyril is worried about his dogs needing to be walked,' she says.

'I have left them tied up outside the back of his house. There was a lot of rope by his sink and I needed to get the dogs out of the way so it seemed like a good solution.'

'Are they still there?'

'They were when I came round. Mostly they were lying down sleeping. The sun was out and I think between the heather and by the wall there is a little suntrap for them. Anyway, they seemed happy enough. But we can walk them if you like.'

'On leads, you think, or loose?' Saabira gets up to put the kettle on.

'Put the pack leader on a rope and the rest will follow.'

'They are not goats!' Saabira laughs.

Chapter 34

Aaman is only gone an hour.

'Done!' he says cheerfully. 'The ground floor is now ready to clean. It should be easy, as there is nothing left in it. You could ask Cyril if he wants to keep the old cooker. It runs off a gas bottle next to it so I am not sure what Health and Safety will say about that. There seem to be rules for everything like this. We have a heater, which is now in the storeroom at work, but we cannot use it because of gas bottle regulations.'

'Is it cold at work?' Jay tries to pull at her hair as she changes her nappy on a towel on the rug in front of the fire.

'No, oh no. They have central heating now. But Gavin was telling me that before they got double glazing there used to be ice on the insides of the windows in the winter.'

Saabira shivers at the thought.

'Was he happy with the bookcase?'

'He was very happy with the bunkbeds and the bookcase. In fact he told to me to thank you again.'

'It is not me he should be thanking.'

'Well, I am going to take a shower and then I will take Jay and the dogs for a walk. Will you come?' He puts his head over the sink and ruffles his hair, brushing off dust and cobwebs.

'I think I might start to clean.' With the guard around the fire she leaves Jay to crawl whilst she takes out a mop, bucket and stiff brush from the cupboard under the stairs.

Aaman sets off with the dogs around his ankles. The sun has found some strength, despite the seasons moving on and the leaves now beginning to fall from the trees. Shielding her eyes with her hand, she watches him walk up the moors until he is an outline against the horizon, Jay on his back, held by her shawl, and the dogs around him. It is not quite the same as the picture she has stored in her mind of him herding the goats in Pakistan, but he cuts a romantic figure to her eyes nonetheless.

'I love you, Aaman,' she says quietly to herself, and another part of her that does not want to speak out loud promises to deal with her jealousy towards his friend Juliet in Greece. One way or another she must resolve that; there must be no more emotional secrets between them at all.

She anticipates the gloom engulfing her as she pushes Cyril's back door open, and so it is with delight that she registers the brightness of the space. The curtains have gone, both the heavy fabric and the thin, greying torn netting. The front room's eye is wide open to view the lane outside, and through its encrusted grime the vivid green bushy mass of the tree opposite is framed and highlighted by the bright autumn sky. Inside, empty of clutter, the room seems dramatically bigger, and the three-legged stool and the small table are dwarfed by its dimensions.

'Oh my goodness,' Saabira says out loud, focusing herself on the task ahead. With her sleeves pushed up, she brushes the floor thoroughly before setting to with a bucket of steaming water. Once the floor is scrubbed she washes and polishes the downstairs windows inside and out. The difference is wonderful and the room is transformed. A fresh coat of paint would brighten the walls but that is not a choice for her to make. It probably isn't a choice for Cyril to make either. That sort of thing costs money. But maybe, if Dawn Todman does not evict Cyril, he could make an arrangement with his landlord. Presumably that is how it would work. She is not sure who is responsible for the walls in a rented house.

She pours the dirty window water down the drain outside and looks out over the moors, wondering when Aaman will get back. The clouds are puffing up white on the horizon now and the midday sun has cooled. Not that it was very hot, just bright.

'Fresh,' she says to herself, and the word seems to apply equally well to the weather and to the newly scrubbed room. The backyard is also clean and clear, apart from the two hutches and a huge stack of wood, enough to see Cyril through the winter.

She leans down and pokes her finger through the mesh and strokes the big rabbit's ear. Its nose twitches but it doesn't move.

'You should have gone for a walk with Aaman,' she tells it. 'You need to exercise. You can hardly move in there, you poor thing.' The rabbit, motionless in its cage, brings to mind Archie's diary – how long has it been still, unmoving? Would it be wrong to read a dead man's diary? Maybe it would reveal more about Cyril, provide a shortcut to understanding the man. She only glanced at it previously, and read the words 'the point of this diary is to set things straight. I will not say it is an apology, Cyril.' What does that mean, and why would Archie be apologising to Cyril?

'No,' she says to herself. If she wants to know more about Cyril she should ask him, not spy on him through someone else's diary. Nevertheless, she goes back inside and up the stairs and into Archie's room to have a good look around. Although tidy, it needs a good clean. The books lies open, the diarist is dead, and she feels very tempted. But as her fingers reach for the volume she forces herself to turn on her heel. She will ask Cyril first.

'How are you feeling?' She puts a cup of tea down on Cyril's bedside table. The back door opens and Aaman's voice floats up the stairs, chattering to Jay, who will need feeding, no doubt.

179

'Not so bad, but I seem to be sleeping so much.' Cyril sits up to put his glasses on, fiddling with them over his ears.

'We must get those repaired. You have someone who does that for you?' Saabira asks, pulling the stool from behind the door to sit down for a moment.

'I don't know. I've had these since Highroyds.' Cyril takes the spectacles off again and holds them very close to his face to examine the broken lens.

'Perhaps when you are better we will find an optician. In the meantime, your home is looking amazing. The downstairs is all clear and clean and fresh. But not much of the furniture was worth saving. Only the three-legged stool and a small hexagonal table, really. Also, Aaman wants to know if you want to keep the old cooker.' Cyril looks up at her puzzled. 'He wonders if Health and Safety will not like the gas bottle,' she explains.

'Oh. It was Archie's cooker. It doesn't work.'

'So we will get rid of it? Then, perhaps, when your leg is healed we can find some new furniture for you somehow?' He nods, but it doesn't really seem as though he is expressing his opinion.

'There is something I wanted to ask you. What about upstairs?'

'Upstairs?'

'Everywhere needs a good clean, but I didn't want to start cleaning the bedroom without making sure you are happy with this.'

'Mine is the one at the front.'

'Yes, I guessed, and the other was Archie's.'

'Yes, Archie's. Nothing has been moved. I left it just like it was.' Cyril rubs his eyes.

'I saw a book by his bed – that was his diary, was it?' She feels she is not being honest. She should either ask if she can read it to understand Cyril more or she should accept that it will take time to get to know her neighbour and his complexities.

'Yes. I look at it sometimes, his writing. It makes him feel close.'

'Have you read it?' Now she is fishing to see if he can actually read, and her cheeks flush at her behaviour, but curiosity keeps pushing her on.

'No.' Cyril looks at his hands, interlocks his fingers, his glasses clenched in his fist. 'He said I should read it. He said when he was really unwell, a day or two before he was dead, that there was something in it for me. He said I would be pleased.'

'So why have you not read it?' Is she being cruel or helpful now?

He shrugs.

'Would you like me to read it to you?' She wonders if she sounds too eager.

He shakes his head, the moisture in one eye increasing so much that it flows over his lower lid and trickles down his face. He wipes his cheek with the palm of his hand and puts his glasses back on. He looks more like himself now. With his glasses off, Saabira struggles to recognise him.

'Would it not be nice to hear what he has written, to know what he wanted to tell you?'

He shakes his head again.

'It would be too sad.'

Saabira nods her understanding. But something is niggling her – those few words she read unintentionally.

'It is very much none of my business, but would you like me to read through the diary to see if what was in it for you was important?'

'I don't really think it would be important. It's just words he wrote.' Cyril picks up his tea.

Did she remember to put sugar in it? He smacks his lips and swallows, fully satisfied, so clearly she did.

'Sometimes words can be very important...'

'Or very bad,' Cyril says.

'What would you like me to do with his diary then? Shall I leave it there or shall we throw it away?'

This makes him turn his head sharply to look at her. They make eye contact and they remain looking at each other for slightly longer than Saabira finds comfortable.

'Not throw it away. I'd like to keep it. Maybe you could read it and if what he says is good you can tell me and if it's bad never tell me.' He takes another sip of tea.

'Okay.' Saabira does not feel she has treated Cyril fairly. She is not exactly sure what she has done, or fully why she did it, but either way she got the outcome she wanted. She has his permission to read the book, but it doesn't feel right. An unsettling thought flashes through her mind, that when she encouraged Aaman to go on his dangerous, and illegal, journey, she was also getting the outcome she wanted, and at someone else's expense. As she stands to leave she reproaches herself. 'You are a manipulator, Saabira.'

The knowledge does not make her happy. Cyril smiles at her and she smiles in return but she feels she has betrayed their emerging friendship.

Chapter 35

As Saabira leaves Cyril's room she can hear Aaman in the bathroom, and judging by the splashing he is giving Jay a bath. Reluctant to disturb them, she slips down the stairs, out of the back door and around to Cyril's house. The clean room takes her by surprise again but she doesn't stay; she walks straight through and up the stairs into Archie's room.

The bedsprings creak in complaint as she sits.

'The Diary of the Final Days of Archie Sugden,' she begins, her curiosity defeating thoughts that what she is doing might not be right, and she tells herself that she will only read the opening page.

'I can feel it in my bones and my chest. This damn disease has got its final hold over me and I am not long for this world. I thought I wouldn't care when it got to this stage. The world itself is diseased, the people a blight. I thought I would be glad to be done with it all, but as my chest rattles and I grow weaker I am rather annoyed to find that my emotions are dominating. I get tearful for no reason and, worst of all, I have started to feel something quite alien – regret!

'Ha! The irony that, as my body decays, my conscience blossoms.

'Well, I don't consider myself a bad man. It's true I don't suffer fools and I have a quick temper, and I am known for my determination to get even if people slight me. That's just how the game is played in this dog-eat-dog world, and people seem to get upset that I just play the game better than them. They didn't see the way the world disrespected and rejected my mother for being a single parent. But then, when she turned her sharp mind to business and amassed her little empire, that all turned into grovelling and simpering. We concluded together, me and her, that it's money that talks.'

Saabira wonders if Aaman has finished bathing Jay. Really, she should go and start the cooking, but first she will read just one more entry.

'Anyway, the point of this diary is set things straight. Make no mistake, though, this is not an apology, Cyril, as that would suggest that I did something wrong. I don't believe anything I have done was wrong. At the time it was right, but as things move on your learning would have you do things differently. Also, if you say my first motivation to have you as lodger was wrong then maybe you would never have moved in and then where would you be, eh, Cyril? The world would never have let you amount to much. I think you got the least kicking when you was with me.

'So, I want to get something out of me system. But as I say, this is not an apology, it's just an explanation about what happened and how things have changed. You see, it was when I was in the council office, where I had gone to complain about me council tax bill. Anyway, the queue was all the way down the corridor and I got talking to this man. Well, he said he had taken in a lodger and the council not only paid this lodger's rent but also a good sum for him to take care of the lad, because he was a penny short of a pound. Nothing serious, he assured me, just someone who was a little bit more gullible than your average man. Care in the Community, the scheme was called, he said, and anyone could offer to be a carer. I made a joke about this, saying that he would end up becoming his lodger's gofer, but he said all he had to do is manage the lad's money and make sure he got enough to eat. I thought it sounded like a good scam and, long and short, that's how it was that you came to live in me house.'

Saabira is not sure what the word scam means. She curls her upper lip at the absent Archie.

184

'What I had not taken into account was that you might stay for some time, and in that time we would find that we got on alright. In the beginning, because you never came out of your room I didn't even notice you was here, except Marion took to sleeping in your bed instead of mine.'

Saabira looks at the picture of the woman in the silver frame, and leans back across the bed to take hold of it. She is a strong-faced woman, but not particularly attractive. She turns the frame over in her hands and twists the tiny flat stoppers that hold in the photo. On the back of the photo is written *Marion Sugden*, and then, in brackets, *Mother*. Saabira looks again at the woman's face and tries to reconcile herself with the idea that Cyril was sleeping with Archie's mother. Puzzled now, but intrigued too, she puts the photo carefully back in the frame and continues with the diary, hoping that reading more will shed light on what seems so far like a very strange way of living.

'I think it was the way she took to you that made me first think twice,' Archie says, and Saabira glances at the picture of Marion again and frowns.

'But what really changed things for me was when they gave you your ridiculous job. It was/is a typical bureaucratic cock-up. Well, not so much a cock-up but just your usual non-thinking, inhuman decision-making of the powers-that-be. I mean, it's so apparent that you are an animal lover and that animals love you. Someone would have to be blind not to see it. Look at Marion! She's always been a fairly good dog but she listens to you in a way that she has never listened to me, and she trusted you completely.'

Saabira looks again at the photograph of Marion, Archie's mother, and this time she smiles.

'But I'll leave this subject for now as I am in the middle of some plans that I am hoping to complete before these bones of mine finally give up on me. I hope what I'm doing will please you, and I'm determined to keep going until it's all finalised.'

The pen changes then to pencil. It seems like a good time to stop reading, and she really should start cooking, but Saabira is drawn in by the first words of the next entry.

'One thing that is finalised is your name. You remember that your work at Hogdykes required you to have a bank account and I took you to the bank? Do you remember that snooty girl at the bank? She was full of herself saying that you couldn't open a bank account without a full name so I gave you mine. Remember? Then she said that I couldn't do that, just give you a name, so I said, "We'll see about that."'

'Well, as you know, we ended up giving Hogdykes my bank details which has worked out fine all these years. (Which reminds me, I've left my bank card on the mantelpiece, and you must remember to go to the bank and get your money from the machine in the wall every week until something new is sorted. You remember the number. It's the year you were born. In case you forget it I've written it in pen on the back of the understairs door.)

'Anyway, back to that girl in the bank. She made me cross and I was determined to get even, so, and I know it has taken me some time because – well, I had that spell in hospital with this damn disease, then I buried myself in things I felt I had to do to ignore the inevitable, and I admit for a while I forgot about it. But anyway, after sending mountains of letters backward and forward to your primary care worker and the Care in the Community team and even the council, I finally registered you officially with the my surname. Mr Cyril Sugden. So that's you now. And I'll tell you what, it wiped the stupid smile off the girl in the bank's face when I went back in there because she still had a record of your signature from the last time.'

Saabira is not sure what she thinks of all this. Archie seems to be rather a pushy, arrogant man. Who names another adult after themselves and why on earth would it be useful? She shuts the book with a snap and a cloud of dust hovers over it.

She must go and put the food on. She carefully puts the book back in its place and leaves the room, but then goes back in and snatches it up. She'll take it with her.

'We've had a bath,' Aaman announces, holding up Jay, who has a huge towel wrapped around her and a small towel like a turban on her head. She is dripping slightly, and there is a striking resemblance to Aaman's father.

'I have cleaned the floor and windows and Cyril says that it's alright to remove the cooker and clean upstairs.'

'Well, the dogs got a little muddy, but I took them through a stream on the way back and I hosed them down before they went inside, so it will still be clean, if a little wet.' He turns to Jay. 'We liked the dogs, didn't we? Do you know,' he continues to Saabira, 'that if you walk straight up out of the back of here you get to an official walk called the Peninne Way? It says it is 286 miles long. I love how England is organised in that way, with walks that have markers to follow. Can you imagine a 286-mile walk, just for fun? That is longer than the Hunza Valley.' Saabira loves it when Aaman gets all animated like this. 'You could do it, couldn't you?' He turns back to Jay.

'Yes, if she was strapped to your back.' Saabira puts the kettle on to start the food.

Archie's diary stares down at her from the kitchen shelf.

Chapter 36

Later, when Jay is asleep, Aaman and Saabira curl up in front of the fire.

'What a day!' Aaman says. He sounds tired but pleased.

'Cyril seems to be sleeping a lot,' Saabira says.

'It's nature's way of healing.'

'I want to show you something.' She gets up to take the diary from the shelf. 'This is Archie Sugden's diary.' Saabira sits on the rug at Aaman's feet as he lounges on the sofa. 'He said that Archie told him there was something in it that was important for him but he hasn't read it.' The room is thrown into high contrast by the fire, the orange flames picking out the folds on Aaman's shirt.

'Do you want me to take it up to him?' Aaman doesn't look like he wants to move anywhere. Dark shadows are deepening under his eyes, and his limbs are without life.

'No. I had a talk with him. I am not sure, but I think he cannot read. But he also didn't want to know what it said. He seems to have this idea that everything written down is bad news.' Aaman strokes her hair lazily as she speaks. 'So I offered to read it for him.'

He smiles and gives a little snort of laughter. 'Is it interesting?'

'I am not sure Archie was such a good man. He took Cyril into his home for money.'

'Go on then, read a little to me.' Aaman lets his head rest back, closes his eyes. The hand that is stroking her hair becomes still.

Saabira opens the book and finds where she had read up to.

'It's not dated. I don't think it's that sort of diary. It is entitled "The Diary of the Final Days of Archie Sugden".'

'Ah, he knew it was his time,' says Aaman fatalistically.

'Shall I not read, then?'

'No, go on.'

'So, this entry starts, "Today I have felt even worse. I don't want to tell you."'

She breaks off. 'By the way,' she says, 'he is addressing all this to Cyril.' Aaman grunts his acknowledgment. 'So, where was I? Oh yes…'

'Today I have felt even worse. I don't want to tell you because I know you will worry, but I can write about it here because by the time you read this I will be gone and I won't be suffering any more. I just feel particularly weak today and this cough feels like it is ripping the lining off my lungs – which for all I know it probably is. The pain is indescribable. I know what you would say. You are all for letting in the witches from the hospice to inflict their smug patronising charity on me. But that is not for me."'

'You are on the moors right now with Marion. What I would give for a last wander up on the tops, with the dog by my side, the curlews protecting their nest with their swoops and dives, to hear the grouses coarse machine-gun calls as they skim the bracken. Just for the clean moor air on my face, the sudden skirmish of startled sheep in the heather, and the endless open space that has always drawn me closer to nature and made me realise how insignificant my life really is compared to the beauty and the longevity of this planet.'

Saabira stops to look at Aaman, who is so still, with his head resting back on the sofa and his eyes closed, that he could be asleep.

'Go on,' he murmurs. She turns back to the book, the light of the flames dancing amongst the letters.

'But as I sit here, pondering the enormity of the cosmos and the speck that I am in comparison, one thing keeps returning to me and lies rather heavily in my mind. I'm sure you remember the paving stone scam? Well, the first year it just seemed like an obvious thing to do. I had rung them and written to them about fixing that paving stone just outside of here. It made me cross the way they never took me seriously. I pointed out someone could trip and seriously hurt themselves, but these council people really don't care. They are just doing a job.'

Saabira stops reading, but she leaves her finger poised under the next word.

'This word "scam", it means to take advantage by tricking someone?'

'Um.' Aaman acknowledges with minimal effort, giving no indication if he knew this or not.

Saabira returns to the book, her finger at the ready, and she slightly alters her voice, makes it lower, gruffer, almost as if Archie is talking.

'So when you did trip it was just perfect timing and I couldn't let such an opportunity get away. I know I pushed you into making more of it than it really was and I know how reluctant you were to sue them. As I sit here, now, thinking in retrospect, I believe it was perhaps not such a fair thing to do. All these emotions are overpowering me these days and they let me see things from a different view, and now I see how it might have been for someone as sensitive and honest as you.

'If I had just done it that first time when you did actually trip I might not feel so bad but when I pushed you into prising up that paving stone the next year and making you play the same scam, and the year after as well, I feel pretty rotten. I thought the compensation they paid me was everything at the time. But I didn't consider it from your point of view, and indeed, until all this recent soft sensitivity I am plagued with, I am not even sure that if I had thought about it I would have been able to understand – not on an emotional level. Not fully.

'So, suffice it to say I understand now.'

An ember spits and the colours twist and flicker in the fire.

'He wasn't a nice man, was he?' she asks Aaman. 'I cannot understand why Cyril was so fond of him when he used him and took such advantage of him. I mean, he took Cyril in for the money he could make and then he made Cyril do this trick for money, and, if you were listening, he talks about *his* compensation, not Cyril's.'

A log suddenly hisses a blue jet of flames which then dulls to a yellow, then flickers and is gone.

'What do you think?' Aaman does not reply, and Saabira is not surprised, when she turns to look at him, to find that he is asleep. Her eyelids are feeling heavy too, and tomorrow she must clean upstairs in Cyril's house. Should she wake Aaman to make him to go up to bed, or bring down a blanket and make him cosy on the sofa? She never had this sort of dilemma back home. They ate and lived and slept in the same room. But also, back home she would not have to find a blanket to cover him.

She shivers as she stands and moves away from the fire. Perhaps she will bring a blanket big enough for both of them.

Chapter 37

Sunday afternoon flies by, and Cyril's house is cleaned from top to bottom.

'He is like a different person upstairs.' Saabira puts the broom, mop and bucket back under her stairs. 'The furniture is all in better repair and there is no sign of his hoarding like in the downstairs room. He could probably benefit from a chest of drawers in his room, though. All his clothes are in an open suitcase on the floor.'

Aaman is encouraging Jay to walk on unsteady legs, tightly grasping his finger with one fist, and with a big grin on her face. Aaman counts each step.

'One, two, three! You are so clever.' Then Jay's legs give way and she sits heavily on the floor, cushioned by her nappy. He looks up at Saabira. 'You have finished then?'

'All done. Upstairs, downstairs. I even cleaned the kitchen cupboards and the cupboard under the stairs. Do you think the skip should be gone before they come to inspect tomorrow?'

'I don't see why.' He claps his hands and Jay copies. 'Can you stand?' Jay dutifully stands. 'Can you walk?' She wobbles, but looks determined. 'Come on Jay, come to me.' He jangles the front door keys. 'Come on, come and get the keys.' Aaman drops the keys into his shirt pocket, out of sight, and Jay's eyes shine. She takes one step, then another, eyes wide open, her eyebrows high and her mouth open in a sustained grin as she celebrates what she can do, gasping at her own abilities. She makes a final lunge and her fingers fiddle with Aaman's shirt until she retrieves the keys and holds them up to show everyone her prize.

'You are so clever,' Aaman tells her. Jay turns to Saabira to see if her mother agrees.

'Who's my clever girl?' Saabira claps her hands and Jay copies, the keys rattling between her palms.

They make their evening food together. Aaman takes a plate up to Cyril and he stays up there for quite a long time, talking. Saabira feeds Jay, who then falls asleep before she is even put down. When Aaman comes back downstairs he suggests that an early night would do them all good, so, after they have eaten, Aaman insists the pots are left until tomorrow and they climb the stairs together, Aaman behind her, his hands on her hips, half pushing, half helping himself up.

Morning brings hazy white mist rolling down off the moors, making everything so much stiller. It seems a little odd that the birds are nevertheless singing; the low cloud suggests that the world should also be silent. After feeding Jay, Saabira sets about making Aaman his breakfast, and wonders if Cyril is awake. He must be so bored of being stuck in bed. Maybe between them they can help him to come downstairs today, if he feels up to it. A change of scenery might cheer him, and not having to run up and down the stairs with cups of teas will cheer her. Not that she needs cheering – clearing Cyril's house has given her such a sense of purpose over the weekend that, now it is done, by comparison, the day that is laid out before her lacks direction. She needs to find something to fill her time apart from Jay. Beautiful Jay. She watches her daughter's eyelids flicker. Her first nap of the day is getting shorter and shorter. She still has her mid-morning nap as well as her afternoon sleep, but Saabira is aware how quickly things are changing. Soon her baby will be a toddler and will be walking freely. They will have to find a way to make the hot Aga safe. They might need a lock for the cupboard under the sink, too, where all the cleaning things are kept.

The sound of creaking floorboard tells her Aaman is up and she puts the kettle on and gathers the cups to make tea. Three cups. One for Cyril.

The crunching of tyres on the cobbles outside and the banging of a car door are a most unwelcome intrusion into the stillness of the beginning of her day. With the street being so narrow, those who live in Lotherton leave their cars down on the main road. It is unusual at the best of times for anyone to venture up this cul-de-sac, except on foot. In fact the only car she has witnessed coming up is Dawn Todman's.

The banging on Cyril's front door echoes in the emptiness of the cleared room. Its clarity through the wall is unexpected and Saabira jumps.

'What on earth is that noise?' Aaman comes down the stairs, his hair sticking up in every direction. He tries to flatten it with his hands, yawning, and rubs his face with his palms. The banging is repeated.

'Is that next door?' They both peer out of the front window into the grey dawn light.

'That is Dawn Todman's car. She must be here to inspect.'

'Why so early?'

'I suppose we had better go round and let her in?'

Aaman does not answer, but heads to the back door whilst Saabira steps out of the front.

'Good morning, Mrs Todman,' she says to Dawn, who is peering into the skip, 'My husband has gone round to open up for you.'

'Is this all from the house?' Dawn says without a word of greeting, still eyeing the skip.

'Yes.'

'There must be nothing left!'

'He has very little furniture now,' Saabira agrees.

'Well, if that Mr Brocklethwaite doesn't get his way and get Septic Cyr... er, and get Cyril evicted, then there are several routes he can go down to get some furniture. There's lots of help available for that sort of thing.'

'Oh.' Saabira feels caught off guard. 'Aren't you helping Mr Brocklethwaite to get Cyril evicted?'

'No.' Dawn sounds emphatic.

'Oh,' Saabira repeats.

'Aye. He's bit of an octopus after he's had a sherry.' She pauses, her lips twitching towards her nose in a sneer. 'And his wife only just in the kitchen as well!'

Cyril's front door opens a crack and Aaman pushes the dogs back to let the woman from Health and Safety in.

'Oh yes! The porch! It's gone!' Dawn says. 'So much better, and no smell. He's not done all this by himself, has he?' She pats Coco and scratches her behind the ears as she goes in.

'We all helped,' Aaman says.

'Well, the transformation is amazing. I have to admit I've not been in here before, but I saw it through the door, just stuff piled high to the ceiling, and the stink.'

Coco pushes her nose into Dawn's hand and she responds by patting her and holding the animal's head against her leg. 'Who's a lovely girl, then?' she whispers.

'Well, I don't think anyone can complain against this.' She is smiling and she looks like another person. 'But,' and her smile fades. 'I don't know about all these dogs. How many are there?' She fusses over each in turn.

'That's Coco, she's Zaza, Sabi, and Blackie Boo is the black one. Teddy Tail, Gorilla Head and Mr Perfect.' Aaman points to each in turn. Saabira feels very proud of Aaman for learning all their names. She only knows Coco, Blackie Boo – and Mr Perfect, because he is so golden, almost orange.

'The trouble is, if they get out they'll go around in a pack. People find that intimidating.' She crouches down to look Gorilla Head in the face. 'Have they all been to the vet recently?' She feels around the dog's ears and under its chin, and it makes a whimpering sound, grateful for the attention, and Dawn pats its flank before standing again.

Saabira exchanges a glance with Aaman. 'I am afraid we have no idea,' she says.

'Hmm.' Dawn crouches in front of Zaza and feels her ears and neck. 'Well, they've no ticks, they're not scratching and they all seem pretty healthy. What's the rabbit situation?'

The image of the large rabbit, too fat to move, tightens Saabira's mouth.

'What is it?' Dawn does not miss Saabira's discomfort.

'Nothing,' Saabira lies, but she does feel concern for the big rabbit. Dawn pushes through the dogs to the back door.

'Well, it's not a health and safety issue but that big one needs a run, or something,' she says, eyeing the creature critically. 'Where is Cyril, anyway?'

'He had a fall, and has broken his leg, so he has been recovering at our house while this one was being cleaned,' Aaman explains.

Dawn Todman looks over incredulously, first at him and then at Saabira. A frown comes and goes on her forehead and her mouth opens as if to say something but then closes again. She looks back at the rabbit, deep in thought.

'That is very kind of you,' she says finally, making eye contact with Saabira. She nods her head vigorously. 'Right. Well, I'd better be going. I'll write up my report based on what I've seen. Tell Cyril that he has nothing to worry about as far as I'm concerned, except he might have to reduce his dogs' numbers. The RSPCA can help him find new owners.' She turns to leave. 'On an unofficial note, and I'm not saying this as a Health and Safety officer, mind, this is just from me – if he wants to relieve himself of the big rabbit, well, I used to keep them when I was little. It might be quite nice to have one again.' She flushes. 'It might be better for the rabbit as well, because I have a little garden at mine and I could make a run.' She pats the dogs again and makes her way back to the front door, where they are all startled to find Mr Brocklethwaite standing with legs wide, elbows out, sleeves rolled up, with an angry scowl on his face. 'Ah, Mrs Todman,' he growls, 'have you evicted him yet?'

Chapter 38

'He can't stay.' Flecks of spit glisten on his lips. Dawn takes a step back into the room.

'Can I help you?' Aaman steps forward.

'I don't see what you have to do with this. All I want to know is when is he going?' Mr Brocklethwaite pushes past Aaman and into the front room. 'Well, buckets of blood!' he exclaims, coming to a sudden halt. Saabira frowns. She has never heard this expletive before, and it clearly is an expletive by the way he spits it out.

'What on earth happened here? Has he gone already?' Mr Brocklethwaite chortles.

'No, Mr Brocklethwaite, he's not gone, and I'll not recommend that he goes,' Dawn says tartly, pulling her shoulders back.

'Aye, I thought you might change your tune. You give a man the feeling that you're friendly but you're not.'

'Mr Brocklethwaite, if you are referring to the other day—' Dawn's tone is indignant.

'Oh no, let's not go there.' Mr Brocklethwaite dismisses her with a wave of his hand. 'You were quick to take me sherry, though.'

'You've got a nerve!' Dawn spits back at him, and Aaman takes a step to her side, Saabira on the other side, their allegiance made plain. 'Forget it,' says Dawn, regaining her composure. 'I have nothing to say to you. Cyril, or rather…' She turns to Saabira.

'Saabira,' says Saabira.

'And…' Dawn turns the other way.

'Aaman,' says Aaman.

'Saabira and Aaman, instead of trying to cause trouble for Cyril, have helped him to make his home a

198

better place and in the process they now have a good, clean neighbour. Perhaps if you had tried to help rather than point the finger this whole issue would have been dealt with years ago.' And with this she turns on her heels and marches out, past Mr Brocklethwaite, who has turned a deep red, and to the car. As she is getting in, fighting with her seat belt, she adds, 'Oh, and let Cyril know about my offer with the rabbit – just in case it is a help to him.' The last half of the sentence is aimed at Mr Brocklethwaite. She then slams her car door shut and backs down the cobbled street at an alarming rate.

Mr Brocklethwaite murmurs something under his breath, which could be 'cow', but Saabira is not sure.

'Well, you can tell Septic Cyril that I do not intend to let it rest here. Old Archie has been dead these two year past, and with no landlord he's nowt more than a squatter. I'll have him out yet.' Pushing past Aaman for a second time, he leaves by the front door, marching – pumping his arms and leaning forward slightly because of the incline – up to his own house next door.

'My goodness!' Aaman says in his usual quiet voice. 'So that was Mrs Dawn Todman and Mr Brocklethwaite! It is certainly not a dull place we have chosen!' He whistles through his teeth. 'Actually, she is not as bad as you made her sound, but he is much worse!'

'She seems to have changed,' Saabira admits. 'Or maybe the first time I met her she was just having a bad day.'

'Well, if this was an example of how her days go then every day must feel like a bad day. And what was Mr Brocklethwaite saying about sherry?'

'I don't really know, but Dawn did mutter something to herself about Mr Brocklethwaite being an octopus when Mrs Brocklethwaite was out of the room.'

'An octopus?' Aaman laughs.

'Really, Aaman, it is not a laughing matter! The man has no respect for anyone, not even his wife.'

'Why so serious, wife – don't you know that you too are married to an octopus...?' and he slides his hand around her waist.

'Aaman, are you never going to grow up?' she says, pulling away.

Aaman's face takes on his sad look, the one that always reminds her of a lonely puppy. She steps towards him and allows his other arm to go around her waist. He pulls her to him, making her giggle, but, as seems to happen more often than not, as if she knows what she is doing, Jay begins to whine through the baby monitor Saabira has on a piece of cord around her neck. She and Aaman sigh in unison.

'I'd better go, anyway,' Aaman says. 'I will be late for work.'

'But you've had no breakfast.'

'It looks like today I will go without breakfast.' Back in their house, Saabira hurries upstairs to Jay, calling down to Aaman, 'It is not good to go without breakfast, you will not work so well.' By the time she carries the child downstairs Aaman is putting on his big coat.

'Take some of yesterday's rotis at least?'

'Ah, my little jasmine!' Aaman kisses her on the cheek, and then kisses his daughter, who pulls away and hides her face. Aaman smiles. 'It is only one meal. It is not even a whole day, and food is assured.'

She knows he is referring to his time in Greece.

'Well, take an apple,' she insists, grabbing one from the fruit bowl in the middle of the table.

He chucks her under the chin and turns to leave.

'I might go into Bradford today,' Saabira says as he puts his hand on the doorknob. 'I thought that if Cyril can be left I might just go to the big library there and see if I can find a book that will tell us what his rights are, in case it is true that he is a squatter. Maybe by paying rent he can become legal again.'

200

Aaman's eyebrows lift. 'You never cease to amaze me,' he says. 'If you do come, find a telephone box and call me.' He takes out a card from his pocket and hands it to her.

'What is this?' she giggles, studying the card. 'You have a proper business card now?' She laughs again and Jay grabs at the colourful card.

'Of course,' Aaman replies. 'I am a proper English businessman now.' He lifts his chin but then wobbles his head from side to side and puts his palms together and raises them slightly, and bows deeply, grinning.

'You are a clown,' Saabira replies, and with a kiss he is gone.

Saabira makes a pot of tea and takes a steaming mug up to Cyril.

Chapter 39

She comes into the room smelling of rich spices and light flowers and, as always, her bracelets jingle as she moves.

'Good morning. I have brought you tea.' She sets it down on the bedside table. 'Did you sleep well?'

'She's been already.'

'Who? Oh yes – Dawn Todman. She was very impressed with your house.'

'Am I to be evicted?'

'Oh no! I do not think so. She will be presenting a favourable report. Her only concern was about the number of dogs, and whether they would not be happier if there were not so many together.'

Cyril frowns. Not so many together? It's not clear what that means. They certainly would not be happier back on the street, where a car might come. 'You know, find them new homes, with people who love them,' Saabira adds, pulling the stool from behind the door and sitting down. Her knees neatly together, she rests her hands on top.

His chin starts to quiver. Are they going to take them, give them to other people? He doesn't want her to see his mouth, which he is having trouble controlling, so he lifts his mug of tea high enough to hide it.

'Anyway, it is not a thought for now.' She dismisses the subject breezily and Cyril's tears, that were threatening, subside. 'Mr Brocklethwaite also came round whilst she was here.'

'I thought I heard him.' Cyril heard him say the word squatter and then his boots clacking against the cobbles as he marched up the lane. Mr Brocklethwaite

202

marched like that when he argued with Archie, he remembers.

'So what's your excuse this time?' Mr Brocklethwaite asked of Archie, a mug of Bovril in his hand. Archie and Mr Brocklethwaite were sitting either side of the fireplace, which Archie had only lit ten minutes before, so it was not very hot. Sometimes it got so hot you had to move the chairs away from it. Mr Brocklethwaite would come round sometimes, and he and Archie would talk about this and that; Cyril understood some of it, but often he didn't really listen to what they said.

'I don't need an excuse,' Archie said. 'I just don't fancy it.'

'Every Sunday you used to come – until he moved in.' He hissed the end part of this sentence, as if he didn't intend Cyril to hear, but Cyril knew that he had wanted him to hear really. Marion came to sit under the kitchen table and Cyril continued to study the jigsaw puzzle that was laid out on top of it. Archie had put all the edge pieces together but then he had said he was bored with it and gone to light the fire just before Mr Brocklethwaite came round. The picture on the front of the puzzle box showed a pair of kittens with bows in their hair, and it made Cyril smile, and he was glad to have something to concentrate on now that Mr Brocklethwaite was here.

'It's nowt to do with him. I just don't fancy it.' Archie pushed his legs out towards the fire, crossed his ankles, his fingers intertwined across his chest, chin down.

'You used to fancy it. Come on, I'll get Brenda to make sandwiches for both of us.'

'No, you're alright, Eric, I'll just stop in. Besides, weather's changing, it's getting a bit nippy out there.'

'And when did that ever bother you?' He stood then and his voice was raised. 'I'll tell thee, you've been a changed man since he moved in.' He didn't try to hide who he was talking about this time, and even jerked his thumb in Cyril's direction to make it clear.

'Leave lad alone,' Archie drawled.

'No, I won't. We've been friends these last years, and every Sunday we go fishing. Every Sunday, mind. Then he runs up and suddenly you've no time for your old pal. Well, things change, and I'll tell you that for nowt! When he's gone, wandered off, got himself lost or locked up, you'll look for your friends then and my guess is you'll expect them to be there. Well, they might not be.' He walked over to the kitchen table and slammed his cup down so hard that some of the Bovril splashed out and some went on the jigsaw. Cyril looked up accusingly but Mr Brocklethwaite just grinned back at him, and it was not a real smile.

Then he left, banging the door behind him, but it didn't close properly and Cyril could hear his boots clattering up the cobbles.

'Shut door, lad,' Archie said to him, and he did. 'You know, in a way it is your fault but not in the way he thinks,' he said, indicating the chair that Mr Brocklethwaite had vacated. Cyril felt his breathing quicken. 'Before you came I went fishing and never thought twice about the fish. Now, seeing the way you are with all living things, the respect you show even the tiniest insect – well, it's made me think twice. Maybe sticking a hook in a fish's mouth is fun for me – but I don't care what folk argue about their nervous system and whatnot, it can't be fun for the fish, gasping and flapping about, now can it?' And that was all he said. After that, Cyril couldn't remember Mr Brocklethwaite coming round for Bovril and a chat.

'I'm afraid that Mr Brocklethwaite is not as easily pleased as Dawn Todman,' Saabira says.

'If there's no landlord he might be able to evict me more easily,' Cyril says, his head hanging forward.

'Maybe we have to face the reality, Cyril. But I am also thinking that, whatever Mr Brocklethwaite can do, maybe I can undo. Who was it that said, "It only takes the good to do nothing for evil to prevail."' She smiles.

'The only thing necessary for the triumph of evil is for good men to do nothing.' Cyril corrects her, but the moment he has said the words he wonders if he has done wrong: she looks shocked, not pleased.

'You know this quote?'

He is not sure what to say. Is she angry?

'No, please, I am interested that you know this quote. Where do you know it from?'

'I read it.'

Her mouth drops open but she closes it quickly.

People often assume he cannot read because he doesn't like to read in front of people. He never has. Being taught to read was the one great gift the children's home gave him. But no sooner had he discovered books then the other children used it against him. They teased him endlessly, stole the books he was reading, drew rude pictures and words in them, and even tore them up when they belonged to the library. He very quickly learnt to hide the books and to hide himself away when he read.

'A politician said it. Edmund Burke.' Like so many other sentences, he had read it and it had stuck. He can still remember the page because, on this one, someone had drawn a little Mickey Mouse in the margin – that had been done before he borrowed it from the library – and because on the second line from the bottom was a typo, which read *form* instead of *from*.

His answer does not seem to have satisfied Saabira, but she asks no more, and he volunteers nothing.

'So I thought that I might go to the library in Bradford today to see if I can find anything out about your position – you know, see if Mr Brocklethwaite can be stopped somehow.' Saabira's tone is kind, and she does not appear to hold anything against him. 'But I will only go if you feel you will be alright on your own.'

'Maybe today I could go downstairs?' He wanted to ask yesterday but as the subject didn't come up he just stayed in bed and watched pictures from his mind on the wall. He used to be able to do that for hours but now he finds it bores him a little, and he prefers talking to Saabira.

'Okay, shall we try?' Saabira is on her feet.

'Can we try in half an hour, please? Your tea is really nice,' he raises his mug slightly, 'And then I would like to put on my trousers.'

'Certainly.' She seems pleased, gives him a little nod and leaves the room.

With Jay settled on the rug, happily taking beans out of the jar and putting them back in, Saabira takes the diary from the shelf.

Chapter 40

Saabira settles down on the rug next to Jay, with Archie's diary. Cyril's flash of knowledge has stirred her up and made her question so many things she has just presumed about him. If she is honest, she has compartmentalised him as being harmless, and kind, but not very bright and consequently unable to read. But that has just been proved untrue. How much of what he shows is just a result of his life so far, and how different would he be if he'd had a loving family around him as he grew up? It is all very fascinating. She opens the diary.

'I feel cold all the time now. It's not really surprising when I have no fat on me any more. I'm down to just bone. My belly is just wrinkled skin, my legs are like sticks. There are odd moments when I feel a little stronger and I think I might recover a bit but I am only lying to myself. I was hoping my mind would go before my body and then I would be unaware but it seems my body is going bit by bit even though my mind still feels strong. Mind you, it was almost worth letting those hospice witches in to get these new pills. They are amazing. At the moment I am completely pain free.

'So, as this is one of my more lucid moments I've decided not to waste it rattling on about myself but to take the time to tell you a few things, Cyril.

'We've got on alright, you and me, these last four years, and I can honestly say you have not been the irritation I thought you might be, at first. You never step over the mark, you are always respectful and polite and you always, always think one step ahead about how the things you do may affect me, or other people in general,

207

for that matter. I appreciate that you are this considerate around me.'

Saabira is interrupted by Jay who wants her to put one of the beans in the jar, then another. She takes a handful and they take turns to put them in the jar. Jay enjoys this, and Saabira tries to read as she flips one bean after the next into the container.

'I digress,' Archie continues, 'I am rattling on about myself when I said I wasn't going to. These strong pills make my mind wander and sometimes I don't notice for ages.

'So, back to what I wanted to tell you. Because you are always so respectful you never asked me questions, which was how I wanted it. But as a result you never found out what it is that I do to make me daily bread. Or should I say what it *was* that I *did* to put brass in my pocket – I have changed the tense because now I will be dead. That is such a strange thing to write, but in a way it makes me feel better, as if I will be talking from beyond the grave when you read this.

'There I go again, talking on about myself when I am trying to tell you what I do/did and what this has to do with you.

'I wish you had known Marion (my mother, not the dog). She was a very strong woman and, in her lifetime, after society gave her such a hard time for having me out of wedlock, she pushed herself and acquired several properties, not just this one that we live in. She also had four terraced houses in Bradford and the corner shop in Greater Lotherton. I've added to this with a couple more in Bradford and a couple more round here. It's a good game, property, 'cause once they are bought and you get a letting agency to take on the running there is little more to do and you get a steady little income.'

Saabira leans back. 'We know you were the landlord, Archie,' she says to herself, 'but who has your house now? Who does Cyril pay his rent to?'

There is a rhythmical tapping above her head. It can only be Cyril.

As the fire is not yet lit and Jay is engrossed in her game, Saabira leaves her to go halfway up the stairs to call to Cyril. He informs her that he is dressed and ready to come down, and would she kindly help him?

Saabira puts kitchen chairs either end between sofa and hearth to make a temporary pen for Jay. Her daughter's little face is concentrating as she tries to take beans out of the jar. If she only takes a few then she can withdraw her hand, but if she grabs too many her fist becomes too big and she cannot get her hand out. She is trying to judge the maximum she can grasp and still get her hand out.

'Coming,' Saabira shouts up the stairs.

Getting Cyril down the stairs proves to be much easier than she expected. He takes his weight on the handrails and hops with his good leg. She is in front of him ready to break his fall should he misjudge. At the bottom he takes a little rest.

'Do you want to sit on the sofa or at the table?' she asks.

'Do you have any jigsaws?' he says.

'No. Shall I get one of yours from next door?'

He heads for the table.

'Can you get the one of the kitten and the one of the cottage with all the flowers?'

'Of course.' And, after a glance at Jay, who is still engrossed, she goes next door and back as quickly as she can.

The bus to Bradford takes a while, winding its way down narrow lanes through magnificent countryside. The greens are like deep emeralds, the heather almost brown now, the sky a rich blue-grey fading to white on the horizon. It always looks like the monsoon weather. She will buy an umbrella today.

Soon, houses flank the road, and the bus goes all the way into the centre of Bradford and drops her at the bus station. She is directed out and up a street where the path goes down a slope and under the ground. Jay's eyes are wide and Saabira hurries her step, but the path widens at an intersection and she looks up at a perfect circle of sky above her, which lets in the sounds of cars, as if the open sky is the centre of a roundabout. She takes the first exit from this junction, up a slope and back out by the road where there are even more lanes and lights and traffic. It's the wrong exit; she backtracks and a few minutes later she is standing outside a large modern building with the word *Library* in relief letters above the doors. The glass doors open automatically and she gazes up at the grand, high ceiling. 'It's wonderful here,' she tells Jay, who is looking out at a group of pigeons fussing and pecking the ground around a woman eating her sandwiches on a bench.

Saabira looks around her, unsure where to start. A girl behind a long desk looks up and catches her eye.

'Hello, can I help you with anything?' she asks. She is wearing a saree.

Chapter 41

The receptionist fusses over Jay and then listens to Saabira, who explains what she needs. 'Come with me,' the woman says with a smile, and leads Saabira to a workstation where she can get online. She leaves, but returns moments later with a book for Jay to look at, which has things to press and squash, and Jay is completely absorbed until she becomes hungry.

By then, Saabira has amassed some information from the government portal, and from a land registry website, and has written it down on a pad of paper.

She has discovered that Cyril's house is owned by a trust company based, not in England, but on a small island off the west coast, halfway to Ireland, called the Isle of Man. A quick search reveals that the government of this island is independent from England, and that it is a tax haven, although it is still part of the British Isles.

'It is more complicated than I expected,' she tells Jay, who is beginning to wriggle and complain and definitely needs to eat and sleep. 'But enough of this now, my little bumble bee. Let us go and have our lunch.'

'Did you find what you needed?' the girl in the saree asks as they pass reception.

'Yes – thank you very much.'

'Aww, such a sweet little thing. Don't cry, baby.' The girl wiggles her long, painted fingernails in Jay's face, which makes her cry all the more.

'She is hungry,' Saabira explains.

'Oh, okay, cafe down this corridor to the right. There is a baby changing unit on your left.' She smiles widely.

'Thank you.' Saabira follows the directions. 'You know what, Jay, if you grow up here in England, which is so organised, you might find Pakistan a bewildering place.'

But Jay is not interested in the sounds her mother is making; she just wants food.

Saabira feels a little disappointed that she did not have lunch with Aaman but it was more logical for her to eat in the cafe with Jay, and by the time they finished his lunchbreak would have been over. Besides, having lunch with him would have involved finding a telephone to let him know she was coming as well as actually finding the place, which might have been a bus ride out of the centre of town. Once Jay is fed she becomes floppy, and the easiest option is to jump back on a bus to go back home anyway.

The bus they take drops them, not at the end of the cobbled lane, but in Greater Lotherton, which pleases Saabira. She relishes the thought of the walk along the narrow roads flanked with drystone walls, with the moors beyond on every side, hearing the call of the birds and the rustle of the sheep in the bracken, and feeling the wind on her face. It is a dramatic change from the city she has just left. Back home, if someone had described this landscape she would never had imagined preferring it to the horizons that surround their village in Pakistan, but now she is here it might very well be that she does like it better.

'It is passionate, like the Brontë sisters' stories. They told stories of love and jealousy,' she tells Jay, who is just waking up but is still slumped against her shoulder. The word 'jealousy' brings the thought of Juliet in Greece to mind. Saabira knows she still needs to deal with her feelings about this. She shakes her head. She still has no idea how.

They walk down the hill, over the railway line in the valley bottom and up the hill on the other side. Just as they

212

are coming to the end of the cobbled lane, a fat raindrop lands right on the end of her nose. She begins to judge the distance to their home but then it is as if the heavens have opened and Saabira makes a dash for the telephone box at the bottom of the lane.

Jay is awake now, her hands reaching out to the windows of the red telephone box, and then she wriggles, she wants to get down. There is nowhere she can escape to so Saabira obliges. Soon the windows begin to steam up. They are there five minutes waiting for the rain to subside before she thinks to use the phone. She has the name and the number, and it will be the quickest way to find out more.

'Hello, Haggle and Gripp, how may I help you?' says a voice on the other end of the line.

'Oh!' says Saabira, suddenly feeling unprepared. 'I would like some information about my landlord, please.' She frowns at her own words, and wonders whether the woman on the other end might consider her question odd, or say something that will make her feel foolish. 'May I take your name, please?' says the voice. There is a pause and the woman asks her to spell her surname. 'And the address?' Another pause, and a rustling sound. 'Thank you, I will see if Mr Haggle is available. Please hold.' The line goes quiet.

She seems to wait for ages, but as Jay is happily watching a beetle that has come in under the door to take refuge from the rain, and as the downpour continues, drumming on the roof of the phone box, she is in no hurry.

'Hello, Haggle speaking, how may I help, Mrs – er...' His tone is clipped and hurried.

'Saabira,' she says, to relieve him of his struggle with her last name. She repeats her request, and tells him the address of Cyril's house.

'Ah, right, yes,' he says, 'Well, the house you are referring to is part of the Noiram Trust.'

213

'If it is a trust does that mean it is a charity?' Saabira idly writes Noiram in the condensation that has gathered on the telephone box window.

'Not necessarily,' Mr Haggle replies. 'Trusts are often used by charities because of the tax breaks they afford, but this is just one application. A trust is a legal entity in its own right,' he purrs, evidently warming to the theme, 'with trustees and beneficiaries. In this case I am one of the trustees and Mr Gripp is another.' She can hear him taking a breath.

'Is there a problem with the house?' he continues. 'The state of repairs or something? If you have any issues with the property it's best to speak to the management company that you pay your rent to.'

'Oh,' says Saabira. She hadn't considered the possibility of there being a management company involved. 'Can you tell me who the management company is, please?' She breathes on the letters she has written on the cold glass and they come up clearer. There's a pause on the line.

'I thought you said you were the tenant.' The voice sounds hard now. 'Who did you say you are?'

Saabira curses herself under her breath for not thinking more quickly, and then chastises herself for using bad language.

'Thank you,' she mumbles, and hangs up hastily.

Jay does not want to leave the telephone box. The rain has just about stopped but she is still fascinated with the beetle and she squats, following its progress across the floor, but not brave enough to touch it. Outside, Saabira waits for her baby to stand. She looks at the child through the glass, and she can also see the letters that she wrote on the inside of the window in the condensation: Noiram. She closes her eyes to think for a moment. Jay stands suddenly and starts to cry. The beetle has crawled through a crack at the back of the box and is gone. She must ask Cyril if he

214

pays rent to a management company. Perhaps they will be able to clarify his situation.

At the house, Cyril is slumped on the sofa, asleep, his damaged leg awkwardly straight and the jigsaw of the kitten and the one of the house covered in flowers both completed on the kitchen table.

Jay immediately wants her jar of beans; Saabira sets it down on the rug in front of the fire, which is not lit. The Aga is keeping the place beautifully warm.

The kettle's whistling does not wake Cyril, although he shifts and his half-broken glasses fall down to the very end of his nose. She must do something about those, find where they can be repaired. It's still early and she can allow herself a moment before starting the food. She takes down Archie's diary and sits with it between the overly fluffy kitten and the overly flowery house. The book feels more personal now that she has done some research. Why did Archie sell his mother's houses to the trust company, and what does that mean for Cyril? Is Cyril actually paying his rent? Maybe through the bank account that Archie set up, and he is not even aware of it. Perhaps he is not a squatter at all. When he wakes up she will ask him. Looking at his bank statements might be the easiest way to sort all this out, and it might also show who the letting agency is.

It occurs to her that she has taken a very long way around to find out some information that is, perhaps, not very useful. And why on earth has she not just asked Cyril some direct questions? She sighs because she knows the answer to this. She has presumed he knows nothing, just like she presumed he could not read, or that he could not take in and recall information like the Edmund Burke quote.

She opens the book.

'My mother might have been sharp but she never really paid much mind about how much tax the government took off her. When she died I had to let one of the houses go just to settle up the death duties. I weren't right happy about that, I can tell you! So I've made it my business to find out about taxes and that sort of thing!

'Anyways, the long and the short of it is that the house is no longer mine so the government cannot tax me on it when I'm gone. It belongs to a trust company now – the Noiram Trust. Ha! I can still live here for the rest of me life, but when I die them buggers will get nowt.

'I won't bore you with the details, but suffice to say this arrangement will save a pretty penny.'

'Oh!' Saabira says quietly to herself. 'I should have just read on a little. But what does it mean for Cyril, Archie?' She turns the page, but the entry ends here, and the next is written some days later, and does not mention the trust.

'Noiram,' Saabira says to herself, and an image of the word comes to mind, written on the window of the phone box. Beyond is Jay, squatting on the ground inside, but the letters come into focus again, reversed, now she is looking in from the outside. Of course! Noiram is simply Marion written backward! It seems so simple. Why didn't she see that immediately? It seems her brain has become sluggish since she stopped studying. Not for the first time, Saabira considers that she must find a way to keep herself mentally more active.

Jay stands, leaving her beans, and tries to climb onto the sofa.

'No, Jay,' Saabira hisses. But Jay takes no notice, and with fists grabbing at the material of the cushions she hoists herself up before Saabira can stand. Once on the seat she crawls across and curls up under Cyril's outstretched arm. He does not wake up and Jay closes her eyes. Saabira smiles at the picture the two of them make, and at Cyril's good fortune, and at the fact that the world can be so nice. She leaves them curled up together so she can read on.

Chapter 42

His arm is all stiff and something is lying on it so he is unable to move. His leg is also at a funny angle but at least it's not throbbing as it was. Without moving, he opens one eye and sees a thousand prisms through his broken lens. He closes this eye and opens the other. The fire has been lit, but that is not where his attention is drawn. It is not alive and breathing like the small child curled in the crook of his arm. He stares at the infant, Saabira's baby. Lashes so long they look like they have been stuck on. When closed, her eyes create a single thick black line, which curves upwards towards her temple. It is like holding a bird in his hand, the feeling of this child sleeping there in his arms, and so special. A baby bird, all feathers and no weight, wild and yet trusting. He feels honoured.

Waking a little more, he becomes aware of voices. One is Saabira's, and after a moment or two he recognises that the other is Aaman's.

'We cannot tell him, Saabira,' Aaman says quietly. Saabira answers; it is too quiet to hear the words, but it is something about a bank account. Aaman murmurs something in return. Their voices are low, as if to hide something, conceal a secret.

'I haven't seen any bank account statements. If there had been any we would have seen them when we were clearing things out, wouldn't we? I think the lawyers might be the best choice, let's see if we can talk to them and find out the truth,' Saabira says, and then something else that he doesn't hear fully but which ends with '...we have no proof that he is not just a sick, insane man.'

He doesn't move. It sounds like they are talking about him, and the words are not kind. He has been called sick, and insane, before, in the children's home, and at work in the abattoir, but Aaman and Saabira seemed different. With them he is sane and well, and they make him feel balanced.

The tightness in his head, which has been gone for weeks, returns, and a familiar confusing mess of emotions and thoughts that are too scrambled to deal with twist through the grooves worn inside his brain. If he moves, Saabira and Aaman will know he is awake and then they will probably hide what they have just said with insincere chatter. Best to wait, frozen, his hurt leg outstretched and their baby in his arms. Their precious child, unspoilt and loved. So very perfect. How happy he was just a few seconds ago, waking to find they trusted him with Jay. If they think he is insane and sick then what sort of parents are they, letting their only child so close to him?

He tentatively strokes Jay's hair from her face, using small, slow movements so as not to attract Saabira's and Aaman's attention. He will let them continue what they are saying, prove that they are like all the rest. People are often pleasant to his face, only to whisper about him the moment his back is turned, as if he is deaf or stupid, or both. He knows people call him Septic Cyril, and some do not even hide the fact and they expect him not to mind. Do they expect him to laugh with them at himself? What do they expect?

His stomach turns over and he swallows his bile. Saabira and Aaman really did seem different.

'We could ask the lawyers to write to him, couldn't we?' Aaman says. If they are talking about lawyers it can only mean one thing – that they too are trying to get him evicted. Saabira has been to the library, and she said she was going to try to help, him but it seems she has just been helping Mr Brocklethwaite instead. Maybe that was why they were so keen to clean his house out, to make it ready for someone else to move straight in.

He screws up his eyes and tries not to make a sound as the tears fall. Saabira and Aaman, after Matron Jan and Archie, have been his first real friends, and he has really considered them as such. But now they are proving to be like all the rest. The hollow feeling that engulfs him takes him back to the wardrobe, curling up in the dark when his mum was out.

He would like to rock now, to bang his head, but with Jay in one arm he cannot move without waking her.

'So one of us must go to the telephone box and call the lawyers.' Saabira says. Aaman mutters something in return and they move apart. Saabira's voice whispers back to Aaman from near the front door.

'Don't mention it if he wakes, let us get it all sorted out first.'

He can hold himself back no longer. The tears pulse free and stream down his cheeks, and he slides his arm from under the warm body of the perfect child and awkwardly squirms until he is standing.

'That's right, get it all sorted first so the simple man cannot do anything!' he shouts at them before he has even turned to face them. 'Treat him like he has no feelings. That's what they all do, even the ones that pretend to be nice.'

'Sorry? What?' Aaman says, but his eyes are on Jay.

'I really thought you were different.' Cyril addresses Saabira. 'You pretended to be my friend, you acted like you liked me. What did you do that for unless you just wanted to be unkind?'

'Cyril?' Saabira's hand reaches towards him.

'To hell with you!' Cyril shocks himself with his language. Jay, who is awake now, starts to yowl. Saabira's eyes flicker from him to her.

'Go, deal with your child, just don't pretend to be one thing to her and turn out to be another.' Holding onto the back of the sofa he hops and shuffles to the back door.

'Cyril – what is going on, where are you going?' Aaman takes two strides towards him and puts a hand on his forearm, trying to stop him.

'Don't.' The tears well again and his nose begins to run. 'Just don't.' He is by the back door now, struggling to open it.

'Cyril, I think you must have misunderstood what we were saying. It is to do with your house and–'

'I know it is to do with my home, I am not so stupid!' Cyril has the door open now. 'Well, you and Mr Brocklethwaite will actually have to get me out first. I'm sick of being pushed around.' The door slams behind him.

The wind off the moors is so strong the tears on his cheeks blow back towards his ears, leaving cold trails that soon dry. The clouds rumble and churn, dark grey right down to the horizon. It is going to pour down.

Using the low wall for support, he manages to make his way to his own back door as Aaman comes out after him.

'Cyril, please come back…'

He does not wait to hear the end of what sounds like it is going to be a speech. More insincere words, no doubt, like he has heard a thousand times. Words like that never lead to anything good. The dogs rush him as he steps into his own house. They lick his hands, and Coco jumps up and he falls against the door.

'Get down,' he says, but as he does so it is he who sinks awkwardly onto the floor, his bad leg walked all over by the dogs, the tears licked from his cheeks as he gently nods his head backward so it bangs repeatedly against the door.

Chapter 43

'He must have heard some of what we said, and misunderstood. Go back round, knock on the door until he answers,' Saabira implores Aaman as she rocks and cuddles Jay, who is screeching at the top of her voice.

'I tried to talk to him, but he has shut his door.'

'Did you knock?'

'Of course I knocked. Maybe we should wait until he calms down.' Aaman strokes his child's head as he speaks over her noise.

'Maybe I should go round. Can you take Jay?' She holds their daughter out to him.

'I think it might be a good idea to go and ring the lawyers again, see if we can find out the full situation.' Aaman gets his fingers caught in Saabira's bracelets as he takes Jay.

'I am not sure they would speak to me after last time... I think he knew that I wasn't being honest about who I was. Perhaps you could call them, Aaman?' Saabira asks. 'As a man they may take you more seriously...' She smiles and steps a little closer to him, her arm touching his. But at the same time she swallows to make her mouth a little less dry. She will be nervous if she has to call the lawyer again. Only bad things come from lying, no matter how big or small the lie.

Aaman's eyes widen at her suggestion, and for a second it appears that her request has made him even more nervous than she is. But he regains control almost immediately, and replies gently. 'My jasmine, of course I would do it, but my English is not as good as yours, and I am not sure that I would be able to make myself clear, as you can. Explain the situation in full, and I am sure it will be okay.' He pauses briefly before adding, 'Besides, what is the very worst thing that could happen? That he refuses to speak to you?'

He has a point. The lawyer is only a man on the other end of a telephone line, not even one in the same room as her. She can always put the phone down.

'Okay, I will go.' She puts her shawl on.

'Maybe by the time you come back he will have calmed a little bit, and he might talk to you then?' Aaman rocks his daughter, trying to calm her.

'Let us hope so. Wish me luck.' Saabira waves before pulling the front door shut behind her.

The sharp wind is ripping up leaves from the shallow gutters where they have collected down either side of the cobbled lane. A lady comes out of a house across the road and bangs a fork against the edge of a tin.

'Spike! Come here, Spike!' she shouts in a raucous voice. 'Hello, dear,' she says to Saabira. 'Right nippy out'

Saabira mutters her acknowledgement and smiles, pulling her shawl around her more tightly. A cat flashes past her, up the street, as she turns the corner at the bottom.

'Come on, Spike,' the woman calls, more gently now, as Saabira yanks open the door of the phone box. The wind plays flute-like around the edge of the door where it does not shut properly. Saabira pulls her shawl around her and takes a deep breath.

'Hello, please may I speak to Mr Haggle?' she says as soon as her call is answered. She does not want to give her name, after last time. The floor of the booth is covered with cigarette ends. She pushes these around with the toe of her sandal as she waits for an answer. Two lager cans stand upright in a corner, one with burnt matches on top.

'Who shall I say is calling?' She recognises the girl's voice from yesterday.

'Yes, I will hold.' Saabira tries to deflect the question and it works.

'One moment please.' The phone goes silent.

'Haggle here, how may I help?' The voice is more jovial today.

'Good morning,' says Saabira. 'I am ringing on behalf of a friend. Two friends, to be accurate, a Mr Archie Sugden and a Mr Cyril Sugden.'

The telephone is quiet.

'Hello?' she says.

'I believe we spoke yesterday.' There is a sound of papers rustling, and the voice does not sound friendly now. 'Perhaps you'd like to tell me who you are, and what exactly it is that you want?' Saabira sighs and takes a deep breath. 'I am Cyril's neighbour,' she says. 'And I am trying to find out who his landlord is…'

'Why?' The lawyer's voice is harsh, and Saabira pictures him in court, with a powdered wig and long black robe, scowling at the defendant over glasses propped on the end of his nose. In this vision she could be in the witness box, and he is cross-examining her. Before she has a chance to reply he continues in the same aggressive tone. 'Yesterday you told me that you were the tenant, and that you wanted to find out who your landlord is. Might I suggest that this is not an ideal way to start if you are expecting a positive result from this exchange?'

Saabira's mouth goes dry at these words, and despite the cold in the phone box she can feel a sweat break out on her forehead. Her instinct is to put the phone down, go home and close the door against the world. But a second picture comes to mind. One of Cyril, in his house next door, now empty of furniture, and probably cold and very much alone. Friendless Cyril, who trusted her and let her into his home, opened up to her, and whom she now feels she has betrayed. How much that must hurt. No, his need is greater, and despite the lawyer's odious nature she will press on and see what can be achieved. Aaman's words return: 'The worst thing that could happen is he won't talk to you.' Well, so far so good – he is talking to

223

her. Besides, compared to what Aaman went through on his journey to Europe this is nothing. She is being cowardly.

'Mr Haggle,' she says, 'I was not entirely honest yesterday. I do need to know who the landlord is, but it is for my neighbour Cyril, not for me.'

'I see,' says Mr Haggle.' His voice is a little calmer now. 'Why do you not ask him directly?'

'Have you met Cyril?' she says.

'No...' His voice is guarded now.

'Cyril is a ...' She is forced to pause to find the right word. 'He is a delicate man, sensitive.'

'I see.'

'He was taken in by Archie, as part of the Care in the Community programme, but he does not manage very well with certain things. Now his neighbour wants to evict him because of the smell in the house, and–'

'Hang on,' the lawyer interrupts, 'you said *you* were his neighbour.'

'I mean his other neighbour, Mr Brocklethwaite ...'

'Go on.' Mr Haggle's patient tone sounds forced, overly practised.

'When Archie died,' she explains, 'Cyril could not manage to look after the house. It was full of things he had collected, and there was a very bad smell.' Has she overdone her description? 'His neighbour... His *other* neighbour, Mr Brocklethwaite, and a woman from Health and Safety are trying to find a way to evict him. I am trying to stop them. You see, he is not a bad person, and I thought that perhaps I could help him by finding out who the landlord is, discover his legal position...' Saabira feels that she is not doing a good job of explaining herself at all. Perhaps it would have been better for Aaman to do this after all; he is very good at speaking in jargon and without involving his heart, despite his English being more basic than hers.

224

'Hm...' There is a pause. 'Well,' the lawyer says, 'he is lucky to have such a neighbour.' But there is no conviction in his tone. 'Regardless, I am bound by the law. I explained to you yesterday that the house is owned by the trust, and that Mr Gripp and I are the trustees. That's all I can tell you, I'm afraid. Why don't you have Cyril contact me, and I'll explain it all to him directly?'

At least his tone is becoming more friendly now, but Saabira wonders if she will ever get anywhere with this conversation. She sighs deeply.

'He thinks that I too am trying to evict him now. He got the stick by the wrong end...' She frowns. 'Also, I do not think he trusts lawyers. Ah, I know.' Inspiration strikes her. 'Perhaps you could write to him, explain the situation in a letter?'

There's a long pause, and Saabira thinks she can hear rustling of papers in the background. Would Cyril read a letter, if the lawyer agrees to send one? Finally, Mr Haggle comes back on the line.

'Here's what I can do,' he says. He sounds tired now. 'I have a copy of the letter that we sent out when Mr Sugden died. It explains Cyril's situation in full. I can't tell you any of the details, as I said, because of client confidentiality and all that, but I'll have Rebecca send out a copy of the letter, and perhaps you can encourage Cyril to read it? It sounds like he hasn't seen the original. At least, we have never received a reply...'

Saabira suddenly feels exhausted, but also relieved that the confrontation did not go as badly as she had feared.

'Thank you!' she says. 'I trust he will receive it tomorrow if you send it out first class?' She knows she is pushing her luck now, but then again this sort of behaviour seems to work in books and in the films, so why not in real life?

'Yes indeed Mrs..., er,' Mr Haggle stumbles. Saabira did not give her name today, and she can tell that he thinks he has been told it and has now forgotten. Perhaps he did not write it down yesterday either.

'Goodbye, Mr Haggle,' she says quickly and waits long enough to hear him say 'Good–' but not '–bye' and then replaces the receiver.

It is Saabira who is knocking on the door. He can hear her sandals against the flags, her jewellery as it tinkles against itself.

'Cyril, can you hear me?' she calls. You do not need to open the door if that is what you prefer. But I just wanted to say that I am on your side, and I do not intend to help Mr Brocklethwaite. I have spoken to the lawyer, Archie's lawyer, and he is going to send a letter to explain your position.'

Why is she saying this? Is it a trick to get him to open the door? So she can tell him face to face he is evicted? Or maybe Aaman and Mr Brocklethwaite are there too, and they will physically pull him out? And why has she been speaking to lawyers?

'Cyril, it is important that you read this letter when it arrives. Can you hear me? It will explain everything, and if you want you are always welcome to come next door and we can discuss it together.'

He doesn't move. Coco is laid over his bad leg, and Blackie Boo is by his side. Sabi and Zaza are alongside him; even little Gorilla Head, Teddy Tail and silky, golden-orange Mr Perfect are all only an arm's length away. But then again, there is nowhere for them to hide now the room is empty, and everything is out in the open.

He doesn't say anything, and after a while Saabira goes away.

Chapter 44

Cyril listens, but there are no sounds to suggest that Saabira, or anyone else, is in his backyard.

The empty room is cold and unfriendly. All the warmth and memories are being squeezed out with this threat of eviction and all this talk of lawyers.

But if he doesn't live here, where will he live? The hospital won't take him and he is too old for a children's home. Archie is gone, the rabbits are mostly gone, and there is only him and the dogs left, and the dogs are half wild.

Maybe he should have gone with Marion when she limped her way out onto the moors, never to be seen again. Maybe she knew what she was doing, that there was nothing left for her here. Well, he will not give them the pleasure of evicting him. He will take control just like Marion did. In a minute he will find a way to stand up. When everything was being thrown out, where did he put his rucksack? In the cupboard under the stairs, or under his bed? Maybe he put it under Archie's bed for safe keeping. No one went in there, did they?

He cannot stand. With one leg stiff and nothing to pull himself up by, it is impossible. When he rolls over onto his stomach it alarms the dogs, who stand and wait, their brows lifting between their eyes, wondering what is happening. Once prone, he uses his good leg and his arms to drag his way across the floor to the stairs. Using the doorframe and the handrail and a great deal of care, he finally stands, but he immediately decides that going upstairs on his bottom might be the better way, and so he turns around and sits down again. It is not as difficult as he imagined and, once at the top, he uses both stair and handrail to stand again. Coco is looking on anxiously, the other dogs all peeping around the door frame at the bottom of the stairs.

'It's alright, girl.' He pats her and shuffles towards Archie's room, holding onto the wall, the door handle, the bed-end. Coco will not follow him in here. None of the dogs will. She sits at the threshold whimpering quietly.

'Ah, there it is.' With one hand he pulls out his large rucksack from under the bed. There is something in the bottom of the bag, and he flings it onto the faded Camberwick bedspread that covers Archie's bed, where he pats it down to discover that, at the bottom, is a lump. Tentatively he puts his hand in and fishes out a pair of still-wet walking socks. Once upon a time they were orange and white; now a mould has grown over the foot sections and they disintegrate as he tries to unravel them. The smell is acrid. Coco backs away from the door.

Cyril dumps the remains of the socks on Archie's clean bedroom floor, and then pulls the rucksack after him into his room, Coco following, and shuts the door.

'I'm going,' he tells her as he takes clothes from the suitcase on the floor. 'I've had enough of them telling me where I can and cannot live, telling me where I must work, what I must do.' With the thought of leaving the abattoir comes a deep intake of breath and a heavy exhalation. 'We'll walk out of the back door and just keep going, Coco. If we get thirsty we'll drink from streams, and if I get hungry I know which berries are safe, which leaves are rich, and you, my friend, will have to catch yourself shrews and rats.' He looks her in the eyes; her whimpering stops. 'But no rabbits!' he warns her.

On Thursdays, Mum would always be up early. She would dress him in his only smart shirt and brush down his shorts, smooth his hair with water and then take him by the hand out of the flat and they would walk the length of the street to go in the double doors with the long brass handles a good way further down that long road. Here, Mum would approach whichever man was free behind the counter. The counter had glass screens with an arched opening, and Mum would lean down to the arch and talk through it, shouting slightly. He never understood what that place was. There were four different men working behind the counters and they never seemed to get the same one twice. Only one of them ever smiled, and the other three looked as if they were permanently in pain. He would wonder what was behind the counter that made them so uncomfortable. Sometimes, Mum would talk angrily to the man, and they would be there a long time. Other times she would be handed a piece of paper with no argument and they would leave immediately. They never left without a piece of paper.

On the way back they would go past the fish and chip shop and across the road and past the pub to the post office. This is where he would see the tramp, standing beside the rubbish bin. People like Mum would walk past and never even see him. He looked like he was a big man, but on inspection he wore a large and heavy-looking overcoat over another overcoat which was over a chunky knitted jumper. If Cyril watched carefully he would get a glimpse of one of the tramp's wrists, or his ankle, and both of these were very thin. A big bushy beard made his face look fat. After they passed, Cyril would look back and his mum would pull him on, hurting his shoulder. But he had to watch because sometimes the man took things out of the bin and ate them.

There is nothing much to take and the packing takes no time at all,. A couple of pairs of socks, a jumper. Bracing his hip against the bed he shoulders the rucksack. It hangs lightly and he wonders if it is worth taking at all.

It scrapes down the wall as he levers himself back down the stairs.

'I'll be slow to start with,' he warns Coco. 'But my leg will heal and then we'll stride out, the sound of grouse in our ears, the vast emptiness of the moors all around us and not a person in sight.'

At the bottom of the stairs his foot slips and he sits with a heavy thump. The dogs gather round.

'This leg is bad timing,' he tells Coco. 'But there's no choice. Gorilla Head?' The mottled multicoloured dog's ears prick up at the sound of her name. 'You and Mr Perfect have been a good pair of dogs but now you'll have to go out and fend for yourselves.' The dog turns its head on one side. Mr Perfect steps to Gorilla Head's side at the sound of his name.

'Now then' – he address all the dogs at once – 'I think today is the day that we all part ways.' He puts his hand on Blackie Boo's head. 'I did my best and you are all well and strong, but now we no longer have a roof over our heads and as I intend to never, ever set foot inside that place again I have no job and I can't take care of you. You can start out with me if you like, but as you get hungry I'll understand if you disappear off to find what you can. Just take care of yourselves.' He puts Sabi's head between his hands and leans his forehead against hers. Zaza tries to push in so he pulls her close too, his own head between theirs; Teddy Tail wriggles underneath and brings her head up and clonks Cyril under his chin but he doesn't mind. They know something sad is happening, and he will do what he can for them as long as he can. But there is only so long he can sit there and put off his going. With a final kiss on each of the dogs' heads he is on his feet again and hobbling towards the back door.

The rain is lashing against the back of the house like a nine-tailed whip. It stings his cheeks and drives into his clothes. Coco immediately backs inside. The other dogs also shrink from the downpour.

'Come on, you lot, I would rather leave of my own accord in a bit of rain than have the humiliation of someone throwing us out.' But the dogs hang back. The sky is not too black; the greys vary from slate-grey to silver. To the north-west, the sky has patches of blue and that is where the wind is coming from.

'It will be over in an hour.' He encourages the dogs, which have now curled up with one another in the middle of the empty room. Tonight they will sleep on the moors. He can imagine it – the sound of rustling and small feet running at ground level amongst the bracken as tiny night creatures come out to carry on their lives. The bracken is so high he will be entirely hidden, the bright moon above in a sky of a thousand stars. He will lie on his back and name them.

The wind bites through his tweed jacket, the hole at his elbow letting the cold in.

'Sleeping bag!' All the dogs start at Cyril's sudden outburst. 'Where did Archie's sleeping bag go?' He looks at the door of the cupboard under the stairs. Crossing the room and rummaging in the dark seems like a great deal of effort. He needs to conserve his energy for walking. The rain picks up and the noise it makes increases. With the back door still open, he can see the clouds rolling over one another.

With the sleeping bag in his rucksack and the dogs around his heels, he slams the door behind him and sets off. The peat is saturated and squelches as he walks but his feet stay dry in his big boots. He pulls his tweed flat cap firmly down on his head and the dogs bound ahead, now unconcerned by the rain. It is as if they sense that they are not setting out on a short walk.

Chapter 45

The sun blazes in through the curtains and the sky is blue in the first light of dawn. For a moment Saabira thinks she is back in Pakistan, which happened a lot in the first few weeks. She would wake and not know where she was, or she would think she was back home. But this is home now. She still misses family and friends, of course she does, but she knew she would. What she didn't expect was that she would fall in love with her new home. She likes the house, the village with its narrow cobbled street, the bleak romantic moors, the choice in the supermarkets, the cleanliness of everything, and all those details that make England so different. The hanging flower baskets, empty trains and buses, public toilets with toilet paper and soap and hot water, metal drain holes in the roads that lead to underground pipes to take the rainwater away, ready-made naan breads and sandals, of such quality and so cheap.

'What on earth!' she says to herself. It is a new expression she has learnt, and right now it fits.

Someone is shouting outside, and there is the sound of a metal dustbin lid being thrown or hit. Aaman, who is sitting up in bed reading a newspaper, stops and looks up.

'It seems there is always something on this street. What is it?' he asks.

More shouting. 'It is Mr Brocklethwaite.' Saabira gets dressed hurriedly and runs down the stairs.

'I have found things out!' Mr Brocklethwaite is screaming so loudly his voice cracks.

Saabira breathes heavily from her sprint. Aaman is right behind her. Mr Brocklethwaite stands on the pavement outside his house, legs astride as if he is about to

232

have a shoot-out and there, facing him, outside his own house, is Cyril, with an envelope in his hand.

'This house,' Mr Brocklethwaite points at Cyril's house, 'belongs to a company. Noiram Trust Limited.' His chest is all puffed out and he sneers as he talks.

'Should we do something, say something?' Saabira asks Aaman.

'Do what? We do not know what the letter says.'

'Well, we can tell him to stop shouting. We can discuss this without raising our voices, surely?' But, looking at Mr Brocklethwaite, there appears to be little chance of him calmly discussing anything.

'Did you know that?' Mr Brocklethwaite seems to be relishing the confrontation and he takes a few steps nearer to Cyril.

Cyril shakes his head. 'Not until today.' He holds up the letter and points to it but Mr Brocklethwaite ignores this gesture.

'Just as I thought. If you didn't know they owned your house then you can't have been paying them rent, can you, eh?' Another step closer.

Cyril shakes his head.

'So, I've got you Cyril Whatever-Your-Name-Is,' he crows triumphantly, and he raises an accusatory finger – takes another step forward to close the gap, so the finger is pointing straight in Cyril's face.

'Sugden,' Cyril replies quietly.

'Are you trying to be funny?' Mr Brocklethwaite's jubilance fades and the muscle above one side of his mouth twitches, lifting his lip. Saabira's heartbeat quickens. They are only an arm's reach apart now.

'Cyril Sugden.'

Mr Brocklethwaite turns pink and then red, his hand squeezes into a fist and Saabira worries for his health.

'You dirty little toerag. First you steal my pal Archie, then you steal the house once he is dead, and now you steal his name. Identity theft, that's what it is. Identity theft!' And before any of them sees it coming he takes a balletic leap towards Cyril and catches him with a blow that is more of a slap than a punch. Cyril stumbles backward, and Saabira turns away to protect Jay, so it is Aaman who catches Cyril to stop him falling. When Saabira turns back, Aaman, shorter than both of the men by half a head, is standing between them, a hand on each of their chests.

'I'll have you Septic-Cyril-Bloody-Sugden.' Mr Brocklethwaite jabs a finger over Aaman's arm towards Cyril's face.

'I must tell you something,' Cyril says.

'You're not right in the head, you halfwit.' Mr Brocklethwaite is spitting down his own chin as he shouts.

'You need to listen,' Cyril implores.

'Do you know what a runt is? Well, you are a runt and a cuckoo. Stealing other people's nests.' He makes another lurch for Cyril, but Aaman stands his ground. Several neighbours down the street have come out onto their doorsteps to see what is going on.

Cyril thrusts the letter towards Saabira.

'Tell him,' he begs, one arm shielding his head from Mr Brocklethwaite. 'Look.' He jabs his finger at the words on the page. Saabira skim-reads the top page of the sheaf of papers Cyril has handed her and gasps.

'Ah, Mr Brocklethwaite!' she shouts, and he stops trying to lash out at Cyril and tightens his mouth into a thin line to try to stop the twitching, but his expression remains murderous. 'Mr Brocklethwaite,' she says again, calmly, and with authority.

'What?' he snaps.

'Well,' she says, 'it seems Archie was a bit of a business man.'

'Smart man, Archie, till *that* got under his skin.' He points to Cyril.

'He was so smart that he put his house into a trust. Noiram Trust,' she says.

'Aye, I just told you that, and he' – he jabs his finger at Cyril again – 'has just admitted he's not been paying rent to them. Squatter. I'll have you out!'

'Ah, but you have missed the point, Mr Brocklethwaite. It says here that Archie owned Noiram Trust and everything in it, and Archie gave all he had to Cyril.' Mr Brocklethwaite and Aaman's mouths drop open at these words. Aaman starts to smile and Mr Brocklethwaite starts to grimace.

'Not only that but he also gave Cyril his name, Sugden – gave him it through deed poll. It is all in the letter.' Saabira is aware this information is goading Mr Brocklethwaite, and as soon as she has said it, she wonders if it was a wise thing to do. His red face suggests he has high blood pressure.

Noises behind her take her attention. Whilst this exchange has been taking place, the other villagers have slowly moved from their respective doorways, inching towards Cyril's house, arms folded, alert to catch every word as if it is a theatre production.

The muscles around Mr Brocklethwaite's mouth continue to twitch, distorting his countenance as he faces the audience.

'So he is not a squatter, and he is not illegal. Actually he now owns his own house,' Saabira continues, and Aaman grins.

Cyril points again to the part of the letter he indicated before.

'I think *you* should tell him that, Cyril,' she says and holds out the paper for him, but he shakes his head.

'Please,' he says. She smiles to let him know that they are still friends despite yesterday's misunderstanding. Lifting her chin, she reads loudly enough for everyone to hear.

'It says here that Noiram Trust owns numbers thirty, thirty-one and thirty-two Little Lotherton,' Saabira announces.

'Thirty?' Aaman says, grinning at Cyril. 'That is our house!' and he offers a little nod of respect.

'Thirty-two! That's my house!' Mr Brocklethwaite splutters. Saabira looks up from the letter.

'Mr Brocklethwaite,' she says, lowering the letter. 'Please may I introduce you to your landlord.' She waves a hand towards Cyril, whose chin is now lifted in a manner that would appear regal were it not for his glasses with the broken lens.

'My landlord,' Mr Brocklethwaite repeats in a thunderous voice. 'My landlord!' He spits it out the second time. He looks around at all the neighbours who have gathered to watch the spectacle. 'I'll not bloody live here with him as my landlord,' he shouts, and turns on his heel.

'Aye, be gone with you!' someone from the crowd remarks, and this is followed by much laughter and some cheering and several people clap as Mr Brocklethwaite retreats up the road. Evidently he will not be missed if he leaves Little Lotherton.

Cyril turns to see who is clapping, and finds the whole street is gathered there. Mr Brocklethwaite's front door slams behind him, and the crowd that has gathered all look to Cyril. But they are not laughing at him, or sneering. They are smiling. Mr Dent winks at him and mutters, 'Way to go, Cyril.' The lady with all the children, who still has on her blue hairnet from the bakery, says, 'Couldn't happen to a nicer bloke.' Even Mrs Pringle says, 'Go on love, you show 'em.' And then they begin to spread out and wander back to their own houses.

Chapter 46

The road is emptying now and Cyril faces Saabira and Aaman.

'This is wonderful news, Cyril – or shall I call you Mr Landlord?' Aaman says. He holds out his hand and Cyril shakes it but he cannot look happy.

'Cyril?' Saabira asks.

'I feel so bad about the way I treated you. I just presumed you were like everyone else. I am so sorry.'

'Ah, it is nothing.' Aaman says.

'Cyril, that is what we all do all the time. People did it to you, people do it to us.' She waves a finger between herself and Aaman. 'It is human nature, but it is not a bad thing.'

'It was a very bad thing,' Cyril says.

'Here I must disagree. We cluster people into similar groups and make presumptions because it stops us wasting time and energy. It's a major part of our self-protection. It warns us off the "baddies."' She smiles. Aaman puts his arm around her shoulder and looks at her with pride in his eyes, his other hand on the baby monitor around his neck.

'Well, I am very sorry.' He puts as much feeling into the words as he can.

'So, does this mean we can continue to be your tenants?' Aaman asks, and they all laugh, and without a word they wander back into the warm house and Aaman runs up the stairs to gather up a now-whingeing Jay. Saabira puts the kettle on.

Sitting at the kitchen table, with a big pot of tea between them, Cyril flattens the letter out on the table.

He got quite a long way onto the moors with his throbbing leg. But the bats swooping low over the heather took his mind off the pain, and so did the lonely calls of the owls in the village, becoming fainter and fainter as he walked on, until there was nothing but silence and the stars, a great wide shimmering galaxy of stars that filled the sky and him, and he was at peace. But then he remembered the rabbits, still locked in their cages. There was no choice; he had to return to set them free.

By the time he got back to the house he was so very, very tired it made more sense to go to bed and set out again the next day.

He was woken next morning by the letter coming through the door – a sound he had not heard since Archie died, or at least not since he had put the wardrobe porch on the front of the house. He picked it up and examined it, turning it over to inspect the postmark, and remembered Saabira's words from the day before, imploring him to read it.

'I'll do you a swap,' he says with a hint of mischief in his voice, which takes Saabira by surprise. She has not heard Cyril joke before. 'You read this and I'll read Archie's diary. My guess is they say just about the same thing.'

Saabira stands immediately and takes Archie's diary down from the kitchen shelf.

'It's your book, Cyril. Your book, your house,' she says, her eyes smiling as much as her lips. Jay, who is sitting on Aaman's knee, reaches across the table to take the book and Cyril surprises himself. Instead of pulling it back, jealously and greedily, he lets her take it.

'Shall I go to my room, or my house?' he asks. It might be rude of him to sit amongst them reading.

Aaman points to the sofa by the fire. 'Here looks like a cosier place to read, I would say.' He smiles again. 'Saabira, can I help you with anything in the kitchen?'

238

Saabira is not sure if Jay is helping Cyril walk or the other way around. The two of them cross the room to the sofa; Cyril sits rather heavily and then helps Jay up, and she crawls to sit in the crook of his arm.

'Shall I read you a story?' he says to her and opens the diary. His head bends down towards Jay's, whose hand comes up and points at his glasses. Saabira remembers that she must do something about that – find someone to fix them. Or perhaps Cyril will do it for himself now?

With Jay's warm body against his, Cyril opens Archie's diary and begins to read in a very soft voice to the child. He knows well that it is not the words that impact a child so much as the tone, so he reads it like it is a fairy tale.

But before he has got very far he forgets to read aloud, as Jay is quite content concentrating on a hole in the hem of his tank top, pushing her finger through and wiggling it as it appears on the other side. Where was he? Oh yes, Archie has just been talking about his mother having houses, and about some others that he had bought. The diary continues:

'I've added to this with a couple more in Bradford and a couple more round here. It's a good game, property, 'cause once they are bought and you get a letting agency to take on the running there is little more to do and you get a steady little income.

'But this is the bit I have been dying to tell you.'

The memory of Archie's voice is so clear Cyril can almost hear it.

'Dying to tell you. Ha! I almost laughed then, but my lungs complained. Dying to tell you – what a suitable choice of words. I would love to not be dead when I told you, just so I could see your face, but I don't want our relationship to change whilst I'm still alive, I don't want your thanks, or for you to feel beholden. I just want us to potter along as we have done these four years, so I'll leave you to find this out when I've gone.

239

'I've made you, Cyril Sugden, beneficiary of Noiram Trust, and because the houses are all in trust there is no inheritance tax, which means we've got 'em, Cyril! We got 'em, and not a penny goes to the government. You are now the owner of five terraced houses in Bradford (as I said, I had to sell one to cover inheritance tax but you won't have that problem), and there is also this one we live in and the ones either side.

'But the shop in Greater Lotherton, well, I've sold that to an old man from Pakistan. He was so old I asked him what on earth he wanted it for – why he didn't just retire? Turns out he wanted it to provide a future for his grandson. I wouldn't have understood this once, this making plans for after you're dead, but I get it now. Anyway, the selling of the shop brings me to the second thing I wanted to tell you. This one I've found harder keeping a secret from you.

It's really going to thrill you, this one. Oh, hang on, I can hear your boots on the back doorstep, so I'll continue this the next time you're out.'

Cyril thinks he can remember the day. The moors had been so muddy that he had scraped his boots for ages to make sure he brought no muck into the house, and Archie seemed to be hiding something under his blankets. He rubs his fingers against the book cover and suddenly yearns so hard for Archie he has to look up and around to see Aaman and Saabira sitting at the kitchen table. The two of them reading his letter, their heads bowed towards each other. The yearning subsides at the sight of them, his new friends, and he returns to the book.

'It's been a fair few days since I've last written. I've felt so weak, even holding a pen is too much. Even thinking has finally become a struggle. To be honest, I wish it was all over now – I'm done with fighting this. I hope you don't miss me too much when I'm gone but I think I will miss you. I'm aware that is a ridiculous thing to say but I miss you already, I miss the world and everything in it before I am even gone. It's the truth.

'Before my strength fails me completely I must get around to telling you about the corner shop in Lotherton. I sold it. I told you that? Yes. I've looked back over my writing. I did tell you that. But I didn't tell you why. The quick answer is, I needed the cash for something else, but I won't tell you about that yet as I am waiting for the last papers to come through and I don't want to put it in writing until I'm sure it has happened.'

There is a break in the writing before it goes on, and when it starts again the handwriting is fainter, the pressure variable, and some of the letters shaky.

'The confirmation letter I was waiting for came today and now I can feel myself letting go. It's almost like when you are very tired and you finally allow yourself to lie down and you know you are going to be asleep before your head hits the pillow. I'm grateful for the stronger painkillers. You were right to let the hospice women in. You were also right when you said that they were very kind and caring. I'm still not convinced that young girl was a doctor, though... (that is meant to be a joke, Cyril). But either way, I'm grateful for the stronger medication, even if I do spend most of my time sleeping now. I hope I am not being a burden on you.

'I saw you sitting by me crying last night, when you thought I was asleep. I'm sorry to be the one to make you cry. I have cried too, for you, because I know it is worse for you. It is you who will be left alone. But, in a strange way we have become brothers, you and I, Cyril, in life and in death. Take strength from that.

'Where was I? Oh yes, the letter came today. The confirmation of what I spent the corner shop money on. The new purchase has gone through. I now own, or rather YOU now own, the Hogdykes Abattoir – or, to give it its real name Windy Lea Mill. Ha! We got them again!

241

'You've just started rocking, haven't you? Well, stop, you don't need to.'

Cyril checks himself. He is not rocking, he is not humming, he is not fiddling. Jay looks up at him and then continues to pull at the loose wool end she has found by the hole in his tank top. He kisses her shiny brown hair and reads on.

'Everything is going to be alright now, because I've just fixed it. You do not own what they do in the abattoir, you own the building. So you can now say what happens in the building. The farmers who lease it do so on a rolling contract – no need to worry what that actually is – for you it just means that you can end it with a month's notice. You can stop what they do there, stop the animals being hurt there, stop yourself working there. It's all sorted for you, Cyril, and I hope this positive event will outweigh my death for you. My lawyers, Haggle and Gripp (who also run the trust company), will help you with this when you are ready so YOU will be the one who ends all the suffering.'

Cyril may not be rocking or humming but his bottom lip is quivering.

'All you have to do is write a letter to say what you want them to do and they will do the rest.

'The lawyers, of course, know that you get everything – that was what all those papers were that we signed together, remember? And it was the real reason I opened a bank account with you.

'Anyway, here is what I thought you could do, unless you have better ideas. It would be wonderful if you set up an animals' home in the old abattoir building, so you can now look after all those strays that you keep wanting to bring home. I've begun all the basic paperwork necessary to make this happen, and again this is all with Haggle and Gripp, so when you give them the word the process should not take long.

'I've also instructed them to write to you when I'm dead in case you don't read this. So make sure you open all the letters that arrive. Anything with the name Sugden on it is now to do with you! I told you having the same name would come in useful.'

Cyril stops and wipes his forearm across his eyes before he continues. He has read all these details in the letter from the Haggle and Gripp but it all seems so much more real written in Archie's hand, heard in Archie's voice.

'So, goodbye my dear friend. You now have money so you won't need to work, and you can open an animal home if you want, so you can take care of every animal friend you find. The only thing I would like to encourage you to do is find some friends – good, caring friends, like you have been to me these last four years.'

Cyril wants to turn to look at Saabira and Aaman – his good, caring friends, as Archie put it. How proud Archie would have been of him. But he does not turn to look at them, as he is nearly at the end and feels driven to read on. He turns the page.

'This, Cyril, will be my last entry in this diary, I can feel it. Over the time we've spent together and by the things you have told me I know how brave you've been in your life. So, to be worthy of your friendship (and I hope you consider that we have been friends), I wanted my last entry to be the bravest thing I've ever done. So here goes.

'Cyril, I love you.

'There, I said it. You'll not often hear a true Yorkshireman say something like that. I reckon I never even said it to me own mother. But I say it to you now and it is the truth.

'Goodbye my dearest friend,

'Archie.'

Cyril cannot help himself, and he buries his face in his hands to smother his sobs. He looks over to Saabira and Aaman who are reading the letter from the lawyers.

243

Saabira is mopping her eyes with a tea towel and Aaman is crying quite openly.

Chapter 47

The removals van creaks up the lane the following Saturday.

'Cyril, the van is here!' Aaman calls over to him.

His leg feels better every day and getting about is much easier since Aaman made him a crutch from some of the wood that was in the backyard. He even bound the piece that sits under the arm with material so it would be comfortable. He can also see a lot better since he went into Bradford with Saabira and bought a new pair of reading glasses, gold and shiny like Saabira's bracelets. They are better than his old round glasses but they are not great. No matter, he has an eye appointment next week and then they will make him a proper prescription pair.

'Coming!' he calls, and he leaves Jay on the sofa with the book about tropical butterflies they are reading. Saabira borrowed it from the library in Bradford.

Aaman is standing outside Mr Brocklethwaite's house.

'Are you sure I cannot help?' he asks, but Mr Brocklethwaite doesn't answer.

'Mr Brocklethwaite,' Cyril addresses him. 'Please do not leave on my account. I have no problem with you staying here.'

'You already said that,' Mr Brocklethwaite snarls.

'And I say it again. I do not think Archie would want us to fight, or for you to leave.'

This stops Archie's old friend in his tracks, and it is his bottom lip that quivers this time.

'Please stay, Eric,' Cyril says with feeling. 'For Archie's sake.' Mr Brocklethwaite's lip quivers again and then he grunts and goes inside, where his belongings are already packed in boxes. His wife Brenda is just inside the door, a lace-edged hanky to her eye. She does not give her husband a kind look as he passes her.

'Come, Cyril,' Aaman says. 'You have done all you can.'

With Cyril's hand on Aaman's shoulder for support, they go back to house number thirty. His house, his friend's house.

'I have just made tea, boys,' Saabira says. 'There is bread and I have also toasted something called crumpets.'

'I love crumpets,' Cyril says and licks his lips to make Jay laugh.

'What are crumpets?' Aaman asks him.

'Er, they are round and they have holes running through them,' Cyril explains, 'So if you butter them while they are hot, the holes fill with melted butter, and you can also fill the holes with honey. And when you pick them up the butter and honey soak though and dribble down your fingers.' He can hear himself chattering but he doesn't care – Jay is laughing with him.

The crumpets are on the table and they eat, Saabira toasting more and more because Aaman seems to like them as much as Cyril does.

'Is someone going to let Jay try one?' she asks, turning another two over on the Aga top.

'I'll get her,' says Cyril, and goes over to the sofa. She is looking at the pictures of the butterflies, their wings spread, showing the colours of rainbows. For a moment he is spellbound by them and he knows that if he wanted to he could stare at them really hard and they would fill his mind and he would leave the world for a while. But, he discovers, he does not want to leave the world any more.

Saabira watches Cyril as he gently closes the book, and Jay reaches her little arms up around his neck so he can carry her to the table. It cannot be easy with a peg leg, but it looks like it is healing, and it will be just a matter of time.

There is a tap at the door. Mr Perfect and Gorilla Head, who have taken to spending most of the time with Aaman, both stand, alert.

'Sit,' she says to the dogs and they do, waiting patiently as she opens the door. 'Oh.' The sound escapes from her. The last person Saabira expected to see standing there is Dawn Todman. She looks different. The grey cardigan has gone, and in its place is a navy-blue fisherman's sweater. The skirt and heels have been replaced with jeans and walking boots.

'Hello,' she says, 'I saw next door is still empty, so I wondered if Cyril is with you?'

'Yes, he is, come in.' Saabira speaks politely but she remains wary.

'Morning.' Dawn addresses Aaman and Cyril. 'I'll just get down to it, shall I?' she says, but her manner indicates that this is not a question. 'Health and Safety also cover what was Hogdykes Abattoir. Well, them men down there are not backward at coming forward and they told me all about your bit of luck, Cyril, and how you've given them notice so you can set up an animal home. The whole bunch of them out of work. That's true, is it?'

Cyril nods but doesn't speak.

Saabira gets a mug down from the hooks under the kitchen cupboard and puts it on the table for Dawn. Aaman pours the tea, and Dawn helps herself to milk from the jug by the fresh plate of hot crumpets.

'Well, I'll tell you something for nothing. That place was a disgrace and should have been closed years back. I can't begin to tell you how much I hated it down there. It was the men that were animals, not the other way round. And I'm not sorry they are jobless – they deserve that and more – disgusting brutes, the lot of them.' She takes a sip of tea. 'Anyway, the point is all you have to do is say the word and I'll hand my notice in.'

247

'What?' Cyril puts down his half-eaten crumpet, looking even more puzzled now.

'Well, I thought you was going to need someone and being as, years ago, I used to work for Nine Lives Cat Rescue, and seeing as you'll need someone who knows all the health and safety regulations it could work out just fine. What do you say?' She points at the plate of crumpets. 'Is one of them going begging?' Saabira, Aaman and Cyril all nod at the same time.

Dawn butters a crumpet liberally and takes a big bite. 'With a bit of application I reckon we could have it open for Christmas and then we'll be ready for all them rotten sods that takes dogs for their kids for Christmas and dump them because they find they are too much work before they even see the new year in.' She licks the butter that is running past her fingers down to the wrist. Cyril and Aaman look at each other, but still they do not speak.

Chapter 48

The sun is out but the day is crisp. The rug Aaman and Saabira have spread over the bracken and heather a little way up the hill at the back of their house undulates over the uneven ground, and Jay is crawling between them, pressing down the springy heather lumps.

From where they are they can see all the way down the hill, through the back door of their house and into the kitchen where Cyril and Dawn are sitting at the table, making plans for the animal rescue shelter that Cyril will create at Windy Lea Mill.

After they had got over the initial shock the other day, Cyril and Dawn started making plans for the shelter, drawing little plans on bits of paper. It seems they are equally passionate about the idea of helping animals in distress. Dawn stayed until the evening, and came back next morning to start talking again, and Saabira cooked for everyone. She enjoyed that, everybody sitting around eating together.

She looks down the hill at the squat stone house. It feels so much more like her home in Pakistan now that there are more people in it.

'You know, Saabira, you are quite amazing,' Aaman says.

'Of course, why else would you have married me?' She smiles.

'Because it was arranged?' He teases her.

'Funny. So, tell me why I am amazing?'

'Look.' He nods down to the house. 'You did that.'

'Did what?'

'What you did for Cyril.' He pauses, reflects and continues. 'When we first moved in, he wouldn't even talk to us, and now he sits at our kitchen table like he is part of our family, chatting to the very person who was trying to help get him evicted. That is a serious Personal Makeover.' He chuckles.

'I don't think I have done much, really. It was really Archie's doing.' Saabira presses down the blanket and lets it spring up, making Jay laugh.

'No, Saabira. You made him food, you gave him space and respect, you took your time to win him over. That is what has made the difference. And all that energy you put into making his house clean so he would not be evicted. Nothing would have happened if it was not for your care and kindness.'

'I still think you are too generous. It was you who did most of the work clearing out his house.'

'Saabira, my jasmine blossom, he would not have let me near his house if you had not prepared the way. And, let me assure you, if you had not done it, I am not sure how long I could have lived next door to him. Maybe we should thank your lack of smell for making it all possible!' He lies back on the rug.

'I think, really, it was because I found him fascinating. I still do, you know. But in the beginning, when I didn't understand him, I felt compelled to find a way to reach him.' She can feel energy flow through her as she says this, as if she is ready to do it all again.

'Yes. But I think others would only have made a small effort. There are not many people like you and Juliet in the world.' He looks up at the sky, at a few puffy white clouds on a blanket of blue.

'Juliet?' She can feel her hackles rising.

'Yes, Juliet,' he says lazily. 'Can you not see?'

'See what?'

He snorts another little laugh and turns his head to look at her, his hair falling over his eyes a little. He is due another haircut.

'You, my love, have just done for Cyril what Juliet did for me.' Jay crawls onto his chest and lays prone, pretending to sleep. 'I was a lost and damaged man in a strange place and as Juliet healed her own emotional wounds she gave me wings,' he says seriously.

Saabira turns this over in her mind. Cyril was a lost and damaged man, but was he in a strange place? She turns her head side to side as she ponders this. On the one hand, he wasn't, really – this was where he lived, just a little piece of his home country. But then, it could be argued that everywhere seemed strange for him back then, that the whole world was a confusing place. Maybe Aaman has a point. But – Juliet healing herself through giving Aaman wings? Is she, Saabira, meant to have healed herself through Cyril?

'So from what am I meant to have healed myself?' she asks. He will say something silly now, something teasing; that is his way.

'Jealousy,' he says.

Her blood runs cold and she swallows hard.

'What, you thought I didn't know?' Now he is teasing. 'I knew, of course I knew, but how could I, of all people, do anything about it? Sure, I could have made you pretty promises, telling you that everything was as it should have been, I could have told you all the things that happened step by step so you could see there was nothing amiss, but if you had doubted you would always have doubted, no matter what I said.'

'So you said nothing?' She is not sure that is better.

'I knew you would find your own way.' He looks her straight in the eye.

'And you think I have?'

'You tell me,' he says, but leaves no gap before going on. 'You have done for Cyril what Juliet did for me. There are differences here and there, of course, but basically Juliet helped me by helping herself, and now, through helping Cyril, you have ultimately helped yourself, because now you can understand Juliet and your jealousy will fade.'

He looks away, up to the sky again. Jay might even really be asleep now; she continues to lie on his chest.

Saabira looks back down to the house to see that Cyril and Dawn are now in Cyril's backyard and Dawn has the big rabbit in her arms.

'Go on, then.' Aaman startles her. 'Tell me how you feel about Juliet now.'

How she feels about Juliet now? That's hard. Or is it?

'What was Juliet's healing?' she asks.

'The only thing there is to heal – hurt. She'd been hurt by her mother, her father, her ex-husband – lots of little side stories along the way. A lifetime of being kicked.'

'That is what Cyril is healing from – a lifetime of being kicked.'

'And you?' he asks.

The concept of hurt or pain immediately makes her think of her firstborn, and then of Cyril's twin. Suffering from postnatal depression, she and Cyril's mother both pushed away the people they loved.

She lies back next to Aaman and looks up at the sky. Aaman's hand finds hers and their fingers intertwine. High above is a tiny black spot that may be a hawk, or some other bird – she has no idea. She holds Aaman's hand tight.

'You are right,' she says, and decides not to finish the sentence unless he asks. They lie a while longer. He doesn't ask.

'I understand Juliet better now,' she says after a pause.

'And the jealousy?'

She tunes into that feeling. 'No, I don't really feel jealous of her any more.' It seems like such a release. She turns her head to look at Aaman's profile. She can love him freely, now – freely and totally.

'Well, that's good timing,' he says.

'Why is this good timing?' she asks, expecting another of his little jokes, his tiny teases.

'Her last email said she would visit us over Christmas.' He seems serious.

'Really?' Saabira can feel her stomach churn, and she sits up.

'Really.'

It is one thing not to feel jealous, but quite another to welcome her with open arms. But the jealousy seems to have shape-shifted into excitement. Who knows – if they are so similar, maybe they will get on very well. Why not? Besides, if Aaman could face the adventures he had and Cyril can face the world that kicked him, then she can face a woman who cares about Aaman. At least they will be starting with something in common.

She lies down again, watching the clouds form and change, and her thoughts drift with them, and as the next cloud forms so does an idea. The cloud swells quickly and becomes dark. But Saabira's mind is stuck on her idea, which is also swelling and solidifying.

'I have an idea,' she says. 'And I am wondering how you are going to feel about it?'

'Tell me.' He sits up, scooping little Juliet into his arms.

'I think I want to train as a psychiatric nurse.'

'Good idea,' he replies, as if she has suggested what they should have for dinner. 'Oh, I forget to tell you,' he continues, changing the subject and scrabbling to his feet with a sudden burst of energy. 'They put my first wage in the bank yesterday, my first British wage!'

'My wonderful husband!' she says. She stands and gathers up the rug. Perhaps it is best to let her idea sink into his mind a while before she brings it up again.

'So, you know what we should do right now?' Little Juliet claps her hands, caught up in Aaman's excitement. 'We should go and pick ourselves out a Christmas tree, buy some tinsel and decorate the house with all the things they do for Christmastime here.'

'Christmas? So we are not to celebrate Eid now?' Saabira scowls at him.

'Oh yes, of course we'll still mark Eid, but we're in England now, so we must also enjoy English rituals and celebrations as well. We must integrate.' They start to walk down to the house.

'In that case, we must also enjoy Chanukah and Ramadan and definitely the winter solstice.' She laughs and pushes him playfully on the shoulder.

'Chanukah, Ramadan, the winter solstice, Mother's Day, Father's Day, Easter, April Fool's Day, Halloween, Bonfire Night, Trooping the Colour. In fact, every day from now on will be a celebration.' They are by the back door now, and he stands to one side and bows deeply to invite her to pass first.

If you enjoyed Saving Septic Cyril please share it with a friend, and check out the other books in the Greek Village Collection!

I'm always delighted to receive email from readers, and I welcome new friends on Facebook.

https://www.facebook.com/authorsaraalexi
saraalexi@me.com

Happy reading,

Sara Alexi

Made in the USA
San Bernardino, CA
03 December 2016